BURDEN
OF BLOOD

BURDEN
OF BLOOD

LAURA D. BASTIAN

CHAPTER ONE

Kaylee climbed higher into the tree to avoid the rocks flying at her. Her borrowed dress caught on a limb. She slipped a couple of inches before gripping tightly with her bandaged hand. A squeak of pain escaped her lips when a rock found its mark. The boys beneath her laughed.

"Nice shot!" one shouted.

"If another rock leaves your hands, you will find an arrow in your back." A man on horseback trotted into the orchard. He jumped off his majestic black horse easily as he neared the mob of boys. They dropped the rocks and scattered, but not before the man snatched one boy by the scruff of his neck and held tight.

"What is the meaning of this?" He glanced up at Kaylee and then stared the boy down. His cultured speech proved he came from a much higher class than anyone she had encountered before. His dark shirt with an embroidered collar, so unlike what most people she'd ever known wore, also spoke of riches.

The boy sputtered and squirmed. "We was just havin' fun."

"What if you killed her?"

"We wasn't trying to hurt her. We wanted to see what would happen when she snapped."

The man raised an eyebrow and looked up at Kaylee with more interest. When his eyes met hers, he took a deep breath as if smelling the air. Shivers ran down her spine. A smile spread across his face under a dark, close-cut beard. He looked back down at the boy in his grip. "She hasn't manifested any powers yet?"

The boy shook his head.

The man looked at Kaylee again. "Foolish way to go about bringing the change. What if she started shooting fire at you?"

Kaylee stared at the man. *How many like me has he met? And what will he do with me?*

"They can do that?" the boy asked.

"Some can."

The boy gasped. His wide eyes stared up at Kaylee until he made eye contact. He whipped his head to the side, avoiding her gaze. "Lemme go," he shouted to the man still holding him. The second the man released him, he bolted to where the other boys had gone.

"Why don't you come down now?" the man said.

Kaylee stared at him. He was tall and muscular. A sword hung from his right side. His black hair stuck up in places, as if he'd run the horse hard at some point. He was too much man for her to deal with after having lived the last three years in hiding. She didn't dare come down to him, but neither did she dare stay in the tree.

"Who are you?" Kaylee asked, peeking through the leaves. A branch brushed against her cheek, so she shifted to avoid getting scratched. He somehow knew her secret already, but hiding her curse was so ingrained in her. She knew she couldn't let him see her blood. "What do you want?"

"Name's Asher." He pulled off his riding gloves and looked up into her eyes. Kaylee's heart clenched in fear again. His eyes flicked briefly to her bald head. He raised an eyebrow but didn't say anything about it.

"No need to postpone the inevitable," Asher called up. He bent down and picked up a rock, bouncing it a couple times in his hand.

Kaylee closed her eyes and braced herself. She didn't want to see when the rock hit. He'd have more power behind it and—more than likely—a better aim than any of those boys. When nothing happened, she peeked down to see him watching her with a smile.

"Come down now and I'll personally escort you to the king."

"The king?" Kaylee squeaked, her voice so tight she was surprised it came out. Her father would roll over in his grave. The monastery had been the perfect place to hide, but they had kicked her out as soon as they discovered she was female. If she hadn't accidentally cut herself, she'd still be living there.

"Hurry it up."

"I won't go to the king," Kaylee whispered, choked with fear. She'd never had to refuse an order from the monks, but nothing could make her agree to go to the king. Her father had forbidden it.

"It's the law, girl. You don't have any choice in the matter." He crossed his arms over his broad chest and looked around the orchard. "Besides, the king takes care of his Blue Bloods. You'll have more riches than you can imagine."

Kaylee looked at her bandaged hand again. The blood had begun to seep through the cloth tied around it, soaked through with a blue as deep as the flowers in the field outside the orchard fence.

She'd grown careless and cut herself on the wagon wheel she'd been helping Brother Osmon with. When he saw the blood pooling in her hand, he'd nearly fainted before he ran to tell the others about her. They'd not spoken to her again. Instead, they bundled up all her belongings, made her change out of the monk's robe she'd become accustomed to, and kicked her out.

Kaylee knew she couldn't stay in the tree forever. Now that the boys harassing her were gone, she could climb down. If only Asher weren't there. Her hand still stung where she'd cut it. She moved carefully, then jumped easily from the lowest branch and stumbled because the dress didn't give her the free range of motion she was used to with the robe. The man took her by the arm and led her to his horse.

"When did you first bleed blue?" Asher asked.

"At fifteen."

"How old are you now?"

"Nineteen."

Asher stopped and looked her over. "Don't look nineteen." He stared at her bald head again and narrowed his eyes as if trying to imagine her with hair. "You've been hiding your gift four years? And you haven't snapped?"

Kaylee shook her head. "Please don't take me to the king."

"Why not?"

Kaylee shook her head. "I don't want to be his slave."

"Slave? Who told you that?" Asher looked at her.

"My father."

"Then he was a fool. The king treats his Blue Bloods very well."

Kaylee stared at him in confusion. No one had ever spoken well of the king in this area. And her father was no fool.

"He will give you more than you could ever imagine." Asher looked her over. "You wouldn't have to hide. You could have your own clothes, maids, carriages, and horses." Asher looked back up at the tree. "You will learn ways to defend yourself from scruffy dogs like those." He pointed in the direction the boys had run.

"How do you know this?" Kaylee asked.

"I find Blue Bloods like you and escort them to the king."

"You're a bounty hunter?"

"No."

"Do you get paid for delivering Blue Bloods to the king?" Kaylee asked.

Asher shifted the rock from one hand to another. "Yes."

Kaylee raised an eyebrow.

"I merely do a service for those who need help getting to the king."

"I'm not coming with you."

"You are. It's the law. Anyone who knows what you are will take you for the reward. The king punishes those who hide one like you." Asher looked up the hill at the monastery sitting peacefully overlooking the green valley. "If you want to make the people who helped you suffer because of your stubbornness, then go ahead. If not, you'd best come with me."

Kaylee looked to the monastery, her home for so long. No wonder they had rushed to get her out of there. She couldn't risk letting the monks be punished if anyone knew she'd hidden there for years. She reached up and touched her bald head. People would know she'd been with the monks if she stayed close.

Kaylee turned to Asher and lifted her bandaged hand. "How did you know what I was? How did you find me?"

"Let's just say I have a sense about these things."

Kaylee adjusted her pack to hold it in front of her. For a moment, she considered running, but she knew it would be foolish. Better to go with him now and find a place to sneak away when she was further from the monastery. She had to protect them, but she would not let him deliver her to the king.

Asher helped her on his horse, her legs straddling its broad back. Her skirt slid up to her knees. Asher stared at her leg a moment. When she leaned down to see what kept his attention, he shook his head quickly. Kaylee looked harder at her leg. Besides the fine blonde hairs and a few scrapes from her time in the tree, she couldn't see anything interesting about it.

Asher mounted the horse behind her and gathered the reins. Kaylee hadn't ridden a horse since she arrived at the monastery with her father. This magnificent beast was smooth and easy and dangerous. The man behind her had complete control of the animal. She felt the difference in the motion of his legs behind her own as he guided the horse. It had been a long time since she'd thought of a man as anything but a monk. Strange sensations bubbled up deep within her belly.

They rode in silence for miles. She took in everything about Asher, from his movements and breathing to his musky scent. He was in much better physical condition than anyone she'd ever met. The monks were scholars with little need to do much physical labor. The garden and a few farm animals they kept for their food didn't take much more strength than what Kaylee had. It wasn't easy work, but she knew it would never produce Asher-size arms.

"How did you manage it?" he asked after they'd traveled for a while.

Kaylee turned her head just a fraction. The stubble from his jaw brushed her bald scalp. She quickly turned forward and kept her mouth shut.

"How long were you there? How did you keep your secret?"

Kaylee shrugged and remained quiet.

"How did you get in?"

Kaylee didn't respond.

"None of them had any inkling you were a woman?"

He leaned back. Kaylee turned her head just enough to see he was trying to size her up.

"You don't have an overly feminine form, but it is obvious you are female."

Kaylee didn't respond. She turned away to look straight and watched the road before her.

"Baldness doesn't flatter you, but your cheek bones are fine. You have very delicate features. Once I get you cleaned up and dressed properly, you'll be much easier to look at."

Kaylee tried not to be offended. She sensed he wanted to egg her on. Silence was her best defense. He chuckled. "Guess the monks there are blind." He leaned to the side and reached around to take her chin firmly in his hand. It didn't hurt until she tried to shake him off. He kept hold until she relaxed. He turned her face to get a better look at it.

"You have a girl's face no matter your lack of hair. Maybe we'll have to send the king's men to question the monks. Find out who knew you were there and helped you hide."

"No one knew," Kaylee said quickly turning her head to make him release her face. She had to protect them.

"So how did you do it?"

"I don't know. I just wanted a place to live."

"So you picked a monastery? And pretended to be a man? Why?"

Kaylee shook her head.

"You could've gone to the castle," Asher said. "Even if you hadn't been a Blue Blood, the king always has room for another servant girl. Whether in his direct employ or as a simple wash woman, you'd have been taken care of better than any other place."

Kaylee clenched her jaw. Would he ever shut up so they could make the journey in peace? Once they made camp, she would escape.

"Why didn't you go to the castle at Inshansi?" Asher pressed.

Kaylee shook her head. When her father found out she had blue blood, he took her as far from the castle as he could. They were simple farmers but learned together how to survive. Her father's words echoed in her head. *We have to keep moving, Kaylee. The king will use your power for his own ends. We can't let him find you.*

"Doesn't matter now," Asher said, pulling her from her thoughts. "You will be there in a few days and your training can begin."

"Training?" Kaylee whipped her head around and knocked into Asher's firm jaw. He grunted in annoyance as he rubbed his chin. Kaylee cringed. She never meant to talk with him.

"What do you think they do?"

Kaylee turned forward again.

"Has no one ever told you what a Blue Blood is?"

Kaylee looked down at her bandaged hand. The bleeding had mostly stopped. The blood on the cloth had dried and turned a strange purplish hue.

"You've seriously never heard of your heritage?"

Kaylee sighed. "Father only said it was rare and I should stay hidden."

"It is rare. But it's a gift. You are blessed with two lives. One as a Blue Blood."

"Two lives?"

"You really don't know?" Asher asked. He shook his head and pulled his horse's reins to slow down.

"You can die, same as anyone else. But until you do, you have a gift that is very valuable to the king. Your abilities are beyond what a normal person has. He pays handsomely for me to bring girls like you in."

"Girls?"

"Only females can become Blue Bloods."

So that was how the monks knew. "What kind of gift?" Kaylee grew more confused.

"Each girl I bring to the king has been different. Mostly the gifts deal with the elements. Earth, fire, water, air. A few are more valuable because of their rarity."

"And I will have this gift until I die?"

"Yes. Then you will live again as a normal being."

"A second life?" Kaylee whispered. "How did this happen?"

"I don't know how it starts. You just are."

"Why do you find people like me?"

"To serve the king."

Kaylee gripped the saddle's front, gritting her teeth against speaking badly about this king Asher seemed to revere. Asher shifted behind her and took the reins in one hand. His movements sent more shivers down her spine.

"Why wouldn't you want to go to the king? You'll be cared for. Protected. You'll be so valuable to him, he'll assign guards to watch you constantly. You would always be safe."

"That is no life."

Asher snorted. "And hiding as a boy in a monastery is?"

Kaylee shook her head and vowed to keep her mouth shut. No one before had gotten under her skin the way this man did. Maybe it was because no one had treated her like a female in such a long time. She'd only been a woman again for less than two days, and she didn't like it.

CHAPTER TWO

After riding for half a day, they approached a large village. Asher slowed the horse and leaned to the side as he looked Kaylee over again.

"Maybe we should get you a scarf or hat to wear. Bring less attention to you." Asher reached into a side bag which held clothing. He pulled out a large white handkerchief and handed it to her. Kaylee stared at it, unsure what to do.

"Here." He took it back and folded it into a triangle. "May I?"

Kaylee shrugged. His warm hand brushed across her head as the cool fabric covered her scalp. He pulled it tight, tying it at the nape of her neck. The motion sent strange shivers down her spine, originating where his fingers touched her flesh. "There you go. You look almost normal."

Kaylee pressed her lips together.

He urged his horse forward again and they entered the village. He stopped in front of an inn with an air of confidence that made her think he'd been here before. Asher climbed down from his horse and offered his hand to Kaylee. She lifted one leg over the saddle horn and, unsure if she would be able to dismount herself while wearing the dress, gratefully accepted his help.

Asher's strong hands gripped her waist and, once she stood safe on the ground, lingered there for a moment. She looked at him with a raised eyebrow. Asher jerked his hand back, turned, and moved toward the inn. Kaylee hadn't seen an inn for years, but the smells coming from it reminded her of traveling with her father. Her heart ached as she thought of his grave in the monastery's cemetery. She hadn't even said goodbye. She wished she could have sat on the grass by his small grave marker one last time.

A boy came from around the back of the building. The youth stared at Kaylee. She resisted the urge to touch her head. The less she reacted, the sooner they would ignore her. Asher looked the boy over and patted his horse. "You look big enough now to handle Denn. Almost a man now, aren't you, Gerry?"

The boy stood up straighter and reached for the reins. "Yessir."

Asher ruffled Gerry's head and handed his horse over.

"Take care of him for me?" Asher pulled his bags from the horse. Kaylee adjusted the bag she held in front of her until it slung over her back.

"Right away, sir." Gerry took the reins and led the horse away.

Asher walked to the door and opened it for Kaylee. She stared at him a moment, unsure what to do until he gestured for her to walk in first. It was darker inside, with one small window on the north facing side, but it was still open and welcoming. The scent of a hearty soup and warm bread made her mouth water as she walked forward.

Asher pointed out a bench near the wall. "Sit down a minute while I get us some rooms."

Kaylee sat on the hard wood, trying to smooth down the confining dress. If only they'd let her keep the robe she'd worn in the monastery. She understood why they took it away. It represented something she wasn't. It would raise too many questions if someone wore it outside the stone walls. Kaylee reached up and adjusted the cloth Asher had tied on her head, to make sure it was still in place and secure. No one could know the monks had sheltered her for so long.

Kaylee met Asher's eyes as he watched her from the counter. Was he worried she'd run, or was he studying her feminine form and wondering more about the monks? His study confused Kaylee so she turned away, unwilling to encourage him. A short man walked into the room with a mostly white towel in his hand. He stopped short and looked her over.

Asher spoke. "Master Rhett."

The man turned to Asher and a broad smile stretched across his face. "Asher Herst. How long has it been since you came through these parts?"

"Near onto a year at least." Asher faced the counter, turning his back to Kaylee as the man slid behind it. "You seem to be doing well still."

Master Rhett nodded and stepped up behind the counter, making him almost as tall as Asher. "I can't complain. We haven't had any issues like a few years back. It's been right nice, now that the king has sent soldiers through here again."

Asher nodded and turned to indicate Kaylee. "I got myself a charge. I'll be needing my regular room."

"Of course." Master Rhett looked at Kaylee with interest, but soon opened a box and got out a key. Asher handed over payment and the coins clinked against each other before disappearing into the innkeeper's large hand. Master Rhett tucked the coins into a leather pouch on his belt.

"Thank you, sir." Asher turned to Kaylee and picked up his bag at his feet. "Come." He motioned to her as he walked past. She jumped to her feet and followed without a word. A narrow hallway to the right of the large staircase led to their rooms. Kaylee had to press against the wall to allow another guest past.

Asher opened a door and stepped inside. Kaylee hesitated in the hallway. She had been trained not to enter another person's room without express permission. Was it the same at an inn? Asher set his bags down and turned around. He raised an eyebrow at Kaylee.

"Are you coming?"

Kaylee took a deep breath and stepped into the sparsely furnished room. *A single bed?* She stared at it, wondering where she'd sleep. She didn't dare look at Asher, afraid of what she might see in his eyes.

A small table along one wall had a bowl with a pitcher nestled inside it. She eyed the fresh, white towel folded neatly to the side, wishing she could use it to clean up. After riding on the horse all day with Asher breathing down her neck, she longed for the cool water to wash away the unsettling feelings deep within her center. A simple wooden chair near the window was the only other furnishing. Maybe she would sleep in the chair.

Asher opened a door in the wall. "This will be yours."

Kaylee peeked in and saw a tiny room, smaller than her room at the monastery. Kaylee hugged her small bag of belongings close, relieved she wouldn't be in the same room with Asher.

"Take a few minutes to relax. I'll be right back. Don't leave this room."

Kaylee longed to pour the fresh water onto the cloth and wipe the sweat from her face and neck.

Would Asher be angry if she used the cloth for herself? She needed to put him at ease so she could slip away when the time was right. Kaylee sat on the chair, picking at the worn fabric of the dress. She owned nothing else. These rags were her only option.

The clothes she wore when she arrived at the monastery were those of a farm boy. The monks had traded them to pay for her robe and blanket. Kaylee hadn't understood why her father insisted she pretend to be a boy until now. And, with his final words reinforcing his demand to stay hidden, she wished she wasn't a girl.

CHAPTER THREE

Asher bounded down the stairs, excited to get a good meal. Cooking his own fare as he camped each night got old. He'd stay in a couple of these places on his way back to Inshansi. It would be good to get some supplies. He considered buying an old horse for Kaylee to ride but changed his mind. Giving her a horse might encourage her to run.

Most of the other Blue Bloods he escorted to the king came willingly and often had their own horses to carry their gear. Kaylee came with practically nothing. He was surprised she had even her small bag of belongings, since monks took a vow of poverty.

Besides, having her on the horse with him was pleasant. She seemed hesitant at first, but once she relaxed he found he enjoyed the feel of her there. She was a sturdy girl, not too thin, but small enough that the horse had no trouble carrying both of them. She didn't talk much. Many of his questions and attempts to get her to open up went unanswered.

He wished he knew why she chose to hide in the monastery. Her father took her there, but where was he now? And why had she stayed in hiding? It would take some delicate questioning to learn the reasons, but he welcomed the challenge.

Asher found Master Rhett in the little alcove off the front room. He sat in a large faded chair reading an old book. He looked up when Asher entered and invited him to sit.

"I can't say how happy I am to see you again, Asher."

Asher gave him a nod. "Thank you."

"Why has it been so long?"

Asher shrugged. Not everyone knew what he did, but he trusted Master Rhett. He used this place many times in his travels. One of the Blue Bloods he escorted to Master Rhett's inn years ago had previously snapped. The girl was able to use her powers, but she couldn't control them. She nearly set the room on fire. Master Rhett handled the situation well, earning Asher's repeat business.

He used to find them quite regularly. Many times he would discover multiple Blue Bloods from one town. He returned to those places every year to search for more, with no success. He began to worry he wouldn't find a new one before the bounty from the last ran out.

Finding Kaylee was like a breath of life. It had been more than a year since his last find. Asher had to be more careful with his money. He couldn't overspend on things he didn't need. He resolved again not to buy a horse for Kaylee.

Emerging from his thoughts, he answered Rhett's question. "My business takes me all over the realm."

"We have a fine stew cooking away, and after dinner I'll challenge you to a game of chess."

Asher grinned. "You sure you're willing to be soundly beaten again?"

"I believe I can handle it." Master Rhett stood. "I'll get the food while you get your young lady."

Asher appreciated the fact Master Rhett didn't ask questions, the sign of a fine innkeeper. Rhett knew Asher would pay for any damages caused by a Blue Blood with powers. *Lucky for me she hasn't snapped.* Asher returned upstairs and knocked on the door, unsure whether Kaylee would be decent.

"Enter."

Asher pushed on the door and walked inside. She wasn't there and Asher panicked even though he'd heard her voice bid him enter. He peeked through the door of the extra room to see her sitting on the small bed in her little closet. Kaylee raised one narrow eyebrow giving him a longsuffering look.

"Dinner is served. Wash up and come on down," he said.

Kaylee stood quickly and washed her hands in the bowl on his small table as if she'd been dying to have permission to use it. She took the towel then dipped it in the water and wiped her arms, face and neck, sighing with pleasure as the cool water wiped away the grime of their traveling. Asher watched her in fascination. Kaylee turned around and seemed stunned he was still standing there. She looked down at the floor.

Asher turned away. Staring at her so blatantly was unacceptable. He had never made blunders like this with the other girls. Why was he so fascinated with her?

"Excuse me, Kaylee." Asher cleared his throat. "I am sorry I didn't ask earlier. Did you need anything?"

Kaylee blinked, but shook her head. She'd probably done without for so long it didn't occur to her to ask for anything.

Asher resolved to find out so he could get anything she needed before they left the village. He wracked his mind for what she might need. A new dress for sure. She would not need a brush immediately, but eventually her hair would grow. Should he get her one now, or wait until later? Of course she would probably be in the king's possession by the time her hair got long enough to need any sort of comb. That thought troubled him.

Kaylee turned away and Asher realized he'd been staring again. "Hurry. Master Rhett has dinner for us."

Kaylee nodded.

Asher left the room before he did something stupid again. He waited in the hallway for her to come out. He needed to control himself. She wasn't even that beautiful. She had a pleasing face to look at, and full lips, but she didn't look like a woman most of the time, but he knew she had soft curves. He'd been highly aware of her each time he helped her mount or dismount the horse.

These thoughts had to stop. Kaylee belonged to the king. She would serve him in whatever way he needed to maintain control of the kingdom. Asher felt jealous of the king for the first time. He hoped Kaylee's lack of hair and her reluctance to act like a woman would help keep her from any overt attentions of the king.

He forced those thoughts out of his head. Kaylee joined him in the hallway and he locked the doors to their rooms. They walked quietly down the hallway and stairs and sat at the table. Master Rhett quickly placed full bowls of soup in front of them, followed by a loaf of bread, two mugs, and a stoneware jug in the center of the table. Asher grabbed a chunk of bread, wanting something to do instead of watching Kaylee. He poured himself some ale. As he reached to pour some in her mug, she covered it with her hand.

"It's not allowed."

"You can't have any ale?"

Kaylee shook her head.

"You know you aren't still a monk, right?" He spoke quietly, not wanting to be overheard by Master Rhett.

Kaylee glanced at the ceiling and sighed, removing her hand from the mug. Asher poured her some ale. She didn't say a word but still refused the drink.

The silence remained as they ate. Asher wanted to know more about her, but Kaylee ignored all his attempts at conversation. Besides, Master Rhett would surely be listening. When they finished, the young boy, Gerry, came in and took their dishes away.

Asher leaned back to look at Kaylee for a moment. He wanted to return to the room and question her. Instead Master Rhett walked in, carrying a chess set. Kaylee's eyes lit up for a moment, but then she ducked her head and turned away from the game. Asher tucked that little bit of information away and planned to get a small set he could take on their journey. He might be able to get her to open up if they were involved in a friendly game.

Master Rhett offered to escort Kaylee back to her room.

Kaylee shook her head. "I can make it on my own, I'm sure."

She was halfway up the stairs before Asher remembered he had the only key. He jumped up and rushed after her. Kaylee didn't say a word as he opened the door to the room. He waited until she entered her room through the small door, and then he locked her in.

She didn't question him at all but the look in her eyes spoke her annoyance. *Why do I care what she thinks of me? It's her own fault I can't trust her to stay here.*

He turned to rejoin Master Rhett.

CHAPTER FOUR

Kaylee slung her pack on her shoulders, prepared to leave after breakfast. Asher must have sent Gerry to the village merchant to gather some supplies because he had a couple of extra bundles he hadn't had the night before, and was praising the boy for his quickness.

Today she rode behind him. It felt better to not be trapped between his arms. The extra items in the saddle bags made her wonder if he'd put her back there for his own comfort.

She waited until they'd gotten a mile or more out of the village before curiosity got the best of her. "What is the king like?"

Asher's muscles tightened at the sound of her voice, so she relaxed her hold on him. He turned just slightly, his eyes narrowed as he studied her. "I have spoken to him only twice. Each time he was kind and fair. He's a powerful man with many years' experience. He's been the king my entire twenty-six years, but he's aged well."

Kaylee didn't speak at first, hoping he would continue. They rode in silence for a while before she finally asked, "What does he do with people like me?"

Asher took a long, slow breath. "He will train you. You have a power hidden within. If we can find out what it is before we get there, it will be easier for you to show him your abilities."

Kaylee stiffened for a moment. Her power made her nervous. Her father had talked about women who did horrible things with their powers, all in the name of the king. If she never learned her power, she would never run the risk of hurting someone.

"It doesn't matter if you don't have your power when you first get there. They will test you to figure out what you can do. Most Blue Bloods have powers similar to one another, although occasionally they surprise the king."

The answer didn't satisfy her. "But what does he *do* with us?"

"Those with battle skills, he uses to protect his country. Those who can influence in other ways are used to—"

"He will use me?" Kaylee interrupted. "In whatever way he desires?" How could someone force another to serve a king against their will?

Asher tried to protest. When Kaylee leaned around him just enough to see his face, he stopped talking. He shrugged. "I guess technically he will. But if it keeps the kingdom safe and in power, don't you think your service to him will be worth it? He will treat you well. He will shower you with gifts and riches for your service."

Kaylee paused for a moment. "Would you serve him?"

Asher nodded. "I do serve him."

"By bringing him girls like me?" Kaylee asked.

Asher sighed. "Yes, but I do more than that."

Kaylee waited for him to elaborate. He didn't. Nothing he said would make her comfortable with being the king's slave. Asher may not think of him as evil, but Kaylee's father insisted he was. Otherwise he wouldn't have hidden her away.

They stopped for camp just before the sun touched the mountains behind them. The long road remained empty after leaving the outer edges of the small village. Kaylee enjoyed the solitude and views of the countryside throughout the day. Lush fields gave way to rolling hills dotted with small herds of sheep. The road meandered around the forest edge, entering the tree line on occasion, but mostly staying just outside it.

In one of those little spots within the trees, Asher decided to make camp.

"Gather some wood for a fire while I get us settled." Asher led his horse to a clump of trees and started removing the packs and saddle.

"You trust me to go out there alone?" Kaylee asked, surprised he would let her out of his sight.

"Where would you go?" Asher glanced at the darkened trees. "I doubt you have much skill in fighting off wild animals . . . unless you've been keeping your gift a secret." Asher looked at Kaylee as if trying to decide if that was even a possibility.

Kaylee didn't say anything, but met his eyes, trying not to give too much away. He could mock all he wanted to. She wasn't completely helpless on her own.

Asher peered into the shadows of the tree line. "Maybe I should get the wood and you can set up camp."

Kaylee smiled, finding his sudden hesitance amusing, but Asher quickly added. "Don't get any ideas. Denn won't let anyone ride him without me." Asher pulled the saddle off Denn and began to rub him down.

Kaylee crossed her arms. "Make up your mind."

"You get the wood," Asher answered after a minute.

Kaylee turned her back to Asher and walked toward the trees closest to them. Dead wood and fallen branches littered the forest floor. She grabbed two large branches, a few inches in diameter, and dragged them back to Asher. His eyes widened as she dropped them at his feet. He muttered something under his breath as she turned to go.

On the second trip, she picked up smaller branches for kindling. She cursed the dress at first, until she discovered she could use her skirt to carry the wood. In the shadows near the clearing she watched as Asher stopped and stretched his back. When he yawned, hope bloomed in her chest. Maybe she would slip away in the night as he slept. She'd take his knife so she wouldn't be defenseless. Her father taught her to throw a knife well, but the years in the monastery had left her out of practice. She'd been skilled enough to keep the wolves away with slings and rocks when she lived at home. Kaylee was good with a sling but better with the knife.

She dumped the pile of branches out of her dress and caught Asher staring at her again.

"What?" Was he on to her plan to run tonight? She brushed off the dirt and bark that had stuck to the fabric, trying to look innocent. Had she been too obvious in her appraisal of the knife at his belt?

"Nothing." Asher shook his head and turned away, busying himself with his pack. He cleared his throat and nodded toward the pile of wood. "That should do for tonight."

"You sure?" Kaylee asked. "I can make one more trip."

"There's just two of us, and the fire needn't be large. We'll just want it burning enough to keep any wolves away."

Kaylee propped the long, dry branch onto a rock and stomped on it, snapping it cleanly in two. She moved the branch a little higher and stomped again. This time it took three tries to break it. She stopped for a breath. "Do you have an axe?"

"Yes, but I'll do it in a bit."

"I'm capable," Kaylee said.

Asher looked her over. "I'm sure you are." He hesitated for a moment before going to his pack and pulling out a small axe. He looked into her eyes for a moment. Kaylee raised one eyebrow and fought a smile. He seemed to relax a little as he handed her the axe, handle first.

Kaylee took it silently and attacked the bigger chunks of the branch. She worked quickly, aware the whole time Asher watched her. When she finished, she returned the axe to him, and he took it without a thanks.

"You have a striker?" Kaylee asked.

"A what?"

"A striker. Something to strike and get the spark?"

"Oh. Yes." Asher moved to his pack and pulled out a small pouch with a stone. He paused a moment before he passed her the knife.

Kaylee got to work. She pulled the dry grass and used a rock to scrape a little hollow in the dirt. She then arranged the smaller bits and put some dry grass to catch the spark. It only took three strikes before the spark caught. Bending low, she blew softly, encouraging the flame.

She leaned back and smiled with pride. Asher crossed his arms over his chest and frowned.

"Did I do it wrong?"

"Maybe I'd better keep an eye on you. Don't want to find you missing in the morning."

Kaylee frowned. By showing she was competent, she'd just ruined her chances of taking off tonight. It didn't matter. She still had a couple weeks before they would reach the king's immediate lands. She would have time to disappear. Plus, if she hung around and put him at ease, it would be easier to learn his traveling habits and figure out the best way to take off without being caught.

Kaylee moved over and sat on a chunk of wood. Instead of offering to help with anything else, she wrapped her arms around her knees. She fingered the dress after a moment and wished she could change out of it.

"Were you serious about getting me something I wanted?" Kaylee asked.

Asher looked up from the food he was preparing. "Within reason."

"I want a change of clothes."

"That shouldn't be a problem. I'm sure we could find a seamstress who could modify some of her stock to fit you when we get to the next town."

"I don't want a dress."

Asher looked her over. "Why?"

"I don't like dresses."

"But you're a girl."

"So?"

"Girls wear dresses."

Kaylee rolled her eyes. "I haven't worn a dress in years and I'm still alive. Having sturdier clothes to travel in would be better. What if I ruin this dress?" Kaylee picked at the hem and held it up. "It's not the strongest material. I'll end up ripping it to shreds."

"The way you treat it, you might." Asher looked at the load of sticks she'd carried.

Kaylee pulled the scarf off her head. "Besides, if I were to wear a shirt and breeches, no one would notice my head. I could pass as a boy for a bit."

Asher looked at her bare head. "But you're a woman."

"So you've said. If I were to dress as a boy, it would be easier traveling."

"You don't understand me. You don't look like a boy. I honestly can't understand how the monks missed it. Your features are undeniably feminine."

Kaylee frowned and tried another angle. "I don't want to wear a dress. They're uncomfortable. They're cold and breezy. It is very difficult to wear it astride a horse. It would only be for traveling. When you want me to wear a dress in public, I would."

"I'll think on it."

Kaylee nodded. She stood and moved over to the packs near Denn. She moved a couple of things out of the way before finding her small bag. Her things were still there, but not in the same place. It was obvious that Asher had gone through it while she gathered wood. She lifted it up and asked, "Find anything interesting?"

Asher didn't even look her way. "What are you talking about?"

"You looked through my pack. Did you take anything?"

Asher whipped his head around to look at her. "I wouldn't take your things."

"Sure you would. You took me without even asking if I wanted to come with you."

Asher stood and crossed his arms over his chest. "You wouldn't have been able to stay there anyway."

"Doesn't matter."

She pulled out her father's book and felt the pages. He said it was important. He charged her to treat it well and keep it hidden from the world. From his fevered rantings, she assumed it had something to do with the history of the Blue Bloods. The one time she chanced a peek at it in the monastery, it hadn't made any sense. The random words jumbled together. Maybe if she read through the book one more time before she got to the castle, she might figure it out. Could she read it while they rode? Kaylee looked at Denn and decided she'd never be able to manage on the horse. It would have to wait.

CHAPTER FIVE

Asher broke a stick and threw the smallest piece into the fire, sending sparks into the air. Heat rolled off the blaze, chasing away the chill descending on the camp. The flames bathed Kaylee in a deep orange light.

Kaylee was different. She didn't act like a girl at all, but she was very much a woman. It surprised Asher how much he felt drawn to her. Four days into their journey, and he was completely lost.

He'd finally relented to her continued begging for different clothes, but with her legs encased in the loose fitting wool breeches and her homespun shirt flowing easily around her arms and chest, he was very distracted. A dress was a much better item of clothing for a woman. Except when Kaylee used hers to gather wood. He had seen more of her legs than he should have. Since then, he couldn't keep his mind off her.

Asher snapped another section of the stick and tossed it into the flames.

He needed to focus on the bounty she'd bring. The professors of lore at the king's castle would help her discover whatever hidden power she had. When he turned her over, she would be fine. They would train her and use her to keep the king rich and powerful.

And a grateful king would reward Asher handsomely. He had personally been responsible for finding more than forty Blue Bloods in his ten years as a bounty hunter. At sixteen, he learned his cousin was a Blue Blood, so he took her to the king. The reward was big enough to pay off his father's farm. He left the next year to search for more Blue Bloods. Every time, it had been easy and straightforward. With his second bounty, he hired a Blue Blood to enchant a talisman that would vibrate, indicating when a Blue Blood stood within a mile of him.

When one of them bled or manifested their power in any way, he could smell it, making it easier to pinpoint which woman he needed to approach to escort to the king. He often wondered if he had some strange gift similar to the Blue Bloods, but he never dared tell anyone he could smell them. He didn't know if the king would take him and keep him to train, or if he'd allow him to continue hunting for more Blue Bloods. He couldn't risk it. He enjoyed moving around on his own.

No one had found male Blue Bloods. Even so, when Asher first learned he could smell them, he'd cut himself to be sure what color he bled. A deep red put an end to his concerns.

It was still a mystery how the Blue Bloods came to be. No one could remember when it first started. Sketchy histories and scholars agreed that Blue Bloods lived among them for close to a millennium. Though the numbers decreased dramatically over the last few centuries, it was still common enough to find some in every section of the kingdom.

Kaylee spread out her bedroll. She lay down on one side of the fire across from where he sat. He didn't trust Kaylee to stay with him. He'd never been unsure of what to do with one of his bounties before. Once he explained the benefits and riches awaiting them at the king's palace they were always willing, even eager, to go. Some went to Inshansi on their own when they learned they bled blue.

Asher stood up and grabbed his bedroll. He placed it next to hers to indicate he would stay close, but he didn't lay in it right away. He moved back to the log near the fire and resumed his study of her.

Kaylee glanced at his bedroll, and she then rolled on her side, away from him. She placed her pack under her head for a pillow. Asher reached into his pocket and pulled out the cord he tied to her pack each night so that if she tried to leave while he slept, he'd know.

He was a light enough sleeper that if she moved much, he would wake. He didn't worry about needing to keep watch through the night. The king's soldiers kept the country free of ruffians and brigands. He'd never been disturbed in all his years of travel.

Soon Kaylee fell asleep. Her breathing slowed and she lay still. When he was convinced she was out, he banked the fire to make sure it continued to burn through the night without risk of it spreading if a wind came up. He quietly climbed onto his bedroll and pulled his cloak over him. He reached over to Kaylee's pack and tied the cord to the strap before he attached the other end to his wrist.

He eased himself into sleep, almost sure he'd be woken in the night to her trying to leave. He hoped she'd either try it right away or wait for at least four hours so he could get a good stretch in.

Denn snorted. Asher sat bolt upright. Immediately he looked over at Kaylee in the soft morning light. She turned to him in surprise, her brow furrowed.

"What?"

"You stayed." Asher blinked.

"You expected me to run?" She glanced toward the trees. "Where would I go?" she asked, repeating his words from the first night on the road.

Asher frowned. She was tough to read. It didn't help that she looked at him with sleepy eyes. Her shirt slipped a little, exposing her collar bone to the morning air. Her skin was lightly sprinkled with freckles under the thin layer of dirt and grime. Traveling was messy and he felt bad for her. He should make sure they stopped near a larger stream soon so she could clean up a little.

Asher busied himself with getting breakfast things ready. Kaylee slipped away into the trees but returned quickly. She carried some berries and wild roots in her clean hands. She must have found them close to the stream and washed them. His mouth watered. It would be nice to have a couple of berries to sweeten up the morning mush heating in his pot.

"Thanks," Asher said.

Kaylee nodded, gathered her bedroll, and packed quickly. Her efficiency impressed him. She knew how to travel and it pleased him to know he wouldn't have to do everything for her. This was definitely one of the easier bounties he'd taken on when it came to traveling in the wild.

They ate quickly, without speaking, ready to travel in less time than Asher would've taken on his own. He climbed onto Denn and reached down to offer Kaylee a hand up. She frowned briefly but got on without complaint. She sat stiffly at first. Asher realized she was probably saddle sore. She most likely hadn't ridden a horse at the monastery. He was impressed that she didn't complain, but Asher wished she would so he'd have a reason to get on her nerves. She talked more when she was angry.

He decided on a different tactic. He started at a walk, then urged Denn into a trot, then back to a walk, then a rough gallop. Denn obeyed without complaint, trusting his master. Besides a few grunts of surprise as the horse moved, Kaylee didn't say anything. Eventually Asher realized he'd tire Denn before Kaylee lost her cool. He slowed the horse down to a walk.

Not sure what to say, he kept quiet for a bit. Kaylee watched the road as they traveled.

"Looking for a place to hide?"

Kaylee snorted.

"What?" Asher asked.

Kaylee stayed silent and continued to watch the road. Asher studied the surrounding countryside. He searched it with new eyes, trying to see everything she might see. Would she run? He wished he could be sure of her.

CHAPTER SIX

Kaylee ignored Asher as they traveled the long, dusty road. When they left the forested area after breaking camp, Kaylee studied the land. How could a king possibly own so much, and yet never come near those areas? Her father had told her the king stayed in his palace and ran the country by sending men he trusted to do what he wanted.

Asher was one of those men. If the king trusted Asher, she knew she couldn't. She wanted to hate him, but he hadn't done anything to her besides taking her on this journey against her will. He'd been even kinder than her own father had been at times.

As they moved through the countryside, she realized she'd read some of the histories of the places they passed through. The monastery kept the records of all the previous kings, of the wars and hardships as well as the prosperity. Time had altered some of the landmarks, but she recognized them.

They stopped briefly for lunch, but were back on the horse sooner than Kaylee wished. It would've been nice to walk and stretch her legs and back, but Asher insisted she ride with him again. Eventually the sight of a tiny village met her eyes. Though it was only late afternoon, Asher decided to make it their place for the night. Kaylee didn't think it would be any different than the one they stopped at before, but this innkeeper was nowhere near as friendly. Asher was cautious and didn't seem to trust him as much as Master Rhett.

Kaylee knew he wouldn't have picked this inn if there had been any other choice, but in a place this small she figured it was lucky they had found a place to stay at all. At least they wouldn't sleep on the trail. The food cost extra at this inn. Master Rhett included it in the price of the room at his place. Asher stood at the front desk, hesitating when Master Nate told him the price of the room. Asher glanced back at Kaylee with a frown.

"We'll take one room."

She kept her mouth shut. She couldn't meet his eyes when he turned to her again. Asher joined her at the bottom of the stairs.

"Head on up," Asher said.

The room was smaller than the one at Master Rhett's. A lopsided bed, pushed against a rough wood wall, didn't look inviting. Kaylee figured she would have to sleep on the floor anyway. She walked in after Asher and placed her pack on the floor near the window and laid her bedroll out.

"You'll take the bed."

Kaylee looked up from smoothing her blanket out and examined the woven mat on the bed closer. Most likely full of bedbugs. "No thanks."

"I'll take the floor." Asher put his stuff down, took her blanket, and tossed it on the bed.

Kaylee sat on the small wooden stool, unsure. Asher put his things down and then washed up. He offered the stained towel to Kaylee when he finished.

"Let's eat."

"Do I stay dressed in these?" Kaylee asked, fingering the boy's clothing she'd finally managed to get from him.

"Probably best. Your hair's still too short to pass for a girl with no questions."

He took her into a noisy common room just off the front of the building where they paid for their lodging. It reminded Kaylee of one of the many taverns she and her father stayed in during their travels together. The serving girl seemed pleasant enough, but she looked tired and acted flippant toward the people she served.

She smiled big at Asher, and Kaylee got a look she'd never received before. Kaylee looked at Asher, unable to understand why he stifled a laugh. She held still and refused to be bothered by the interest of the people who watched them come in. Asher sat at the table and Kaylee joined him. He ordered dinner for them both but made sure to only ask for one mug.

Kaylee nodded her thanks.

"Where you from, stranger?" a small man at the bar asked.

"Come from the north," Asher said.

"No kidding. What you come down here for?"

Asher shrugged. "I like to travel this way now and again."

"You travel everywhere in the kingdom?" the man asked. "Ever been in the king's city?"

Asher nodded and let his gaze roam the room.

"What's the king gonna do now that he ain't the only royal wanting to run things?"

"What?" Asher asked, turning back to the man and looking at him more closely.

"Ain't you heard?" the man said after taking a big drink from his mug. "Rumor has it that there's someone claims she has the right and he don't."

"I haven't heard that yet. And a queen no less?" Asher turned his chair and looked the man over, trying to look unimpressed, but Kaylee was sure he was very interested in what the man had to say. "How long has that rumor been running?"

"Probably two or three months ago when I heard it first."

Asher looked confused for a moment. He didn't say anything until the man left the counter and came over to their table. He sat down between Kaylee and Asher. Kaylee slid over and ate in silence. She didn't feel the need to participate in the conversation, although she listened to what they said.

"Name's Zeb." He held his hand out to shake.

Asher took his hand and replied, "Asher."

Zeb looked over at Kaylee expectantly. She looked at Asher and he said, "That's Kale."

Zeb nodded but didn't offer his hand. "What happened to your head?"

Kaylee looked to Asher.

"It's none of your concern," Asher said.

"Did you have nits?" Zeb looked her over again. "Nasty things, they are. Only sure way to get rid of em is to cut all yer hair off and pick em off one by one."

Kaylee narrowed her eyes. She'd never heard of nits before. Zeb shuddered and turned away to face Asher again. Kaylee, relieved, let the two carry on without her.

"What do you think it would mean if the king isn't the true ruler?" Asher asked.

"Means you ought to decide which side would have the best chance of survival and join them," Zeb laughed.

"The king has Blue Bloods. I doubt this new challenger will be able to fight against him." Asher leaned back against his chair. "No one has bothered Inshansi for hundreds of years."

"If she had Blue Bloods she could."

"So this woman has her own army of Blue Bloods?" Asher looked at Kaylee briefly. Zeb looked at her too, with more interest this time. Asher turned back to Zeb. "What made her think she should be the ruler?"

Zeb shrugged. "I don't know that now, do I? I'm only saying what I heard said before."

"Three months ago?" Asher asked.

"At least." Zeb motioned for the serving girl to bring him another drink. She poured more into his mug and asked Asher if he wanted more. He refused but gave her a smile, which she returned eagerly. A flash of anger crossed Zeb's face, giving Kaylee a moment's concern. He quickly smiled for the girl, who turned and ignored him. Zeb's eyes turned dark.

"The king isn't doing much good for most of us around here," Zeb said.

"The king keeps the peace in the realm."

"At what cost?" Zeb said. "He taxes everyone. Insists on making any Blue Blood a slave. Had a friend once who lost his daughter to the king. He never sees her, though she's still alive. He's tried many times to visit her, but they always turn him away. The king rarely sends his soldiers here to do anything other than take our money." Zeb took a long drink from his mug. He glanced around the nearly empty room and leaned closer, speaking low. "Now, if you ask me, maybe this queen would be a better ruler."

Asher shook his head, but took a bite of his dinner instead of responding.

"Where you going after you leave here?" Zeb asked.

Asher turned to look at Zeb. "West."

Kaylee's eyes widened and she looked at Asher. Had he changed his mind? She ducked her head when she caught Zeb staring at her.

"I wish you well on your travels." Zeb stood and took one last drink from his mug. After he set it heavily on the table, he tossed down a small copper coin and walked out of the room. Kaylee couldn't understand Zeb's strange behavior. She studied Asher. Besides glancing in the direction he'd gone, Asher didn't seem bothered.

Asher leaned back and studied her in turn. She met his eyes, searching for any clue to his thoughts. Would he think Zeb a traitor to the king he seemed to worship? Or would this open his mind to the possibility the king was wrong?

Back in the room, Kaylee tried once more to sleep on the floor. Asher stopped her and lay down quickly. "Unless you plan to sleep snuggled up next to me, I suggest you take the bed."

Kaylee turned away and moved to the bed. She was tired and sore from riding the horse again all day, but she doubted she could fall asleep very easily with him so close. It hadn't been like this when they slept by the fire. Why did having walls around them make it feel so different?

In the early morning hours, Kaylee woke to the familiar sound of the rooster crowing. The sound reminded her of early hours at the monastery and studying in silence. She longed to do the same now, but all she had was her father's book. The monks forbade her to keep anything from her past. She didn't know how her father managed to hide this book from the monks when they first arrived. He told her where to find it in his room just before he died of the morbid sore throat. She hid it from the monks. Knowing she could freely look at it now sent gooseflesh down her arms.

She saw the book only once before her father's death. She found it in his room at home and started reading it when he caught her. That was the first time he'd ever lost his temper. He struck her across the face and ripped the book from her grasp. "Never touch this again." The harsh tone of his voice, nothing like what she was used to hearing, frightened her. Kaylee numbly nodded as she held her cheek. The sting of his words hit harder than the slap. Kaylee placed her hand on her cheek, remembering the pain.

She'd run from the room and hidden under her covers. Soon after, Kaylee's father came to her and held her close, whispering things she didn't understand. Two days later, they left, taking only what they could carry.

She quietly pulled the book out, turning it over in her hand to examine the worn leather binding. The leather, though cracked in places, felt soft to the touch. Kaylee ran her fingers over the swirl branded into the leather. A few small scars crisscrossed the cover.

Kaylee opened the book. She touched the pages inside. They felt stiff and fresh, as if she had formed the pulp and set it herself. She lifted the book to her face and breathed in deeply. No musty smell clung to it like the books in the monastery. It was a contradiction in ancient and new.

A rush of excitement surged through her as she ran her fingers over the words. The watered-down blue ink looked so different than what she knew. She helped make the ink the monks used. The ink they used would have been much darker had this been made of the same substance. The large words dwarfed the ones she wrote with the quill in her labors as she copied down the religious volumes the monks so carefully crafted.

It was like the ink had bled slightly as it touched the page. Some of the words were odd and unfamiliar, but most of them were very easy to decipher. Many letters had long tails and swirls. The writer seemed to jot down things at random. She couldn't really see any form that made sense. Kaylee turned the page and examined it. The same disorder filled each page. Kaylee continued to turn pages, looking for something that might make sense. In the upper corner of each set of pages, tucked into the spine of the book, appeared an unfamiliar symbol. At first she wondered if they were numbers, but they didn't resemble any she knew.

The jumbled symbols didn't appear to be individual letters. Triangles with slashes through them. Circles with curving lines. An open box with a triangle nestled inside. Another box with an upside down triangle, and another with a circle. So many different shapes in various designs. Their beauty mesmerized Kaylee. She studied them in fascination.

She was so immersed in the book, she started when Asher stirred and moaned as he woke. She closed the book, tucking it under her blanket. She didn't want him to ask about it.

Asher stood and stretched, rubbing his hip. His messy hair sticking up made Kaylee glad her hair was gone. However, she hadn't used any of the paste on it for days now and the brown stubble on her head had begun to grow. It was soft in one direction yet prickled her fingers when she rubbed it the other way. At least she didn't have to wear the scarf anymore. She was surprised when Asher finally allowed her to wear men's clothes. It made things easier as they traveled.

Asher turned and looked at her sitting on the side of the bed with her back to the wall. He cleared his throat. "Do you need some privacy?"

Kaylee considered him for a moment.

"To change, or freshen up?"

Kaylee nodded and Asher left the room. She pulled the book out and tucked it back into her bag, reluctant to let it go. Something about it made her feel whole.

She longed to talk with her father about the book. If he were still alive, he'd never let her read it. She closed her eyes against the sting of tears as guilt washed over her. He told her where to find the book and made her promise to keep it hidden as well. He'd be so disappointed in her for getting kicked out of the monastery.

Kaylee quickly used the chamber pot and threw its contents out the window. She didn't need to do much to change. She pulled her socks and boots back on and longed again for the comfort of her robe. Although she was becoming more used to them, pants felt strange. She admitted that she liked it better than the bulky dress. When she stepped out of the room, Asher stood waiting by the door.

"I'll be right behind you." He stepped into the room and spoke over his shoulder. "Go on down."

Kaylee moved slowly down the stairs, surprised to find the main room empty. A side door opened. Kaylee turned toward it.

"What can I get you?" The serving girl from last night blocked Kaylee's way. The girl smiled at her with wide eyes that blinked repeatedly.

Kaylee resisted the urge to rub her head self-consciously. She glanced up the stairs expecting to see Asher, but she remained alone with the girl. She shook her head and mumbled a response in as low a voice as she could. "Nothing."

"Oh, come now. I'm sure you'll be having breakfast."

Kaylee shook her head and looked back toward the stairs again. Where was Asher? She wanted to eat, but she didn't dare order a meal until he was there to request it himself.

"If you want to slip into the kitchen with me, I'll make sure you get something good." The girl put her hand on her hip and arched her back just slightly. Kaylee wondered if maybe she was having some back pains, but the look on her face was all smiles and winks.

Kaylee ducked her head and looked away. She found an empty corner and tried to move out of the way, but the serving girl stepped into her path.

"I'm Melina." She smiled big, blinking rapidly. Kaylee wondered if the girl had something in her eyes. "What's your name?" she asked as Kaylee tried to slip past her again.

Kaylee cleared her throat. "Kale."

"How long you been working for Master Herst?" Melina moved closer.

Kaylee took a step back and looked behind her again. Where was he? "Not long."

"Is he a good master? I'm sure if you wanted to, you could get hired on here real easy. Master Nate could always use a strong man like you to help around the inn." Melina took Kaylee's arm and squeezed the muscles, sending an uncomfortable shiver through Kaylee. Melina seemed surprised for a minute, and Kaylee wondered if she finally realized Kaylee wasn't a boy. Was that why she'd been talking to her so much? When Melina didn't remove her hand and stared at a spot over Kaylee's shoulder, she worried something was wrong.

Kaylee took Melina's hand off her arm and tried to get her attention. Melina stood still, barely breathing. She stared, not looking at anything Kaylee could see. Kaylee looked around the room for help, but they were still alone. Should she slip away and hope Melina snapped out of it, or should she try to wake her?

Kaylee tapped Melina on the shoulder, but it elicited no response. A terrible thought crossed Kaylee's mind, and she wondered if maybe her powers had manifest. What if she hurt Melina by touching her?

Kaylee snapped her fingers, trying to get her to make eye contact, but Melina still stared. Kaylee walked around Melina, finally deciding to pull her toward a chair. If Melina lost her balance, the fall would hurt. Maybe she could put her somewhere out of the way until whatever happened to her wore off.

Taking her by the upper arms, Kaylee pulled her backward, and Melina crumpled. She grunted as the full weight of the serving girl nearly pulled her down as well. She managed to drag her over to a wooden bench by one of the serving tables and hefted her onto the seat.

"What did you do?" Asher asked.

Kaylee straightened quickly and shook her head in bewilderment. "I have no idea what happened. She was talking to me non-stop, but then touched my arm and all of a sudden she just froze."

Asher narrowed his eyes. He moved quickly to her side and examined Kaylee first before he turned to Melina. "Is it your powers?" he whispered.

"I don't know. She grabbed me to keep me from walking away and then she just stopped."

Asher took a step back and frowned at Kaylee. He opened his mouth. When he tried to speak, he was interrupted by Melina's voice. "What do you say, Kale, you want to—" Melina jumped up from the bench, looking around the room as if she were confused. When she saw Asher, she squeaked and bobbed a quick curtsey before she rushed from the room.

Asher watched her leave, his mouth open, and then eyed Kaylee. He swallowed slowly and took a step forward, hesitating midstep, and then touched Kaylee's arm where Melina had touched.

Nothing happened. A flood of relief washed over her. Hopefully it wasn't her powers and Melina would be fine.

Asher gave Kaylee one more long considering look. Without a word, he walked to the common room.

It was no surprise they left quickly after breakfast. Melina kept giving her strange looks and Kaylee couldn't wait to put some distance between them. They broke for lunch on the side of the road. Kaylee walked around, trying to ease the aches out of her back and the stinging in her legs, grateful she insisted on breeches. If her legs hadn't been protected, she'd be highly uncomfortable.

Asher pulled out some dried meat and hard bread. They ate in silence. Kaylee smiled to herself when she realized he was tired of talking without getting any response from her. If she weren't mad at him for giving her no choice, she'd probably enjoy having a conversation. He seemed bright enough, but a little cocky.

CHAPTER SEVEN

As Asher prepared the horse to move after lunch, he watched Kaylee with interest. She eyed Denn with wide eyes, frowning. Her movements were stiff, but not as bad as when she'd first dismounted. Deciding to take pity on her for a moment, Asher started to walk, leading Denn forward. Kaylee fell into step with him.

"Thanks."

"Not a problem," Asher said. "It will do Denn good to not carry both of us."

Kaylee looked at the big horse as if she didn't believe it, but she didn't call him on it. Asher fought a smile.

"Tell me about the monastery."

Kaylee looked over at Asher. "What do you want to know?"

It was nice that Kaylee actually spoke instead of her usual grunt. Maybe he should be nicer more often. "What did you do there?"

"I copied a few different books. And I was involved with the crops."

"What did you grow?"

"Mostly vegetables and some grains. We didn't have money to buy from the village."

Asher debated within himself if he should ask more questions. He couldn't tell from her body language if Kaylee would welcome more discussion. Deciding it was best to ease into things with her, he didn't press. They walked in silence for most of the afternoon. Although they hadn't spoken more than a few words since lunch, Asher felt like he had made progress. She didn't scowl at him and the few times he did speak, she gave a simple answer instead of ignoring him.

The countryside was quiet. No other travelers going toward the king's city. A small tinker's wagon stopped to offer something, and Asher looked over the man's wares. When his eyes rested on the small box similar to Master Rhett's chess set, Asher asked to see it.

"Here you go, sir," the tinker said. "Made in the king's city itself. Carved by a master. Only seven coppers."

Asher shook his head. "Seven? That's ridiculous. I know this carver you speak of and he only charges two."

The tinker shifted his weight from foot to foot. "Well, tis true the carver charges less, but I do have to feed Peach here once in a while. Makes it only fair for me to charge a bit more for all my work in bringing it out to these parts."

Asher handed the chess set back to the tinker. He heard Kaylee sigh next to him and vowed to do what he could to talk the man down. He could get it cheaper in Inshansi but by then, Kaylee would no longer be with him to play. He felt an unusual desire to please her, to test that mind of hers and see if she were truly different from all the other women he'd known.

"Perhaps you'd be interested in a bit of dried fruit to supplement your food supplies. I recently replenished my stock. You'll get first pick."

Asher glanced at Kaylee. She didn't speak, or even lean forward to see the items the tinker was talking of, but the look in her eyes made him sure she was tired of their regular fare.

"Show me what you've got."

The tinker quickly placed the chess set back in its spot and moved a few cases around, and then he pulled out a small trunk and opened it. Inside lay cloth bags, neatly placed in rows. The smell of a blend of fruits Asher hadn't eaten in ages impressed him. He didn't dare ask the price. Hoping his face had remained passive, he looked at the tinker.

"Besides these, I have some nuts and crocks of honey. I'd bet they would add much to your meager supplies." The tinker looked at the bags on Denn's saddle.

"How much?" Asher asked.

The tinker met his eyes, and Asher knew he was being judged. He glanced at Kaylee, but her eyes roamed the wares inside the wagon.

"For three bags of fruit, one bag of nuts and this crock of honey—two gold." The tinker opened the honey and held it up for Asher's inspection.

"One gold, and two silvers," Asher countered. "I pick the fruits. And you throw in the chess set."

"Done." The tinker replaced the lid and Asher had a sinking feeling he'd countered too high.

Asher pulled out the bags of fruit and nuts and placed them on top of the chess set. The tinker held his hand out eagerly. With a mental shrug, Asher pulled out the coins from his small pouch on his belt, making sure to show the tinker he didn't have more than a few coppers left. The bounty Kaylee would bring would more than make up for the overpriced goods from the tinker. And the way her eyes kept straying to the box in his hands, he knew he'd get a bit more interaction from her now.

Asher took a few nuts from the bag and shared them with Kaylee before stowing things away on Denn. They resumed their journey in the same companionable silence as before. To Asher, it seemed like Kaylee wanted to speak.

He forced himself to wait for her to bring it up. His constant questions had been an obvious irritation to her and he vowed to change tactics. He was disappointed but not surprised when she remained silent for the rest of the afternoon.

At their camp for the night, Asher unloaded the packs off the horse and watched as Kaylee got right to work gathering up the wood and starting the fire. Asher had stayed at this spot before. An active stream a few yards from the roadside offered the perfect place to fish. He pulled out his line and hook, and set about to catch some dinner. Before long, two good-sized trout lay still in the grass, gutted and ready for roasting over the fire.

Asher cleaned himself up in the stream then started dinner, mixing some flour with a few of their new supplies from the tinker, happy it wasn't more of the same hard bread mixed with dried meat and a couple of things Kaylee managed to gather from the surrounding area. This time he'd have a little sweet cake to go with the fish.

Kaylee moved over to the stream. Squatting beside it, she cupped the water in her hands to wash her face and neck. Her delicate hands rubbed up her arms to just above her elbows. A flush of heat hit Asher that had nothing to do with the fire he was cooking over. He forced himself to look away. To give her privacy. It was hard to keep his distance from her. He had to remember she belonged to the king.

And once her powers manifested, she would be able to exact revenge on him if he treated her wrong on this journey. If she snapped, Asher would have no way to force her to come. He was sure only his threat against the monks made her agree.

Kaylee started eating and pulled out her small book again. *Why does she look at it so often?* It didn't look like any he'd seen before. Not many people read, but the book seemed important to her. He fought the urge to move next to her and read with her.

"Tell me about that book."

Kaylee closed it and tucked it under her shirt. "It's nothing."

"Of course it's something. Where'd you get it?"

Kaylee shook her head and refused to answer. He sensed her discomfort. Better to take it easy and learn what he could over the next two weeks.

CHAPTER EIGHT

Kaylee lay in her bedroll and felt him tie the cord to her pack again, but she didn't move. The information Asher gave her about the king and what he had planned for her as a Blue Blood still worried her. Was another ruler really trying to gain power? Asher didn't seem to give the man's complaints at the inn much thought, but with this news, how could Asher still take her to King Inwer?

Kaylee also worried that whatever power she was supposed to have would not be useful. Or worse, what if it were so powerful that the king would use her as a weapon? Asher said some of the Blue Bloods he'd traveled with had already snapped and knew what they were, as if they understood it intuitively. She thought for sure the situation with Melina had something to do with her power, but why didn't Asher think so?

She eased into sleep, wondering what kind of power she might develop. Asher turned, brushing up against her briefly. A shiver ran down her arm. His breathing was slow and steady. A man sounded different when he slept than when awake. He didn't quite grunt or moan, but he made noises she didn't understand.

Kaylee drifted between sleep and wakefulness until something out of the ordinary caught her ear. Denn shuffled his hooves a little but didn't make any sound of alarm. Kaylee opened her eyes to peer into the darkness. The fire behind her helped illuminate the clearing. The trees just beyond the rim of light loomed large and dark. Was something there? Denn didn't seem bothered at all so she decided it must be nothing and closed her eyes.

Sleep had barely overtaken her when she jerked in surprise at Denn's snort of alarm. She sat up, then scrambled to her knees as a dark shadow reached for her. She dodged the attack and felt arms miss her.

"Asher! Wake up!"

The shadow that jumped for her quickly struck Asher, whose body spasmed and lay still.

Had the shadow killed him? Kaylee's stomach dropped. She debated between trying to help Asher and running. When the huge, shadowed man turned toward her, she grabbed her bag and bolted. The cord tied to Asher's arm brought her up short. She yanked at it, cringing when Asher's arm raised and jerked but the cord didn't break.

She dropped the pack and ran but strong arms grabbed her from behind. A large, rough bag covered her head. Someone shoved her hands roughly behind her back and tied them. She felt herself thrown over a horse's back and grunted hard as the air rushed out of her lungs.

She kicked and struggled until Denn shrieked and reared back. Kaylee rolled off, unable to use her hands to stop herself. She fell hard. Her arm cracked underneath her a moment before her head struck something hard, knocking her unconscious.

Asher woke up and immediately vomited. His head pounded worse than the few times he'd gotten drunk. The mid-day sun hurt his eyes. He squinted to cut out the painful glare. Moving slowly allowed him to take stock of his situation. He reached up and gently probed the back of his head, feeling a contusion larger than the three fingers he explored it with. Dried blood matted his hair, giving proof to a wound in the lump.

Had he been attacked? Asher looked around carefully. Denn was gone. Asher brought his fingers to his mouth and whistled for his horse. "She took him." Asher cursed loudly. He should never've trusted her. "She fooled me." Asher crouched for a moment before trying to stand. Once sure of his balance, he straightened up. Not daring to move until the vertigo passed, he looked around. Kaylee's bedroll and the pack he was tied to lay on the ground. Asher bent to grab her things, nearly blacking out. He dropped to his knees and picked up the pack. It was still closed but the folded over flap was untied and the small bundle on the top had nearly worked its way out. She would never have left without that bag. It held everything she possessed.

After a few minutes, his dizziness subsided enough for him to search the campground. There had been a struggle. Stones from the fire pit were out of place and grooves in the dirt from where a foot dragged at one point disappeared into small bushes.

There were at least two bandits who'd attacked them. Kaylee must have fought hard. He cheered silently, knowing whoever took her was probably roughed up as well. He followed the footprints in the dirt leading to Denn's spot. The horse had reared back. Someone tried to ride him. The saddle and the blanket were gone, but his bags remained where he tucked them under the bushes.

A dark spot on the ground caught his eye. Blood in the dirt and a smear on a rock jutting up. As he touched it, panic hit. The blood was blue. He searched for more, finding some near Denn's hoof prints. What happened to her? He didn't see her footprints again among the scattered prints as he wandered the area near where Denn had been.

Asher couldn't think. He whistled once more for Denn, hoping the horse had taken off when they'd been attacked and would return to him. They could've stolen the saddle. One like that would be worth a lot. He reached for his coin purse, relieved to find it still tucked away under his shirt. Asher sat down on his blanket and opened his pack. He didn't have much for medicine, but he did keep a flask of whisky for emergencies. This was the perfect time for a swallow.

Asher took a few moments trying to figure out what to do. Without his horse, the village was three days away, if he could manage to walk that far with the headache that wouldn't let go. He'd buy another horse from someone there and decide what to do next. He doubted whoever had taken Kaylee would go to the village. He had no way to track them on foot.

Asher rolled Kaylee's blanket into his, tucked her pack into the top of his and picked up his things. If he ever found Denn, he'd give the horse a good rub down and make sure he got some extra feed the next time. It was horrible to carry so much.

As each laborious step progressed, Asher's hopes dimmed. He set the packs down and reluctantly sifted through them. He could only carry the necessities. He put what he'd need to survive in one bag, and things of comfort or convenience in another. As the chess set found its way in the bag he would leave, Asher shook his head. It was too bad he hadn't been able to use it. *Wonder if I ever will.*

Thoughts of Kaylee raced through his brain. Her, up in that tree with a stern face and full lips. The way she carried those branches, the gentle touch of her hand on his back as they rode on Denn. An ache formed in his chest as each thought whizzed by. She was more than just his bounty. She was his friend, and he was determined to get her back.

CHAPTER NINE

When Kaylee woke, the pain in her arm almost matched the pain in her head. The jarring of the horse she was draped over forced a moan from her before she slipped into unconsciousness again.

The second time Kaylee woke, she knew she was lying still. Someone pulled on her arm. Pain shot through her body. She screamed before blacking out once more. The third time was not nearly as bad. Her arm still ached horribly but it felt much better in a way. Her head demanded all of her attention now. The slightest movement caused her to hiss in pain and clench her eyes shut.

A deep voice spoke. "You alive?"

Kaylee mumbled, "Yes." She opened her eyes and looked at a huge man squatting beside her.

"Good," a nasally voice said.

Kaylee focused on the smaller man standing behind and to the left. He looked familiar in a strange sort of way, but she couldn't figure where she'd seen him before. A narrow nose and close set eyes could have belonged to lots of people. He glanced over his shoulder. "We need to be off soon. Can ye ride?"

She focused again on the large man. He didn't look like the kind to take no for an answer, so she tried to sit up. The movement sent a jolt a pain through her arm and shoulder.

"Don't move it like that. You broke it when the horse threw you," the big man's voice rumbled. He reached for her arm as if to examine her. Something about his gentle eyes put her at ease. Although they were the ones who had attacked the camp last night, she didn't fear them.

Kaylee vaguely remembered being on the back of Denn before he threw her. Her head throbbed as she recalled Asher being struck during the attack. Had they killed him? It shouldn't matter to her. He'd basically taken her against her will, even if he had been kind. Still, she hoped he was alive. Not because she expected to be rescued, but because he didn't deserve to die.

Kaylee fought the tears and clenched her jaw so she wouldn't cry out in pain again. She gingerly touched her left arm, feeling her way through the aches. Each place she touched felt tender and sore, but when she moved to the next section of arm, the previous location no longer hurt. She reached back up to her bicep and touched a little harder. It no longer felt the same as it had a moment ago.

Kaylee quickly moved her hand down her arm feeling every little pain. As soon as her hand brushed over the area, the pain flashed stronger than before and miraculously felt better. Kaylee placed her hand on the back of her head where the pain there centered. An intense pain shot through her head. She nearly fainted again. Just as suddenly, it was gone. A gasp from the man to the side of her gave witness to her own thoughts. She was healed. Somehow her touch had healed herself.

"That's your power?" the little man asked. "Healing?"

Kaylee turned, eyes wide and mouth open. Somehow her powers had manifested. Breaking a bone must have been enough of a shock to her system that the *snap* had occurred.

"You didn't know?" the huge man who'd woken her asked. He leaned back and crossed his arms, making his biceps look twice as big.

Kaylee shook her head.

"We helped you snap?" the little man asked.

"That might not be a good thing, Zeb," the large man said.

"But, Dolf, the queen will pay big for something like this," Zeb said.

Kaylee looked closer at Zeb and realized where she'd seen him before. He was the one who talked to Asher about a queen at that last inn.

"Where are you taking me?" Kaylee asked. "Who is this queen?"

Zeb grunted. "She ain't from here."

Dolf rolled his eyes. "Quiet."

"Why?" Zeb asked. "She already knows some. Why not tell her?"

Dolf scowled at Zeb and motioned for him to shut up. Dolf squatted in front of Kaylee still sitting on the ground. "What do you think of King Inwer?"

Kaylee frowned. Getting into a discussion about politics was never a good idea. Yet, these men seemed to be backing a queen willing to oppose him.

"It's plain to see you don't want to be a slave to the king. And a slave is what you'd be." Dolf hitched his head to indicate the direction they'd been traveling from. "With that bounty hunter, I doubt you had any choice in the matter. Not us. I'll ask you right now. Will ye come with us to Queen Sherr? She has some mighty strong reasons to see the king dethroned. And with your help, you could make it happen."

"Won't I just be a slave to this new queen?"

Dolf looked deep into Kaylee's eyes and smiled. "Naw, Queen Sherr would give you true authority. Let you make your own decisions. And being her only Blue Blood, you'd have more to offer than if you were just one of the king's many women."

Zeb stood quietly, watching the trees behind them. How could Kaylee decide? She could never allow herself to go to the king, but would a queen be any better? Would she be able to help others with her new powers?

"Where is this queen? How far from King Inwer's lands?"

"About as far as you can get without falling in the ocean." Dolf smiled, making the skin around his eyes crinkle. "Ever seen the ocean?"

Kaylee shook her head.

"Ah, that right there is reason enough to come with us."

Dolf took a step closer, his intimidating size looming over her. His deep voice rumbled softly. "Queen Sherr is a good woman. She'd take care of you."

Kaylee considered things for a moment. She could never allow herself to be taken to the king. Her father had been so adamant about it. If going to a queen were the only sure way to do it, then that's the way things had to be.

"I'll go."

CHAPTER TEN

A sher walked for hours. It was slow going even with his lighter packs. His head could only take so much. He pushed through his exhaustion but eventually collapsed, hitting his head on the ground. He didn't lose consciousness, but the pain made him wish he had.

As he steadied himself to stand, a familiar sound reached his ears. Hope leaped in his chest and he whistled again. The object on the edge of his vision galloped toward him. Denn had returned.

The horse trotted forward and shook his mane as he stopped in front of Asher. Asher took a couple steps forward, then hollered for joy. He could begin his search immediately.

Asher reached up and took hold of his muzzle, placing one hand on the space between Denn's eyes. He rested his forehead on the horse, trying not to become too emotional. He'd worried, knowing whoever had taken him wouldn't care for Denn as well as he could. He couldn't help laughing when he imagined the way the thief would have been bucked off when he didn't expect it.

Asher considered going back to where he'd left the extra pack hidden under the bushes at the camp ground, yet he knew he had to follow and find Kaylee soon. If they got too far away, he'd be tracking them blind.

Denn waited patiently for Asher to load him with the packs he did have. "Sorry, boy, but I'm glad you're here to take these off my hands. When I can, I'll find you something good."

Vertigo attacked when he moved to mount too quickly, but he eventually got on. Denn was in a hurry to move. Asher pulled him back to slow him down. He turned the horse around and followed his tracks. It would be easy enough at first to return to where Denn had left the kidnappers, but after that it would depend on what he found. The talisman would let him know when he got within a mile.

Kaylee had never met anyone who smelled as bad as Zeb. It wasn't just an unwashed body. He had an odor about him that made Kaylee wish she could stop breathing. Having him riding behind her made it difficult to find relief. At least the forward movement of the horse kept him mostly downwind.

Their speed indicated they were in a hurry. The bouncing of the horse would have been excruciating before, but with her newfound power she was actually enjoying the ride. If Zeb weren't behind her, she might have even loved it. She no longer had to worry about being saddle sore. Though she'd almost become accustomed to it with Asher, she merely needed to place her hands on her aching muscles and she felt better immediately. Kaylee wondered on the extent of her powers. Was she able to heal anything? And was it just her, or could she affect another person? She couldn't wait to learn.

When her stomach rumbled, she placed a hand on her middle. There was only one way to heal hunger and her hands wouldn't do it. "How much longer until we'll stop?"

Zeb chuckled. "Can't you handle the ride?"

"I could use some food."

Zeb let go of the reins with one hand and pulled something out of a saddle bag. He pushed it forward and Kaylee took it gratefully. It was more of the same type of dry bread used for traveling but it was better than nothing. She ate the entire thing and wished for more.

Zeb kicked his horse slightly to catch up to Dolf. "Will we stop in the usual place?" Zeb asked. "She's hungry."

Dolf nodded and urged his horse forward into a gallop.

"Hold on," Zeb said as he kicked his own horse. Kaylee had ahold of the mane, but still bumped against Zeb's chest. He grabbed her around the middle for a moment while she gained her balance, and then let go to hold the reins better. It was awkward to gallop two on the horse with her in front. She didn't understand why she wasn't riding behind him. Soon she got the rhythm of the horse's movements, almost feeling like she wouldn't fall off. Maybe they'd get her a horse of her own. They seemed more reasonable than Asher.

They moved off the main road and into a densely wooded area. Dolf went first and soon dismounted his horse. He moved a section of bush out of the way, revealing a cleverly hidden cave. The large opening allowed the horses to enter riderless. Zeb got off and pulled Kaylee down. She followed Dolf into the cave at Zeb's direction.

It took a moment for her eyes to adjust to the darkness of the cave, but Dolf quickly struck a spark and ignited a torch soaked in something flammable. Kaylee looked away from the flame toward casks of whisky lining the corner. Leather satchels hung from protrusions in the rock. Some roughly carved stools and a pile of hay lay to her right. A bulky table had some metal plates and cups stacked upside down neatly in the center. The cave looked almost as comfortable as her cell in the monastery.

Zeb spoke quietly with Dolf for a few minutes. Kaylee heard her name mentioned as well as that of the queen. Dolf shook his head, but Zeb seemed intent on his purpose. Dolf looked at Kaylee, studying her for a moment. He finally nodded and Zeb let out a little whoop. Zeb walked past Kaylee. "Come sit down."

Kaylee followed him and sat on the smaller chair. Zeb eyed her across the table. The way he looked her over sent goose flesh across her skin. "Here's how I see it. You have a power that is untrained. If you let us help you learn your abilities, you'll be able to do a lot more. And when the queen sees your value, she'll offer you a lot in return."

"How do you plan to teach me about my powers?"

Zeb smiled. "By practicing, of course."

"You want me to heal things?"

Dolf dropped a saddle onto the floor near the table and sat on it.

"Dolf, you game?"

Dolf raised one eyebrow for a moment, and then he shrugged. He pulled his sleeve up, revealing dark curly hair on a large forearm. He lay his arm on the table. He nodded to Zeb. Kaylee flinched when Zeb took his knife and sliced a thin gash down the length of Dolf's arm. Dolf didn't breathe any differently than he had before the cut, but Kaylee knew it had to hurt.

Zeb looked at Kaylee. "Heal him."

"What?"

"We need to see what you can do."

"I don't know if I can."

"Try," Zeb said.

Dolf didn't speak, but he looked at Kaylee patiently. She made eye contact, surprised to see pain deep within. That was the only reason she reached forward. The slickness of the blood as she placed her hand on his arm was disconcerting. The hair tickled her palm until she pressed down. Having no clue how to heal him, she hoped just placing her hand there would do it. Looking expectantly into his eyes, she realized there was no change.

Dolf looked down at her hand on his arm. Kaylee lifted her hand and instead touched the cut with her finger.

The edges of the wound began to swell as the tissue bled out, Kaylee couldn't believe Dolf didn't show more indication of pain. What kind of training or experience taught him to behave like that? Kaylee focused her attention on his wound. Blood pooled in the gash. Although Zeb hadn't cut deep enough to damage the muscles, it still bled freely. Something like this should be quickly wrapped to stop the blood, but they didn't seem to be in any hurry.

Kaylee tried to remember what she had done to heal herself. Nothing concrete came to mind. She had just hurt and then touched where she felt the pain. After touching it, the pain melted away. Even her arm that had been broken as far as she could tell had healed quickly with no sign of any injury.

Kaylee looked back into Dolf's eyes. He pressed his lips together but didn't speak.

"Any time now," Zeb said.

"I don't know how to do it. I don't understand how it works."

"We know it works on you." Zeb pulled her hand off Dolf's injured arm and slashed across her knuckles with his knife. Kaylee squeaked in shock and yanked her hand out of his. Cradling her wounded hand in the other one, she squeezed and the wound healed.

Dolf stood and took Zeb's knife, stabbing it into the table top. "That was uncalled for."

Zeb ignored the larger man and leaned forward, taking Kaylee's hand to inspect it. "How'd it work? Make it work on him."

Kaylee reached for Dolf's arm again and tried to do whatever it was she had done to herself. Nothing happened.

"Maybe you can't heal another person." Zeb sounded sad. He turned to look at Dolf. "Sorry, man."

Dolf shrugged and pulled a dirty cloth out of his shirt. He pressed it to his cut and Kaylee cringed.

"Here," she said. "Let me clean it up first."

"No need, miss," Dolf said.

"I insist." Kaylee took the rag then stood and looked around the cave room. "Do you have any water?"

Zeb jerked his head toward the corner. Kaylee rushed over to the water barrel and dunked the rag in it. She squeezed it out onto the floor and then dunked it in once more. On her way back to Dolf, her foot found an uneven spot in the cave floor and she tripped. She hit hard on her knee just feet from the table.

"Ouch," Kaylee grunted. Dolf offered her a hand to stand and she took it as the throbbing pain began. As soon as she made contact with Dolf, a strange tingle developed in her hand that left quickly. She grabbed her knee to rub away the pain just as Dolf whistled.

"It's gone," he said.

"What?" Kaylee looked up. Zeb stood and moved around the table.

Dolf held his arm out for both of them to see. The blood still smeared across his arm, but the cut had closed.

"You healed me," Dolf said.

"How?" Zeb asked at the same time Kaylee did.

"When you touched me just now, as I offered to help you up. It happened so fast I didn't know it at first." Dolf rolled his arm back and forth, wiggling his fingers and twisting his wrist.

Kaylee offered him the wet rag. He wiped the blood from his skin. "Amazing." Dolf looked up and smiled at Kaylee.

"Let's do it again," Zeb said.

Dolf shook his head.

"Come on. Once more." Zeb reached for his knife.

Dolf pulled out his own blade and motioned for Zeb to offer his arm. Zeb considered it for a moment before he said, "Another time."

After riding for hours, Asher wondered if he could ever catch them. He let Denn take the lead. He watched for the trail occasionally, easily spotting Denn's hoof prints and the flattened grass as they backtracked along the road.

When they returned to the forested area, it got harder to see where Denn had been, forcing Asher to pay closer attention. He dismounted a few times, but soon resumed his place on Denn's back and they continued on. If Asher were unable to get Kaylee back, he wouldn't dare tell the king he lost a Blue Blood.

Asher camped for the night in a protected area, making sure his fire was small and sheltered. He didn't want a repeat of the attack. It was odd that it happened in the first place. This part of the country was never known for bandits. The king made sure his entire kingdom was protected.

Traveling injured exhausted him. He worried about staying awake or waking up quickly enough if someone attacked. He kept Denn close, so if anything else out of the ordinary happened, the horse would alert him.

Asher kept his bow and knife close to him. He rubbed the back of his head where the bandits struck before. He didn't even know for sure how many of them he was dealing with. He never saw a thing. He thought of the blood on the rocks near where Denn had been tied up. The amount of blood didn't bode well for Kaylee.

CHAPTER ELEVEN

Three days into their journey away from the cave, Kaylee finally had her own horse. Zeb was more tolerable at a distance. The odd man seemed to enjoy their practice sessions. Sometimes he was fast with the knife, other times he ran it slowly down her skin as if he were being careful to apply just the right amount of pressure. She healed herself easily enough, barely registering the pain, but the look in his eyes concerned her.

Each time she bled, the blue still seemed surreal. She rarely had reason to see her own blood. Living a pretty sheltered life in a monastery, injury was a rare thing. And since the blue blood had manifested at fifteen, she'd been extra careful in order to stay hidden.

Dolf frowned every time they practiced. More than once, she heard Dolf talking in a quiet voice to Zeb, who only laughed and pulled his bone handled knife out again. Dolf never cringed away from the knife, but he stayed away when it was out. His actions made Kaylee wonder if she should be more careful not to upset Zeb. Dolf seemed to be the one in charge, but only by a fraction.

Zeb sat near the fire and trimmed his fingernails with his knife. Kaylee's eyes were drawn to the glimmer of light on the blade, fascinated by the knife. She had seen it up close plenty of times, so she couldn't quite understand her interest in it.

She wanted to hold it. To take it out of his hands and do to him what he'd done to her. Kaylee started when she realized where her thoughts had gone. She was a monk, or had been trained as one. She should forgive those who hurt her. She had no reason to hold any anger toward Zeb. She healed herself each time he cut her. Master Falon would be disappointed in her.

But each time Zeb came close, she wished she dared cause him the same kind of pain. If it had something to do with her powers manifesting, she didn't want these powers.

When Zeb tucked his knife away, Kaylee met his eyes. He watched her with an expression she didn't understand. Lately, each time he looked at her so intensely, her skin crawled.

Dolf moved closer to Kaylee and handed her a plate with food on it. She gratefully took it and kept her eyes on the meal, hoping Zeb would quit looking at her. Dolf remained close, his large presence comforted her.

He was strong and slow to anger making it easy to relax. It was impossible to be calm near Zeb. His blade wasn't the only thing that made her nervous. The way his eyes traveled over her sent shivers down her spine.

Kaylee took a bite of the meal and asked, "What is this meat?"

"Rabbit today," Dolf said.

"How'd you get a rabbit?"

Dolf patted the leather strap tucked into his belt. "Sling."

Kaylee nodded. She'd used one of those before she'd gone to the monastery. Her father taught her enough to survive if needed. Maybe Dolf would let her try it. "Dolf, can I help next time?"

"No need." Dolf pulled on the strap. "I'm a good shot."

She hated being so dependent on these men. She would much rather be back in her little protected life at the monastery. There she had felt useful. Valued. Now, she felt too much like a possession.

Kaylee lay on her bedroll and looked at the stars peeking through the canopy of trees above her. She didn't understand why she always thought of Asher as she went to bed. She missed hearing his breathing next to her. Dolf stayed away from her and made sure he was always close to Zeb. They took turns on the watch, leaving Kaylee to sleep through the night.

The howl of a coyote in the distance woke Kaylee. She turned, her back to the fire so she could look out into the trees. Nothing seemed immediately threatening, so she allowed herself to relax. She shifted into a more comfortable position and caught Zeb watching her closely. She suddenly wished to be surrounded by coyotes instead.

Asher was close. The fire's remains in the pit were less than a day old. He'd lost the trail for a bit a few days earlier until he found a cave where they had camped. It was luck that he found it in the first place. Asher had gotten off the horse to look for tracks when Denn stopped in front of some branches. They moved differently than the surrounding bushes. Through further inspection, he discovered the cave's entrance and spent a few minutes going through it. He'd found traces of blood. This time it was red. He searched everywhere for any indication of blue blood, but luckily he found none.

He took some dried food that'd been tucked up high off the ground in stone jars. The whisky barrels and other goods were of no use to him now, except to refill his bottle. This spot looked like an occasional hideout, not something that was frequented. He'd have to remember it if he ever came through this area again.

Asher turned his attention back to the fire pit. He could see the place the kidnappers had buried the remains of the animal they'd eaten for dinner. They were cautious, but not overly. He would do well to learn some of their tricks if he were going to avoid people like them in the future. Asher remounted Denn and followed the trail as quickly as his throbbing head allowed. It was easy enough to track three horses. More so than the two they'd started out with.

After following the trail for a couple of days, he found a homestead with signs of the two horses heading there. Not daring to approach it without more information, he circled the farm, looking for signs of them leaving. The sight of three distinct tracks surprised him. Did they trust Kaylee enough to give her a horse? Or had they gained another companion?

The signs were even more obvious now. Snapped branches here and there. Broken blades of grass that had been munched on by the horses in their passing were not dried off on the edges. He mounted Denn again and rode quickly enough to cut the distance between them without losing the signs of their passing. They didn't seem to worry they might be followed. He wondered if they thought him dead. It could easily have meant his death. Maybe they figured he wouldn't be able to track them without a horse since they'd taken Denn.

Good thing I trained Denn to accept only me as a rider.

Near evening, Asher slowed Denn to a walk, paying close attention to the trail he followed. They stayed relatively close to a stream. If they had traveled in the water, he would have never found them. If he intended to take Kaylee from these men he would have to do something like that sooner than he thought.

For the first time, Asher wondered what he would do when he found them. He needed that bounty, but he wanted to make sure she was all right. He wanted to see her again. To see what a few more day's growth had done to her hair. He wanted to see her smile again. To see the light in her eyes when she saw something that interested her.

Asher pulled the horse to a stop. He stared into the trees, surprised by the thought. He had been pining for her. He didn't even know her. He had never thought it would come to this. He was no longer interested in her as a Blue Blood. He found her desirable as a woman. And this would put him at odds with the king and his way of life.

Asher clicked the reins and hurried forward. He fingered the amber talisman, wishing it would vibrate to show he was within the mile. He needed to find her. When he got close to the camp, he'd watch it from a distance to see what he could do to get her back.

CHAPTER TWELVE

Kaylee stood when Dolf grabbed a few small rocks and measured them in his hand. She walked over to him and hesitated a moment.

"Dolf?" Kaylee spoke softly so he could ignore her if he chose.

Dolf lifted his head from his inspection of the stones. "Hmm?"

"May I come with you?"

"Come with?" Dolf repeated as if he couldn't understand why she would want to.

Kaylee nodded and waited patiently.

Dolf considered for a moment. He looked at Zeb, who was busy setting up camp. He glanced at Kaylee again and then nodded. "You can come."

Dolf tucked the stones in a small pouch hooked to his belt. He took a few steps forward, raising his voice enough for Zeb to hear. "I'm taking Kaylee with me to look for food."

Zeb waved to acknowledge he'd heard and Dolf slipped away into the forest. Kaylee rushed to catch up, but Dolf held his finger to his lip. He motioned for her to walk carefully. She followed him easily and more than once Dolf glanced back to make sure she still followed.

Before long, Dolf pointed out a trail in the underbrush that looked like it was used by animals regularly. Dolf looked up and down the trail. After a moment's pause he turned right and followed it. Kaylee stepped carefully, making sure to remain silent.

Dolf motioned with one hand for her to stop. He lifted the sling and placed a stone in it. In a motion too quick for her to follow, Dolf swung the leather strap and let the stone fly. A squeal, and then silence let Kaylee know he hit his mark. Dolf moved forward without the same care he'd shown when stalking his prey. He reached into the bush and pulled out a dead rabbit. It was longer than the ones she had cared for at the monastery but didn't look as plump. Dolf skinned it and cleaned out its entrails much quicker than she'd ever done. His movements were sure and practiced. He handed her the stripped carcass, and Kaylee held it upside down to let it bleed out.

"Can you teach me to use a sling?" She spoke quietly again.

Dolf considered her for a moment. He looked her over and then focused on her eyes. "Why do you want to learn?"

"I haven't been able to practice any kind of self-sufficiency for a while now. Where I lived, we worked hard and grew crops and raised small animals. I never had to go looking for my food. Seeing you find your own food like this drives home how unprepared I am for life."

"You won't need to know how to hunt for your own food where we're taking you."

Kaylee frowned. She didn't want to depend on others. She wanted to have a skill that would help her be useful as well.

After a moment, Dolf surprised her by saying, "I don't think you'll ever need it, but it can't do any harm to let you practice."

A smile spread across Kaylee's face.

Dolf held his sling up for her to see. "This one will probably be too big for you, but it'll do for a bit." The center of the strap had a wider cut of leather to set the stone in. He placed his rock in it, gripped the ends, and spun it around slowly. "You swing it a couple of times, and at the right moment you let it go." He released one strap of the sling and lobbed the rock a couple feet.

"The speed you swing it and the place you release will determine how far and fast it flies. You want to aim low for small animals on the ground. You'd be shooting higher for the medium sized animals. Something big isn't likely to go down with one of these unless you hit it in the head just right, but you could injure it enough to slow it down. Or even scare something away if you're desperate."

Kaylee nodded.

"I'll show you a couple more times, and then you can try." Dolf showed her slowly and then picked up the speed with each subsequent example. Time after time, Dolf hit the same tree, no matter what his speed.

There's no way I'll get that good.

He handed her the sling and instructed her step by step. The first time, Kaylee couldn't figure out how to release the stone at the right place. When it finally broke free of the strap it'd flown around almost half the rotation. The rock hit a tree above her, sending leaves raining down on her head.

Dolf chuckled. "Try it again."

Kaylee tried. Eventually she learned where to release it and managed to at least hit a tree close to the one she'd aimed at.

On her third hit, Dolf said, "I think that's enough for today. We should get back before Zeb starts to wonder what we're up to." They walked back along the path they'd trodden before. After a few minutes, Dolf motioned for Kaylee to stop and quiet down again. He waited for a moment. She looked around, trying to see what he saw. Just as quickly as before, Dolf had another stone in his sling and spun it around, sending the rock flying. The squeal this time was much louder, and the cry lasted longer. Dolf reached into the bush to pull the rabbit out. He quickly put an end to the kicking with his knife. He cleaned it up as quickly as before and handed the carcass to Kaylee. She held it out further from her body, since it would need to drain as they walked.

Zeb looked up as they entered the camp. When he saw Kaylee holding the rabbits, he got a strange look on his face.

"Did you try healing one of them?"

Kaylee shook her head. The thought had never occurred to her. An animal intended for food shouldn't be healed, especially if she planned to kill it and eat it afterward.

"Shame. You should try next time."

Kaylee frowned. An animal was out of the question. Practicing on herself was one thing. On Zeb it was tolerable, because at least he felt the pain willingly. The look of satisfaction in his eyes when he slid the blade down his skin and then hers made her flesh crawl. He obviously enjoyed it.

Dolf took her elbow in his large hands. "You don't have to continue with this." He refused to be a part of the practice himself after that first experiment and limited the sessions to once a day.

"I have to learn how to use it. To know what my limits are. What good I can do." Although she didn't enjoy the pain, she reveled in the knowledge she could do something good with this curse forced upon her.

Kaylee could almost block out the pain she knew was coming before Zeb cut her, but in order for her to heal him, she needed to feel the pain. She tried to pinch herself to heal their cuts, but it didn't work. She needed to feel something comparable.

Since they hadn't practiced yet, Kaylee decided to get it over with. She set the rabbits down near the fire and stepped closer to Zeb. She held her hand out to him. His smile of pure joy sank Kaylee's heart.

"Let's try something different. I want to know if you can reattach something that's been cut off."

Kaylee paled at the thought. She pulled her hand back and held it close to her.

Dolf moved to stand behind Kaylee, placing his hand on her shoulder.

Zeb chuckled. "I'm not gonna cut your hand off. But I will take my toe. You will attach it or I will take yours off as well. We know you need to feel pain, so I'll let you decide what kind to make sure it works for you."

Kaylee turned to Dolf. He looked worried, but didn't say anything. *At least he respects my decision.*

The most painful trial was when Zeb took her arm and peeled her top layer of skin back. She knew it was easy enough to heal, but since it was over such a large area it would probably work best and be the fastest to heal. She offered him her arm and said, "Peel it."

Kaylee could only describe his expression as one of glee. She closed her eyes and focused inward. She would let him cut her and ignore the pain for as long as she could. When he injured himself, she would embrace the pain and heal him.

The sting as the blade separated layers of tissue was almost too much to block out. She hissed while Zeb sighed in satisfaction. She turned her head away from her arm, trying not to look at it. She longed to place her hand on the wound and heal it right away but resisted. She had to know her limits.

Kaylee looked at Dolf. His eyes met hers and she found solace in their depths. He seemed to feel the pain with her. Kaylee jumped when Zeb brought his knife down quickly and his howl of pain made her whip her head around. His big toe was no longer attached. The blood spurted out in rhythm with the pain in her own arm. Zeb dropped his knife and grabbed his foot holding tightly.

He wailed through clenched teeth. "Do it. Quick."

Kaylee picked up his toe. She had to brush off some dirt that turned to mud. She motioned for Zeb to hold his foot higher. He groaned as he lifted it. Kaylee placed the bloody ends together. She wrapped her hand around it and willed it to reattach. She felt warmth as the blood flowed from the stub. Was she not feeling enough pain? Kaylee focused on her own skin flayed.

She imagined the way it would feel if it were all over her body. She looked at the pain in Zeb's eyes. She turned to Dolf, afraid that she wouldn't be able to heal Zeb.

The concern in Dolf's eyes made her ache. He would do what he could to protect her, but Zeb was unstable. He would probably maim her more if she didn't heal him. The wealth of emotion and pain came together, and Kaylee felt the force of her power flow out of her hand. Zeb immediately gasped. She sighed as he released the hold he had on his foot and shouted.

She sagged in relief, placing her hand on her own wound. It healed with little more effort than her thoughts. Even the missing blood was replenished. She felt a little tired, but not weakened.

Dolf took her to the side and wiped the blood away from her arm. Zeb stood and hopped around on his previously injured foot.

"Amazing. Is there anything you can't heal?"

"No more tests," Dolf said. He stood firm with Kaylee behind him.

"What are you talking about?" Zeb looked shocked to see Dolf defying him.

"No more. You push it too far." Dolf shook his head. "It ends now."

"We will keep practicing. She must get faster at it. Queen Sherr will want her to be the best she can be."

Dolf shook his head. "If we test, I'll do it. Not you."

Zeb moved forward, but Dolf just crossed is arms over his chest and stared him down.

Zeb seemed to finally believe him and turned away in defeat. He rubbed his foot in the dry, matted down grass to clean off the remaining blood and grime before putting his sock and boot back on. He moved quietly to the fire and picked up the rabbits. Kaylee watched in relief as he shoved the roasting sticks into the carcass of each rabbit and placed them over the fire.

She turned to Dolf, who hadn't moved. "Thank you."

Dolf only nodded as he moved to his saddle bag. He pulled out a section of leather and seemed to measure it. Kaylee sat down and watched as he carved designs into the surface. She was more afraid to do the testing with Dolf. At least with Zeb, she didn't worry about any pain he might feel.

Asher could smell the blue blood when his talisman started to hum. She was close. He couldn't tell her personal scent, but he doubted there was another Blue Blood in the area. Each place they camped, traces of blood were obvious. Some was blue, some red. The amount and frequency the blue blood angered him.

What were they doing that she would bleed in each place? Was she injured? Were they not taking care of her? Was she trying to escape and being stopped each time?

Asher felt sure there were only two kidnappers and Kaylee, given the foot prints at each camp. If he used his wits, he would come upon them without being seen. They weren't taking efforts to hide their passing. He was surprised he hadn't caught up till now. They'd taken Kaylee from him twelve days ago, leading him farther away from the king's city than he'd ever traveled. He found himself in an unfamiliar area. He doubted any of the king's soldiers ever came this far north. He had seen no villages, homesteads, or farms for the last six days.

Dusk settled upon them, but with enough light left for him to see. Certain the kidnappers would've set up camp by now, Asher rode Denn carefully as he approached the forested area. The smoke from the fire was strong, but so far he hadn't gotten a whiff of fresh blood.

He hoped she was well, but the blood from the other campsites worried him.

Denn's ears perked up. Asher listened closely. They stopped for a moment. A horse snorted in the distance, and Asher reached for his bow. He urged Denn to move forward, the horse seeming to understand the need for stealth. Once the trees pressed closer around him, making it difficult for him to maneuver silently, Asher dismounted. He pulled his bow and an arrow from his quiver, setting one on the string without pulling it tight.

His knife was easily accessible if it came to close quarter fighting. He would save Kaylee.

Asher moved slowly through the trees. The smoke grew thicker and stronger. The smell of meat roasting over a flame reached him. If they were eating, he could sneak up on them more easily. He wasn't sure if he could take on two at once. Staying back until they went to sleep might be a better idea. He would decide when he actually saw them.

Asher took a step, making sure his feet didn't hit anything that would make a sound. A stray leaf or branch cracking would give him away. Another slow step. He was so close to getting her back. It was no longer about the money she could bring.

He had failed her. He needed to make it right.

The glow of the fire's light grew visible as he neared the trees in front of him. The normal sounds of a camp reached his ears. The horses shook or snorted occasionally. A deep voice spoke, low but not like they were trying to be quiet.

Through the leaves, he saw two men. A large one and a smaller man with his back to Asher. The small man leaned over the fire as if checking on something cooking. It smelled good. Much better than the dried meat he'd had so often over the last few days.

Kaylee stood and approached the fire, the big guy following her, never letting her get more than an arm's reach away. He must be the one hurting her so often. The smaller guy ignored her, whittling a stick with his knife. Kaylee looked in pretty good health. He saw no injuries or bandages on her. But how had he seen the fresh blood yesterday? In the dirt, he saw more of the red blood than he'd seen at any other place. They wouldn't clean their kills in the same place they camped, so he couldn't understand the blood. And why the lack of injuries to them? Asher examined the two men from his hiding place.

The big guy had a large knife strapped to his belt, but otherwise looked unarmed. A large bow was propped up against the rock nearest the big guy. It looked more powerful than Asher's bow, but he was a good shot. He wouldn't miss tonight.

He studied the two men, wondering who to shoot first. The one carving with the knife first, and then the big one before he could throw the knife on his belt or reach that bow. Depending on how fast they reacted, he might not get the second shot.

Asher hesitated. He watched Kaylee. She sat quietly. She didn't look like she was enjoying herself, but she didn't look frightened. The way the large man kept her close, she was obviously a prisoner, but she seemed more at ease than he expected to find her.

The small man shoved his knife into its scabbard. "It's time." Something about his voice tickled the back of Asher's mind. He could have sworn he'd heard him speak before. He hesitated to move to a better place to see his face, worried that any movement would give away his location so he waited, hoping for the small man to turn.

Asher moved forward slightly, trying to get a better angle, but when he saw the large man pull out a knife he froze. Had they heard him? His panic at the thought of discovery turned to horror when the big man brought the knife down slowly to Kaylee's arm.

She held her arm out, her eyes closed like she expected it. What was she doing? The big man put his knife to her flesh and pressed.

Blood bubbled up from her skin as the knife moved down her pale arm. Rage rippled over Asher. He would stop this now. He pulled his bowstring tight and took careful aim. It would mean taking the man in the back, but if he was hurting Kaylee, he didn't deserve a warning.

Asher let the arrow go just as the man pulled back. The arrow struck him in the shoulder, forcing the man to fall forward onto Kaylee. The small man stood at the shout of pain from the big guy, knife in hand. He looked around in confusion. Asher charged in with such anger that instead of drawing another arrow, he swung the bow and caught the small man across the temple. As the wood struck, vibrations shot up Asher's arms. When their eyes met, he finally registered how he knew this man. Zeb from the last village before Kaylee had been taken.

Zeb dropped to the ground. Asher turned quickly to Kaylee, expecting her to run to him. Instead she held the large man, easing him to the ground. How could she be caring for this man?

Kaylee looked up at Asher as he ran to her. He offered his hand, hoping to pull her away quickly before Zeb woke up. Kaylee stared at him like he was a monster.

"What did you do?"

"I'm saving you."

"You could have killed him!" she shouted.

"He cut you." Asher pointed at her arm, but there was nothing wrong with it. He stared at it in shock. He had seen it cut.

The big man moaned as he moved, jarring the arrow deeper into his body.

"Shh, Dolf." She leaned closer to him and held his face, forcing him to look at her. "It will be okay. I can fix this."

Dolf nodded, his face twisted in pain.

Kaylee looked at Asher. "Help me."

Asher shook his head still staring at her perfect arm. "How?"

"Asher!"

He looked up into her eyes. She was fine, with no injury. Had he imagined it?

"Help me," she said again. She tried to pull the arrow out, but it had lodged so deeply she couldn't move it. Dolf groaned in pain but didn't scream until she yanked back on it again.

Asher shook his head. "You can't pull it back out. You'll have to push it through."

Kaylee paled at first, but then she nodded. She placed her hands on Dolf's shoulder and looked at Asher. "Do it."

Asher squatted down and grabbed hold of the arrow, wondering why he was willing to help this man who'd kidnapped Kaylee. Asher looked at her the demand clear in her eyes. He looked at Dolf. "Ready?"

Kaylee focused on Dolf. "It'll be okay." Dolf nodded again, and Kaylee looked to Asher. "Do it."

Asher pushed. Dolf screamed again.

"Shh. It will be over soon." Kaylee pressed her forehead against Dolf's for a moment, sending a flash of jealousy through Asher. "We just have to get the shaft out first."

Dolf held his breath. Kaylee nodded to Asher again and he pushed once more, breaking through the front this time. Dolf's huge body convulsed. Kaylee lost her balance falling onto him. Asher broke the fletching off the arrow. He gripped the shaft just below the point before he pulled it out completely. Kaylee quickly scrambled up and placed her hands directly onto Dolf's shoulder.

Asher searched for something to stop the blood from flowing so freely but saw nothing close by. Kaylee grabbed the arrow from him and raised it high, bringing it down on her hand. She cried out in pain. Asher yanked it away from her, tearing more of her flesh. She had a gaping wound, but she ignored it and placed both hands on Dolf's shoulder.

Dolf groaned as she touched him, but he soon relaxed. When Kaylee took her hands away, the only signs of the injury were the blood staining his clothes and the hole through the fabric. Kaylee placed her other hand on her wounded hand. When she removed it, all damage was gone.

Asher stared at her. "You're a healer?"

Kaylee nodded. "Apparently."

Asher sat down, hard. This would bring his bounty price to an unheard of range. The last healer had been found years ago, and she was living her second life somewhere on a farm as an old woman now. Asher looked at the now healed Dolf, stiffening. Would he have to fight him? Kaylee might keep him from dying if it came to that, but he'd prefer to avoid any more conflict.

Asher looked over at Zeb, who still lay motionless on the ground near the fire. Kaylee noticed his gaze. Standing quickly, she glanced back at Dolf. He stood slowly and then lumbered over to Zeb. Asher and Kaylee followed him. Dolf leaned over Zeb's body and looked at Kaylee.

"Don't know if even you could fix that."

Kaylee knelt down and touched Zeb's neck. She brushed her hands over the huge lump on the side of Zeb's head. Asher watched her closely to see what she'd do. "He's alive," she whispered. She picked up Zeb's knife, which had fallen from his hand when Asher attacked. She placed the blade against her skin, but Asher pulled it from her before she broke through the flesh.

"What are you doing?" He tucked the knife into his boot between the lining and the outer shell.

"I have to feel pain to heal something." Kaylee looked back at Zeb lying motionless. "It doesn't work otherwise."

"Then don't do it."

Kaylee looked at him with pity in her eyes. "He's one of God's sons, too. I must do what I can." She picked up a rock and smashed it onto her fingertips of the hand still on the ground. Asher heard the crunch of her bone and dropped to his knees next to her. He tried to take her hand in his. When they touched, his lingering headache from the blow to the head was gone. He blinked in surprise, amazed at how wonderful it felt. Kaylee's eyes pinched with the pain, but she hadn't made a sound after the first gasp when the rock hit.

Kaylee pulled her hands from his and touched Zeb. Gently, she placed the fingers of her uninjured hand on the swelling by Zeb's temple. The color immediately changed and the bruised tissue disappeared. Zeb's breathing became easier, but he didn't wake up. Asher made sure Zeb's knife was still tucked away and pulled out his own. He wanted to be prepared just in case Zeb decided to retaliate.

Dolf hadn't moved, but once Zeb looked better he pulled Kaylee to her feet away from him. "Take care of you now." His voice was gentle and concerned. Asher wondered what Kaylee thought of the man in return.

Kaylee healed her finger while Asher stared, again in awe at her powers. Before he had time to react, Dolf reached out and grabbed Asher around the neck with one hand. Asher clawed at the big man's hand, trying to get some air. He pounded on Dolf's hand with one of his own, but it was as useless as brushing away smoke.

Dolf pushed Asher against a tree, lifting him enough that Asher could barely touch the ground. The weight of his body made it that much harder to breathe.

Asher struggled and heard Kaylee protesting on his behalf.

Dolf loosened his hold just enough for Asher to take a hissing breath. Dolf leaned his face closer to Asher's. "I should kill you for what you did."

"Don't. Please," Kaylee begged.

Dolf seemed to waver for a moment. Asher choked, trying to speak. He couldn't get enough air to make a word.

"Why did you attack?" Dolf asked.

Asher tried to answer but still nothing passed his lips. Black spots crowded out the red on the edge of his vision. Asher could barely make out Kaylee behind Dolf. It looked like she was pulling on Dolf's arms but he couldn't tell.

The pressure was soon gone, and Asher fell to the ground. Kaylee dropped to her knees beside him. She touched his neck, but Asher pushed her away. He didn't want her to try to heal him if it meant she would have to hurt herself. She frowned and moved away slowly, not meeting his eyes. Asher tried to speak, but couldn't stop coughing and gasping for air.

Rough hands pushed him against the tree again and wrapped a rope around him, trapping him next to the tree. Kaylee tried to pull the rope away. Dolf stopped her. Asher couldn't help noticing how careful he was with her, but he was firm and didn't let her get in the way.

"Who are you?" Dolf asked.

"Asher."

"Why did you attack us?" Dolf asked.

Asher looked at Kaylee. "You stole her from me."

Dolf turned to Kaylee. "He's the bounty hunter?"

Kaylee nodded.

Dolf snorted. "She's no longer in your possession."

Asher tried to sit up straight. "I have authority from the king to bring anyone like her to him." Most people would find that enough to leave Asher alone.

Dolf smiled, revealing a missing tooth which indicated he was accustomed to fights. "I have authority from the queen to do the same."

Asher shook his head. "What queen?"

Dolf shrugged. "She rules not far from here."

"This is the king's land."

"Not any longer."

Asher didn't know what to think. The king hadn't done much to ensure he maintained all of his land this far north.

"How did you find us?" Dolf asked.

"You weren't that hard to track."

Dolf raised his eyebrows.

Asher struggled against his bindings. "I insist you release me—and Kaylee—and let us go on our way."

Dolf looked at Kaylee. "You want to go with him to this king?"

Kaylee shook her head.

"Do you want to go with him?" Asher asked.

"At least I have a choice with him."

"I gave you a choice," Asher said.

Kaylee raised one eyebrow and folded her arms over her chest. How could she want to go with them? They had been torturing her. Asher had seen the blood at every campsite and caught them in the act moments ago.

Dolf grinned down at Asher. "Apparently you must not be as wonderful as you think you are. The queen will be much better for her than that pathetic excuse of a king." He bent down to whisper. "Don't get any ideas. I won't hesitate to kill you. And I'll do it so quick she won't have a chance to heal you."

Asher nodded and leaned his head back against the tree. He knew he was stuck there for now, but eventually he'd get free. Hopefully.

CHAPTER THIRTEEN

Kaylee watched over Zeb with concern. He still hadn't woken or even stirred. She was sure she'd healed him. The way it felt when the bruising went down was unmistakable. He would've died if she hadn't stopped the swelling to his brain. Even the bones had knitted back together under her touch.

Had there been too much damage done inside his mind? Kaylee knew that an injury to the head was hard to recover from. She'd known a boy who had been kicked by a horse when he was very young. They were surprised he had actually lived, but he was never the same.

Kaylee sat on the ground next to Zeb. She looked at Asher still tied to the tree. His eyes were fierce. She understood why he was angry. He came to save her from these men, but she couldn't let either of them die. And now he was a prisoner because of her.

Without Dolf and Zeb, she wouldn't know her power yet. She was a healer. But what exactly did that mean? Could she heal more than wounds? Could she heal sickness? Could she heal someone who was starving? That's why she was willing to submit to Zeb's tests. She wanted to know what would happen each time.

She looked back to Zeb and placed her hands on his head again. Was there damage she'd missed? Kaylee closed her eyes and let her senses discover for her what was wrong. She felt something but had no idea what it meant. Almost as if the smoothness of thought was interrupted. Something was wrong with his mind, more than the way he got pleasure out of using his knife.

Could she heal something like that?

She stood up slowly and returned to her blanket, grateful Asher brought her things with him. Dolf had found Denn and brought him into the camp. Kaylee opened her pack and looked through it. She was sure all of it was still there. It didn't look like Asher had searched it.

She looked at him again, wondering if he'd ever forgive her.

Kaylee pulled open her father's book and flipped through the pages. Things still didn't make sense as she read separate lines from different pages. The symbol in the top inside corner drew her attention. She touched the symbol with a triangle inside a square which was inside a circle. Two wavy lines crossed in the middle of the square, breaking the triangle into smaller shapes.

Kaylee was so absorbed with the book she didn't notice Dolf approach. He sat down and handed her a bowl of the soup he'd made with the remains of the rabbit.

"What do you think about him?"

Kaylee looked over at Asher, surprised Dolf would ask her opinion on him. "I don't know."

Dolf followed her gaze and shook his head. "I mean Zeb."

Kaylee blushed. "Oh."

"He still ain't woke up yet."

Kaylee looked back at Zeb. "I don't know what's wrong. I tried to see if I could figure it out, but I can't feel it the same way I feel when flesh tears, bones break, or muscles separate."

Dolf nodded and lifted his chin toward Asher. "What'd he do?"

"He struck him with the bow. Zeb dropped like a rock."

Dolf looked at the bow he had taken from Asher. "It's made of fine wood. Could do a lot of damage to a head."

Kaylee nodded. "It did."

"Guess we'll have to wait the night and see what happens in the morning." He took a bite of his food. "Finish up and go to sleep."

Kaylee watched him move to a place where he could prop himself up against a tree and keep a good eye on Asher. She wondered if he would sleep at all. Asher couldn't be comfortable tied up like that, but she knew Dolf wouldn't let him loose.

When Kaylee finished eating, she took her bowl and Dolf's to clean them out. Asher watched her every move, sending strange shivers down her spine. Kaylee turned back to Dolf. "Has he eaten?"

Dolf shook his head.

"Can I give him some?"

Dolf turned to Asher and looked him over.

"I'll feed him, so you don't have to loosen him."

Dolf nodded, and Kaylee bent down to the pot. She scooped some food into one of the bowls she'd just cleaned and approached Asher slowly. "Would you like some?"

Asher scowled at her. "I'd hate for you to do something against your will."

"I don't mind feeding it to you. But if you'd prefer, I can put it back. You could wait until morning and decide then."

Asher's anger seemed to fade. He nodded. Kaylee knelt down in front of him. She tested the soup to make sure it wasn't hot by placing the spoonful against her lip. She licked it off as Asher watched her closely.

She brought the spoon to his mouth and waited for him to open. His lips were full, the bottom more so than the top, but they were well defined. His beard was beginning to come in again, reminding her of the way he'd looked when he first found her in the tree. Shaving probably hadn't been easy to do as he tracked them. She'd left the monastery more than a month ago, so her head was covered in a thick brown fuzz. It felt strange to have a covering of hair.

Kaylee scooped more of the soup and brought it to his lips. He opened his mouth. She nearly spilled down his chin. He leaned forward to help catch the food. The next spoonful was easier to take, and the one following. They soon got a rhythm down, and Kaylee was able to look away from his mouth to his eyes. His dark brown eyes were nearly hidden in the deepening of the night.

A strange combination of emotions crossed his eyes. He looked upset with her, but she saw something else there she hadn't seen when they traveled together. A flutter, low in her stomach, bubbled up to her chest. She looked away to focus her attention on the bowl in her hands. It was almost empty. Part of her was reluctant to finish it off too fast. She wanted a reason to stay close to him. Sitting next to him made her feel comfortable and warm. Her heart skipped a beat every now and then when she met his eyes.

She lifted the spoon to his lips, focusing on the bowl to avoid his eyes. She missed and spilled most of it down his chin. His shirt was open a few inches, so much of it got on his skin. Kaylee quickly wiped it with her bare hand and froze when her fingers touched his chest. The coarse hairs tickled her fingers. She pulled her hand back and looked frantically for something to wipe the sensation off her fingers. The only thing she could think to do was wipe the food off onto the grass.

Asher cleared his throat. Kaylee couldn't meet his eyes. "I'm sorry."

Asher cleared his throat again but didn't reply. He seemed as bothered by it as she did. How could she have done that? It was improper to touch a man in such a way. She wished she could take it back, but having lived so long among men as one of them, she was too comfortable in some ways. In other ways, she didn't understand a thing about them.

They treated her so differently when they discovered she was a woman. She much preferred to be a man. She wouldn't have this curse of blue blood. It wasn't fair.

Kaylee quickly finished feeding him the soup and rushed away to clean up the bowl. She returned to her blankets without looking at Asher. When she got comfortable, she told herself she wouldn't turn to look at him. But the rock under her hip forced her to move. She rolled over and shifted until the rock was no longer an issue. Asher's head rested against the tree. Dolf had covered Zeb with his blanket, also wrapped with one where he sat.

It bothered her to see Asher without any covering besides his clothes. He was too far away from the fire to get any warmth from it. She stood up and went over to Asher's packs. She felt Dolf's eyes follow her, so she picked up the blanket and met Dolf's eye. When he nodded slightly, Kaylee returned to Asher.

She unfolded the blanket and wrapped it around him, tucking it around his shoulders. She looked behind the tree.

"I can't make it reach around to your hands."

"Thank you," Asher said.

Kaylee nodded and moved away, slower this time. She hated to see him this way. He didn't deserve it. So much happened to him because of her. Yet, he brought most of it on himself.

Kaylee returned to her blanket and wrapped herself in it. She didn't have a problem facing him. He would haunt her dreams either direction she faced. She might as well face it head on. Maybe she could have a little control that way.

Morning broke cool and damp. She was grateful for the blanket she had. She sat up slowly, noticing Asher was asleep. She looked over at Dolf. His eyes were open, but he looked as if he'd gotten some sleep.

Kaylee put more logs on the fire and slipped into the forest to take care of her needs. On her return, she checked Zeb again. He still felt different than what she expected. Somehow she thought it was an improvement over the night before. Maybe he would wake up. She squeezed his shoulder, but he didn't stir. A gentle shake resulted in no response as well.

Dolf spoke, his voice thick. "Any change?"

"In a way, but I don't think he'll wake up any time soon."

Dolf shook his head. He looked down at Zeb as if contemplating what to do next. Kaylee couldn't imagine how they'd be able to travel with him like this. She supposed they could tie him over the back of the horse.

Dolf gave Asher, still asleep against the tree, a look of speculation. It didn't look comfortable at all. She looked back at Dolf, surprised to see what looked like compassion in his eyes.

"What are your plans?" Kaylee asked.

"Haven't decided yet."

"You could let him go."

Dolf raised his eyebrows.

"I don't think he'll bother us anymore. He wanted to take me to the king and thought I was being held here against my will. Now that I'm going with you to the queen, he can't stop me."

Dolf crossed his arms over his chest as he looked down at Kaylee. "You are a naïve one, aren't you?"

Kaylee furrowed her brows. "He said he was doing me a service by taking me to the king."

"Might be true, but he'd be getting paid for it too. None of this was for your benefit."

"I'm not incapable of going on my own. I didn't have to heal you. I could have left with him, but chose to go to this queen instead. I want to make my own decisions. I believe you will let me have my own say."

Dolf shook his head. "I don't want him to come after us trying to take you back again."

Kaylee heard Asher moan as he woke and shifted his position. "Let him loose." It was a plea for mercy.

Dolf huffed, causing Kaylee to chuckle about the sound. He walked over to Asher. Squatting in front of him, he pulled out the knife Zeb had been so fond of from Asher's boot. Dolf rubbed the blade with his thumb before he turned the blade back and forth to give Asher a good view of it.

"It's a good thing you didn't try to use this last night."

Asher stared at Dolf as if surprised he knew about the knife.

"If I let you loose, what you gonna do?"

Asher shook his head.

"I don't have any problem hurting you. And I won't be letting her heal you either." Dolf nodded toward Kaylee.

"I won't do anything." Asher's voice sounded sincere to Kaylee. She hoped Dolf would relent.

Dolf hesitated a moment longer, and then he untied the ropes binding Asher. As he moved, Asher groaned. He rubbed his wrists and shoulders as if trying to get the circulation back in them.

"You can take care of your business." Dolf pointed toward the bushes. "But I ain't letting you get too far."

Asher nodded, moving stiffly to slip behind some trees. Kaylee waited anxiously for him to return. She watched the trees hoping he wouldn't try to run. Denn was still tied up next to the other horses.

She busied herself with trying to get something ready for the morning meal. Zeb continued to puzzle her. While she had limits to her healing abilities, she thought there had to be something more she could do.

As the mush heated in the pot, she returned to Zeb and knelt down beside him again. Asher's footsteps alerted her to his return. She glanced up at him as he moved close to the fire. He held his hands to the flame and rubbed them together.

Asher looked down at Zeb and up to Dolf quickly. Did he feel bad for the injuries he caused? Did he wish he had killed them outright to begin with? Was he the kind of man who would easily kill someone, or did his actions pain him?

Kaylee tried to put Asher out of her mind and instead focused her attention on Zeb. She placed her hand on his head in the exact location the bow had struck. Nothing was wrong with him on the surface. She felt no problem with his skin or blood, or muscles above the bone. The bone itself had knitted back together as if the crack never existed. But she couldn't feel anything through the bone. Everything underneath was hidden from her.

Kaylee slid her fingers over it again. If she had known before, she would have paid close attention to the inner workings before healing the bone and other stuff. She closed her eyes and thought of what might be under the skull. She never really thought about it before. Any animal she killed was quickly skinned, gutted, and the head cut off as well.

She slid her hands along Zeb's head and face. His thick, greasy hair wasn't overly long, but her fingers snagged in the tangles and mats throughout. His skull had some lumps and bony protrusions. Scars riddled throughout his scalp. It was obvious he had lived a hard life and been struck in the head more than once. She didn't feel anything that gave her hope of healing him. She pulled her fingers out of his hair and instead focused on his face. She placed her hand on his cheekbones, trying to be gentle yet thorough.

Even with her eyes closed, she knew Asher was still close. His breathing and the movements of his hands as he rubbed them over the fire were obvious. Dolf's heavy footsteps came close, and she knew he stood in front of her across from Zeb. She forced them out of her mind again and let her fingers explore.

When her hands moved over his eyelids, she felt a slight movement of his eyeballs. So he wasn't completely gone. The lack of bone in the eye socket gave her a flash of what might be wrong. Through it, she felt a difference in the flow of blood inside his skull. She was almost sure that could be fixed, but what kind of pain did he feel? How much did she need to feel to be able to make any kind of difference?

He wasn't in any danger of dying immediately. She might have time to do an experiment of her own. No reason to cause herself more pain than necessary. Could a slap of the hand bring enough? Or was his injury within so bad she'd need to be in agony to make any difference for him? She would only find out by trial and error. Keeping one hand on Zeb's eyelid, Kaylee slapped her face enough to make it sting. She noticed the hand remaining on his face felt a slight burst of power, but it obviously wasn't enough.

Asher cleared his throat. She held her hand up to stop him from disturbing her. Dolf whispered for him to remain silent.

Kaylee looked around for something that could cause her a little more pain. She didn't want to bother with knives yet. Maybe the pot sitting in the hot ashes. She reached for it and placed her little finger on the edge until she felt the burn. Her hand still on Zeb's eye gained a little more power and she thought perhaps it was making a bit of a difference. She placed two fingers on the pot a little longer than the first and pulled it back with a hiss of pain. The flow of power from her fingers into Zeb's eye was much stronger, but nothing like what she had done with crushing her own hand or stabbing herself with the arrow.

She placed both hands back on Zeb—one still on his eye, and one on the side where Asher struck him first. There was an improvement, but would it be enough? She was hesitant to try again. She didn't want to feel the pain herself. And she couldn't help feeling anger toward Zeb. He hadn't been cruel exactly, but he'd never been nice either. He was nothing like the other two men watching. Dolf protected her from most of the pain Zeb tried to inflict, but he couldn't stop him in all things.

Asher had treated her in a way she hadn't felt in years. He confused her, but she knew he was a good man. He'd come all this way for her. He tried to save her from the men who had stolen her from him, and now he was paying the price for his nobleness.

Kaylee brushed her burned fingers against the ground, sending a flash of fresh pain. It sent another burst of power through her fingers into Zeb's eye socket. She moved to the other eye and did it again. She placed both hands on his head again. The change was evident. She didn't feel anything wrong with his mind anymore, but she was curious. Did she truly know what it was supposed to feel like? She stood up and moved over to Dolf. He leaned back in surprise, but she grabbed his face between her hands, her fingertips resting on his closed eyes. Everything in his mind seemed fine. She sensed no hesitancies like she felt with Zeb's. She moved over to Asher, who reacted much the same.

He tried to take her hands in his, but she slapped them out of the way and placed her hands on his face. She could feel the aches in his shoulders, back, and wrists disappear immediately as she touched him. She hadn't meant to heal him, not realizing he was in pain, but she forced that out of her thoughts and focused on her original intent. His mind seemed quick and smooth. No hesitancy either. In fact, it felt much stronger than Dolf's. She returned to Zeb and once again felt his eyes. A slight glitch was still there, but it was much better than before. She placed a finger on each eye and once again rubbed her burned fingers on the ground. The tender flesh protested, and she relished the jolt of power it brought to her. A wave of energy entered Zeb's eyes and that last glitch vanished.

She leaned back from him to get a better look. Would this wake him? She expected it to happen quickly, but nothing looked different. She knew he was better, but didn't know what to do next. She touched her own injury and felt the throbbing burn disappear. She looked up, embarrassed at the looks the two men gave her.

"We'll have to wait and see what that does." She walked over to her pack and gathered her things. She wanted to be ready to travel if they were going to leave today.

Asher and Dolf exchanged glances without words. She was grateful for that. She didn't want to discuss what happened. It was still so new to her, and she felt protective of her secrets. She didn't want everyone to know how it worked.

Dolf leaned over Zeb as if expecting him to move any second. When nothing happened, he went about his business getting things packed up.

Asher didn't move from the fire, but he still stirred the mush. He watched Zeb. As Dolf watched him, Kaylee knew they needed to figure something out with Asher. She didn't worry about Dolf letting him come if she asked, but what would Zeb think when he woke up?

She didn't want to think about what he might do. She was glad Dolf had Zeb's knife. She knew Zeb was dangerous with it. He could probably fight without the knife too, but it was still a comfort to think she wouldn't have to worry about it.

They ate in silence, all of them close together as they waited to see what would happen with Zeb. After the meal was finished and they'd cleaned up, they saw no change.

Dolf shrugged. "What do you think? Can he travel if we tied him to his horse?"

Kaylee turned around to face him. "I don't think it would hurt him."

Dolf nodded. He turned to Asher. "And what will you do?"

Asher looked between the two of them. "What are my options?"

"You can leave peacefully with the promise to never follow us again," Dolf said.

"Or?" Asher asked.

"You could travel with us," Kaylee offered. Dolf's eyes widened, and he shook his head. She crossed her arms over her chest. "He's good with a bow. He's strong. He'd be helpful."

"You trust him?" Dolf asked.

Kaylee looked deep into Asher's eyes. "Yes." She answered Dolf when she was sure she saw what she was looking for. Asher wanted to come with them. She didn't know why exactly.

Dolf nodded. "Or you could come with us."

CHAPTER FOURTEEN

Asher didn't know how to answer. Kaylee sat in front of the fire waiting for his response. She had changed in the short time he'd been tracking them. She seemed more introspective and quieter, if that were possible, but she radiated an undeniable power now. It wasn't just that she could heal injuries. What she'd done to Dolf's and Zeb's wounds was nothing short of miraculous, not to mention she'd taken away his headache by touching him.

If she were in the king's employ, he would expect too much of her. The soldiers in the battlefield would be healed immediately, but at what cost? Asher flashed on the memory of her bringing the arrow down on her hand to heal Dolf's shoulder. Then the rock that crushed her finger when she healed Zeb. She did it willingly as if she expected it of herself. She looked powerful, but haunted.

He couldn't allow her to be placed in the hands of the king. No matter what that might mean to himself, he would have to make sure she never had to serve someone like him. And if this queen Dolf spoke of was anything like the king, he would have to take her away from there.

"I want to come with you," Asher said.

"Why?" Dolf asked.

"To make sure she's treated well."

Dolf shook his head. "No need. I'm keeping her safe."

"Right. That's why I saw you cutting into her."

"She agreed to it."

Asher shook his head. "Doesn't matter. I'll come."

Dolf started to speak, but Kaylee interrupted. "Let him come." Her words had finality about them, but Asher knew he hadn't won the battle. Instead, he worried about what he may have gotten himself into.

He needed to be with Kaylee. He couldn't describe it. He couldn't even define it for himself. It wasn't just that he wanted to make sure Kaylee made it there safely. He felt something for her he had never felt for any other woman. He had to stay close. He had to see if she could ever feel for him the way he felt for her.

They cleaned up the camp and loaded the horses. Dolf easily lifted Zeb onto the gray horse. Kaylee helped get him situated and tied in place. Asher's eyes opened wide as Dolf let him get on Denn without any restraints. He even gave him back his bow.

Dolf met his gaze. "Don't know why she trusts you, but since I owe her my life, I will give you your freedom." He held up a finger. "If you throw away my gift of trust, I *will* kill you. No matter what she says." He didn't remove his hand from the bow until Asher nodded.

"I understand." Asher pulled the bow from Dolf's hand when he released his grip on it.

Dolf nodded and climbed on his horse. "You'll be in front."

Asher urged his horse forward slowly. Kaylee tapped her heels into the horse's sides to follow, leading Zeb's horse. Dolf brought up the rear. Asher was alert, looking for any sign of danger in the forest in front of them. Since he'd been attacked by Zeb and Dolf he knew there were dangers he should be cautious of.

An itch developed between his shoulder blades. Kaylee had erased all the aches from sleeping bound to the tree. He actually felt more rested than most mornings. No, the strange sensation in the center of his back was all in his mind. Dolf probably had an aim on him, ready to kill him the moment it looked like he might do something wrong.

Asher glanced back every few minutes until Dolf hollered up to him. "Just keep going on this trail until you get to the place it splits."

Asher nodded and relaxed slightly. He still looked back, but less often. Kaylee seemed to be doing well.

Zeb apparently hadn't given her any trouble. She didn't look concerned at all, but deep in thought. He wished he could talk to her about how healing worked. Maybe he would have time when they stopped again. Or sometime on their journey.

It took until mid-day to get to the place Dolf indicated. Asher climbed off his horse to get lunch. He moved over to help Kaylee get down, but she brushed him away. Dolf untied Zeb and laid him on the ground. He was gentle, given the size of the man, but Asher never want to have to fight him one-on-one. It would not end in his favor.

Kaylee moved around for a moment. She didn't look stiff like she had before, but then again, she'd been traveling for more than a month. It showed in more ways than one. Her hair was coming back in. She still looked odd, but the fire in her eyes and the beauty of her expressions were enough to make him forget she had little hair.

If only she had continued to wear the dress. It would've been easier for him to remember who she was. He'd allowed himself to get too comfortable. In treating her so casually, he had passed a threshold he set up years ago. He turned away from her, knowing he had to reestablish his rules.

Zeb remained unchanged for the entire day. Kaylee looked concerned but seemed to accept the fact they would just have to wait. She rode carefully, never moving faster than a walk. Dolf didn't seem to mind the pace, forcing Asher to slow down to keep from getting too far ahead.

When they set up camp, Asher was relieved Dolf didn't plan to tie him to a tree. As he watched Dolf place Zeb on the ground again, Kaylee gathered wood for the fire. Asher looked around, wishing for something to do.

"Do you want me to start making something for supper?" Asher asked.

"You can cook the rabbit." Dolf tossed a carcass he'd killed with his sling on their journey. Dolf's skill with the sling made Asher even more careful about not upsetting the man.

Asher busied himself with cutting the meat off the bone. He found the pot they used for the meals and tossed it in. He'd been able to gather some things as he'd tracked Kaylee earlier. It would help to extend the rabbit into a full meal for the three of them. Asher looked over at Zeb. He hadn't eaten or drunk anything for nearly a day. If he didn't wake soon he'd starve and there would be no worrying about what to do with him anymore.

They ate their meal quietly. Asher wanted to ask about where they were going, but didn't know how to broach the subject. He wanted to know more about this queen. Could he work for her? Would he want to? Zeb raved about her back at the inn.

"How much farther do we have to travel?" Kaylee asked. Grateful for the question, Asher listened intently.

"I'd figure about a week more, depending on our speed. We're moving pretty slow."

Kaylee looked at Zeb. "I think we could probably move a little faster. He seemed to tolerate it well enough today."

Dolf smiled. "Maybe the jolting of the horse will wake him up. Shake up what's inside him until it all falls back into place."

Kaylee smiled. Asher couldn't help smiling as well.

"This is the farthest north I've been in my life," Asher said. "Is it this barren the whole way?"

"Mostly. There are a few places where groups of farmers have branched out. They'll be getting closer together by the end of the fourth day from now. Then the day after that, you'll begin to see more of what you're used to."

Kaylee asked, "How big are this queen's lands?"

"Not sure," Dolf said. "Zeb knows more about her than me."

"So why are you taking Kaylee to her?" Asher asked.

"She hired us to find her some Blue Bloods. She's not been able to find any in her area. But she knows about them. Knows lots about them." Dolf looked off into the distance as if trying to solve something in his mind.

"There aren't any in her kingdom?" Asher asked.

"Don't seem to be."

Asher wondered if it was something about their own lands that made the Blue Bloods appear. No one seemed to know what it was that caused a girl to become one. They manifested at different ages. Lots were young. Most were in their late teens. A couple snapped as early as twelve, but it wasn't common.

"But she knows all about them, you say?" Kaylee asked.

"She explained to Zeb how to find someone like you," Dolf said. "Once he met you in the inn, he told me he'd found you."

"How?"

"Don't know. His secrets are still his own. He didn't like telling me too much." Dolf looked down at Zeb and everyone's gaze followed.

Asher may never get the answers he needed. They cleaned up and went to set out their bed rolls. "I can take first watch," Asher offered.

Dolf looked at Kaylee, who nodded. It irritated him that he was dependent on Kaylee's approval. But if it allowed him some freedom, he'd take it.

Dolf put his hand on Asher's bow and quiver of arrows. Asher would watch weaponless. Dolf held a knife in one hand and the bow in the other. "Wake me at the half."

Asher positioned himself as the others settled into their blankets. Dolf would be tired after staying up through the night. It could be the best time to take off if he wanted to, but he knew he wouldn't. Kaylee would stay with Dolf, so Asher would stay too. Dolf fell asleep quickly, but Kaylee lay on her side looking into the fire. She seemed lost in thought. Asher took the opportunity to study her.

She was undeniably beautiful. She'd changed over the few days he'd been away from her. She was more sure of herself. Did having proof they could do something powerful make Blue Bloods see themselves differently? The possibilities open to a Blue Blood were endless. Kaylee could heal any injury to herself, and she'd healed him twice. Seeing the arrow wound in Dolf's shoulder disappear was more than amazing. And he'd struck Zeb with a killing blow. He felt it in the way the man dropped. The fact he was alive now was a miracle.

But he hadn't moved on his own since the blow. Asher knew Kaylee was concerned that she wasn't able to heal him, but she also exuded confidence that she had done something for him. It would be interesting to see if he ever woke from his sleep.

Asher blinked, Kaylee's face coming into focus. She was looking directly at him. How long had he been staring at her without being aware? He shifted a little, breaking the eye contact. She seemed curious as to why he'd been watching her. He adjusted his position and looked around the campground. The horses had settled into sleep. Kaylee had picked very dry wood, which helped keep the smoke down. The calming sounds coming from the small stream to their left might lull him to sleep if he weren't careful.

Kaylee turned her back toward the fire, away from him. Asher admired the curve of her shoulder down to her waist. Her hips flared up gently and sloped back down as he followed her legs down to her feet. If she knew he looked at her like this, she would probably be angry.

If he were smart, he would've taken the offer Dolf gave him to leave.

He knew it would've never happened. He couldn't get enough of watching her. He noted when her breathing changed, indicating she was asleep. Dolf slept soundly as well. Asher even tried to take his attention off Kaylee by watching Zeb. He breathed normally but had yet to move at all.

Asher relaxed against the rock he'd settled next to and looked up into the sky. It was hard to see much with the trees overhead, but he saw some stars visible above the trees. With the fire burned down to just a small blaze, it didn't interfere with his view. He always enjoyed seeing the stars, but they couldn't hold his attention tonight.

Asher's thoughts returned to how Kaylee healed him instantly. When she touched him, it was gone. He doubted she even realized what she'd done. She seemed so focused on studying his face and Dolf's. What she learned was still a mystery to him. He hadn't dared ask her about it. She looked so closed that he doubted she would've answered.

Asher heard someone move behind him. He turned quickly to see who it was. Kaylee still rested in the same position. Dolf lay on his back. Asher couldn't remember what position he'd been in earlier. Just as Asher started to turn back, he heard the movement again. He stood up and stepped closer to the fire. Zeb had moved. He still lay flat on his back, but his arm was no longer by his side. His foot looked like it had shifted a bit. Asher watched closely, waiting for the next movement. It didn't come and Asher relaxed. He would wait until morning to tell Kaylee about it.

She'd be excited to see a difference in Zeb. The rest of Asher's watch passed without incident. Zeb twitched once more a couple hours later, but other than that, didn't move. Asher figured he'd given Dolf at least half the night to sleep. He moved over to the large man. The sound of his foot touching the ground near him caused Dolf to wake quickly.

He sat up straight without a sound and nodded to Asher. Asher quickly moved back to his bedroll. It wasn't far from Kaylee or Zeb. He turned his back to the two of them and settled into sleep.

Asher woke to pressure on his neck. He opened his eyes to see Zeb's angry face staring down at him, his hands closed tightly on Asher's throat. The crazed man leaned forward, putting his full weight into the attack. Asher tried to push him off, gripping Zeb's arms, but couldn't get enough force to push him away.

He couldn't shout for help so he searched frantically for Dolf or Kaylee. Both were gone. Had Zeb done something to them?

Asher was losing the battle. He'd die if he didn't get air soon and doubted Kaylee could heal him from that. Asher brought his heels up, struggling to gain purchase with his boots. He needed to get some leverage to break away from his attacker. His maneuvering bought him some time as Zeb's hold broke for a moment. Asher took a gulp of air. Zeb jumped up and stomped on Asher's stomach.

Asher rolled over onto his side, curled into himself. He saw the boot coming, giving him time to cover his head with his hands. The force of the kick broke his hand, though that saved him from more damage to the head.

Asher tucked himself in tighter and cradled his head in his hands. Another kick found its mark, sending a blast of pain through his skull. His ears rang. He almost blacked out. He waited for the third blow, but it never came. He moaned in pain as he looked for his attacker. He saw a flash of movement. Expecting another kick, Asher flinched. Instead, gentle hands touched his hand and face.

He waited for the pain to disappear, but it remained. She pressed her fingers to his eyelids making Asher wonder what she was doing. Her hands moved to the back of his head, and then they were gone. At her gasp of pain, he felt horrible that she had to hurt herself to help him. He tried to protest, but the immediate relief he felt when she healed him made him ashamed for his weakness.

He grabbed her hands as she tried to take them from him. He didn't know what she had to feel to do what she did, but she did it willingly. She caused the pain to herself for his benefit.

"Thank you." He couldn't express his gratitude adequately. There was no way to repay her. He couldn't take her pain away.

Kaylee blinked in surprise.

"I'm so sorry you had to do that." Asher didn't want to let go of her hands. Such amazing hands. He looked down at them. She hadn't healed herself yet. He cringed and let go. Once again, he'd caused her unnecessary pain. She placed one hand on the other. The skin closed quickly, and the swelling disappeared. He lifted the newly healed hand and kissed her knuckles.

"How can I ever repay you?" he whispered.

Kaylee's eyes opened wide. "Try not to get hurt again."

He looked over at Zeb, restrained by Dolf near the fire ring. Asher nodded. "I'll try my best."

Asher stood with her help. He was reluctant to let go of her, but she pulled her hand from his and turned to Zeb. Dolf had Zeb's arms pinned behind his back. The rising sun shone on Zeb's face, illuminating his confusion at this turn of events.

"Why did you do that?" Kaylee asked.

Zeb looked at the two of them with wide eyes. He shook his head as if he couldn't explain what he had done or why. He looked at Dolf with pleading eyes and Dolf released him.

"What happened to me?" Zeb asked.

CHAPTER FIFTEEN

Kaylee examined Zeb again after he tried to kill Asher. His mind didn't feel off like it had at first, but something still felt slightly different about him. Dolf and Asher allowed her to compare their vibes to his again, but she didn't know what to make of it.

Dolf convinced Zeb that Asher was no threat but told him in no uncertain terms that he was now in charge and Zeb would have to follow his lead. Kaylee was shocked when Zeb agreed to it. Was he really injured enough that he'd give up control, or was he waiting for the right time to strike?

Kaylee watched him closely as they began their travels again. The rest of their journey was much the same as when Zeb was unconscious. Zeb still didn't seem to have much of his mind with him. There were times when he would act like things were completely normal, but other times he would start to scream at Dolf or Asher. He rarely raised his voice to Kaylee. She wondered if it was because she healed him, or if he didn't remember her much. Either way, it didn't matter. Dolf kept him occupied, and Asher watched Kaylee. She still couldn't figure out why Dolf was so willing to have him come with.

Three days after Zeb woke, Kaylee pulled her horse to a stop as they crested a hill. She turned to Dolf. "This is where the queen lives?" A rough castle with outer walls in various stages of completion sat about a mile inland from the largest body of water Kaylee had ever seen. Out in the distance, the sun reflected off the water. A village sat nestled between the castle grounds and what Kaylee assumed was the ocean. Small boats floated on the water.

Dolf nodded. "They've made progress since we left."

It was a castle, barely. The disrepair was obvious. Why would the queen live there if she had any sort of funds to provide for a better place? The bastions of the castle still stood, but looked to be in such poor shape she doubted any soldiers would dare occupy them. Scores of men worked on fortifying the walls. Even the monastery had been better protection than this place. Asher looked over the area with the same interest she had.

And Kaylee was supposed to help some woman overthrow a king?

Dolf turned to look at Zeb, who had taken this moment to start singing a lewd song to himself. Dolf reached over and took the reins from him.

Zeb easily gave them up to Dolf and hummed. When they reached the doors of the castle's outer wall, Dolf shouted their arrival. A small window opened, the shutters swinging forward. A head poked out to look them over.

"What's your purpose?" the man in the window shouted.

"We've returned from the assignment Queen Sherr gave us."

The man blinked, and then quickly closed the window. Shouting and sounds of scrambling came from inside. A moment later, the huge door squealed as it opened. It took four men to push the heavy wood allowing entrance. That was one good thing if they were ever attacked. This place worried her. The forest felt safer. She shook off her unease and followed Dolf in. Asher brought up the rear, looking more comfortable than Kaylee felt.

A young man, probably fourteen or fifteen, came out of the main building and stopped in front of Dolf. "Her majesty wishes for you to attend her now."

Dolf nodded and dismounted. Kaylee did the same. She looked down at her travel-stained clothes and wished she had been allowed time to clean up first. She'd never met royalty before. Kaylee slapped her legs, trying to force the dirt off her leggings, but it didn't change much. Nothing she could do about it now. She pulled her small pack from the horse and slung it over her shoulder.

Asher took a moment longer before sliding off his horse. Zeb remained mounted and twisted the horse's mane in his fingers. Dolf tapped Zeb's boot. Zeb sighed as if it were an inconvenience. Swinging his leg forward, high over the horse's neck, he hopped down.

Zeb stumbled slightly then started walking to the door the runner had come from. The messenger rushed to get in front of Zeb, glancing back a couple times to make sure they were still following him.

The inside of the main building was better than the outside, and it seemed like there had been many efforts made to improve on what had been damaged over time. It was more comfortable looking than many places in her monastery. It felt warmer inside, but that could be because they weren't in the higher mountains here like the monastery was. Near the ocean, the air felt different. Heavy and almost wet. She took a deep breath, enjoying the unusual smell.

Kaylee looked at the bare hallways and felt comfort in its similarity to the monastery. She saw more men and women in this castle than she imagined there would be, judging from the state of the outside. Perhaps she worried too much.

The messenger stopped at a pair of doors. One man stood guard. He was almost as large as Dolf, but rougher looking. The scars on his face and neck and the parts of his arms uncovered by a thick leather tunic showed he had known pain. And, most likely, he caused a lot of it in return.

Dolf clasped him by the arm, their large hands splayed across each other's triceps. "It's good to see you, brother." The man by the door spoke in a deep growling voice.

Kaylee looked closer at the two men, not surprised to see a resemblance.

"And you, Tige." Dolf slapped the other man on the shoulder and they stood close, looking into each other's faces.

"Who have you brought?" Tige looked at Kaylee and Asher. He only glanced at Zeb.

"A gift to Queen Sherr."

I'm a gift? She bristled at the thought.

"Enter." Tige moved slowly, but pushed the door open by himself. It seemed to move as slowly as the heavy outer door did. At least the queen wouldn't have to worry about being attacked very easily in this room.

Kaylee didn't know what she expected when she entered the room and saw the queen, but it definitely wasn't what she saw. The tiny woman before her didn't look majestic at all. Her fingers were so petite that when she raised her hands to beckon them all forward, Kaylee was sure her own hands would dwarf the queen's.

As they got closer, Kaylee noticed she was smaller around the waist than a little girl she had seen at the last inn. Kaylee glanced over at Asher. His mouth was open, his eyes wide. Queen Sherr smiled at them.

"Dolf, Zeb, you have returned." She looked at Kaylee with eyes full of excitement and then she turned to Asher. "And I see you have brought me Asher Herst as well." She reached for his hand. He hesitated before allowing her to take it.

"I bet you never expected to see me," Queen Sherr said. She winked at Asher. When he blushed, Kaylee burned with curiosity. They knew each other?

"How?" Asher stopped and shook his head. "What did you do?"

"That will be for another time. But how fortunate for me that they brought you. I am in need of finding more Blue Bloods. This one here looks like she has much potential. The message Zeb sent to me once he discovered her power has brought me much joy."

Kaylee met the queen's eyes but Queen Sherr looked at Zeb soon after. "I'm surprised it took you so long to return to me after you found her."

Dolf stepped forward. "We had a little difficulty on the trip."

"Explain." Queen Sherr returned to the chair she'd been sitting in when they entered the room. Dolf moved closer and described their encounter with Asher. Queen Sherr chuckled pleasantly at the end of the story.

"And you couldn't heal Zeb?" Queen Sherr looked directly at Kaylee.

Kaylee felt the shame of the question. "Only partly."

"Explain."

Kaylee shook her head. "I don't know if I can."

"Try."

Kaylee placed her palms together and rested them gently in front of her. She tried to describe how she felt the problem in someone's injury and how she had immediately tried to heal Zeb. "The bruising and the broken skull were simple enough. I thought things would be fine from there. It wasn't until he refused to wake up that I found out there was still something wrong with his mind. I tried again, but either too much time had passed and the damage was already done, or I just can't heal an injury like that in the first place."

Queen Sherr looked at Zeb as if she was disappointed. "We may yet have use for him. Maybe you can try again."

Kaylee didn't think anything she did would make a difference, but she doubted the queen would accept that as an answer. She nodded her head slowly.

"Now, show me what you can do." Queen Sherr pulled out a pen knife and handed it to Kaylee.

Asher stepped forward as Kaylee accepted it. "There is no need for a demonstration. I have been healed multiple times by her. I can give you my testimony of her power."

Queen Sherr frowned at Asher. "I believe you. I believed Zeb's letter. I still want to see it." Kaylee wondered when they had sent a message to the queen. Of course, it could have been at one of the farm houses they'd stopped at. She was sure she had seen one that had pigeons.

Asher and Dolf both shook their heads. Kaylee's heart swelled with fondness for the two of them.

Queen Sherr huffed. "Would it be easier if I cut myself and allowed her to heal me?" She reached to take the knife back from Kaylee.

Kaylee stepped back so she couldn't take it. "No, there is no problem for me to show you." She placed the knife on the palm of her hand and slid it across the soft flesh. It stung, but she held her hand out to the queen to see. Queen Sherr leaned in closer. When Kaylee placed her other hand on top to heal it, Queen Sherr stopped her.

"Wait." The queen moved over to her tray from lunch that had not been removed yet. She wiped the goblet out with a napkin and, gently taking Kaylee's hand in hers, she poured the puddle of indigo blood into the cup. She wiped the remaining blood from Kaylee's hand with the napkin and then nodded for her to continue. Kaylee was curious at the queen's actions, but she pushed it out of her mind and focused on her hand.

She placed her finger on her palm. The power of the pain infused her until her skin knitted itself back together.

Queen Sherr's breath caught. She took Kaylee's hand in hers once more. "There is no scar." Her voice was almost reverent. She looked into Kaylee's eyes. "It is truly amazing."

Kaylee bowed her head and nodded her acceptance of the praise, although she knew it wasn't by any effort of her own.

"Kaylee, I'm so happy to have you here with me." She took her small hand and placed it on Kaylee's arm. "Together I hope we can do many things. But for now, I will have your things taken to your room. I am sure you would like a chance to clean up, relax, and recover from your journey."

Kaylee nodded her thanks and followed the messenger who had brought them to the queen. Asher attempted to stay, but Queen Sherr pushed him gently out the door. "I think you and I will have much to talk about, but later. I have something else I must do now. You go and get settled in your rooms."

Asher left with Kaylee. She glanced back and saw the queen had returned to the cup containing her blood. Her small hand wrapped around the goblet and lifted it up, but Tige closed the door before she saw what was done with it.

Kaylee turned her attention to Asher. "How do you know her?"

Asher blushed again. He looked behind him as they walked, as if he didn't want to leave. "I found her once."

"Found her?" Kaylee asked.

"She was a Blue Blood."

Kaylee frowned. "She's not one now?"

"I don't know. I believe not."

"How is that possible?"

"You know how it works as well as I do. She must have lost her first life."

Kaylee looked back at the doors with Tige standing in front of it again. "What will she do with you?" Kaylee asked.

Asher shrugged. "She may have me hanged." He said it easily, as if it didn't matter. Kaylee's stomach dropped at the thought. "Or she may hire me for my services to find more Blue Bloods for her cause."

"What is her cause?" Kaylee asked.

"I don't know."

"What will you do?"

"It depends." Asher glanced back down the hallway once more before they reached the corner where the messenger led them.

Their guide stopped at a room about halfway down this other corridor and said, "Sir Herst, this will be your room for your stay." He waited until Asher moved into the room. "I will come for you in a few hours when dinner is served."

The servant motioned for Kaylee to follow him. She met his stride and soon they reached her room.

"Thank you," Kaylee paused. "What is your name?"

"Jayshon," he replied. "A serving woman will be up soon to help you bathe."

Kaylee looked to where he pointed. A huge copper tub rested in the corner. It currently held no water, but she knew it would be filled soon.

Jayshon moved over to a huge cabinet. "The queen didn't know your size so she had a variety of dresses made for you. You will find them in the wardrobe here. Find one that suits you and dress for dinner. I will come for you in a few hours."

CHAPTER SIXTEEN

Kaylee placed both fists on her hips as she stared at the huge piece of furniture. She wasn't looking forward to wearing a dress again, yet it would be better to please the queen from the beginning. She didn't need to wear breaches now that traveling through the countryside and forests had ended. She wouldn't give them up completely, though.

She stepped over to the wardrobe. Might as well get it over with now. She had just opened the door when a quick knock from the outside was followed by a parade of serving girls carrying buckets of steaming water. They poured the water to fill the bath, and then they stripped and bathed her with no regards to her complaints. A large woman stood in front of the tub and looked Kaylee over as she submitted to being washed. Kaylee was embarrassed at first until she realized the woman was taking her measurements. She stood in front of the wardrobe for only a moment before pulling out two dresses. She held them both up, looked between Kaylee and the dresses, and kept the cream colored one.

Relief washed over Kaylee when the shimmering green dress returned to the cabinet. She didn't want to wear something so fancy. It just seemed wrong to wear such a color.

She was pulled up out of the water and dried quickly. One of the serving girls commented briefly about her short hair, but the other women quickly shushed her. They stood her in front of the large woman holding the dress and Kaylee found herself being covered first in some soft undergarments the felt totally unfamiliar. As one of the girls started cleaning up, Kaylee caught her gathering the traveling clothes with the towels.

"Leave those," Kaylee said.

Everyone stopped. Kaylee stepped closer to the one holding her breeches and shirt.

"I . . ." the girl ducked her head, as if she were afraid of what Kaylee might do to her.

"I don't want them gone. Wash them here in the tub."

The girl looked to the large woman as if asking for guidance.

The large woman moved closer to them. "Miss Kaylee. We will take good care of them."

"I don't want them lost," Kaylee insisted.

"They won't be lost," the leader of the women said.

"Exactly, because you will leave them here."

"But we can't wash them in these tubs." The woman crossed her large arms over her chest.

"Then I will wash them. They are not leaving my room." Kaylee was surprised to find herself standing with her hands on her hips. The other girls cowered away from her. Even the large woman seemed to cave.

She turned to the girl holding Kaylee's clothes. "Wash them here, Hannah."

Kaylee nodded.

"Yes, Trae." Hannah turned back to the tub, immersed the clothes in it, and scrubbed. Kaylee watched for a moment until Trae spoke.

"Miss Kaylee." Trae held up the dress she'd picked out and Kaylee glanced down to find herself standing in just a shift.

She moved forward and allowed them to dress her. She was pleased that these women would do what she said, but knew they would expect certain things from her as well.

When one of the girls brought some ribbons to Trae, the older woman shook her head. "Where are we going to put those?"

Kaylee reached up to her hair. "I don't need anything like that."

When they finished their ministrations, they left, but Kaylee made sure they left her travel clothes to dry in her room. The window was small, probably to keep any archers from being able to shoot into the room, but with enough air flow that Kaylee was certain they would dry eventually.

Kaylee returned to her bag she hadn't had time to unpack. There had to be a place she could put her things without worrying about servants looking through her belongings. Kaylee picked up the book and stroked the worn leather before opening its pages again. She brushed her hand across the book and let her thumb linger on the now familiar symbol in the corner. She wished she could make sense of this book. Maybe here she'd be able to study it. She closed the book and tucked it under her pillow, vowing she'd find a chest to lock her personal stuff in. Surely the queen would allow her some privileges.

Jayshon returned to escort her to dinner. Asher was with him and they walked quietly down the hall. Asher cleaned up well. She'd seen these clothes before, so he obviously didn't get a new wardrobe, but he looked better than she'd seen him yet. Enough to send an unfamiliar flutter through her middle.

The dining hall was smaller than expected, given the size of the castle. The large table only had three place settings, though it could have held twelve comfortably. Kaylee glanced at Asher. He returned her look, walked forward, and bowed slightly before the queen.

Queen Sherr waved away the bow and invited them to sit. "I am glad for your company. I tire of eating alone."

Asher sat down on one side of the table and Jayshon led Kaylee to her place directly across from Asher. Jayshon slid the chair out for Kaylee and helped her sit on the right side of the queen. He left and three servants entered the room carrying trays heavy with food.

A girl, smaller in size than Kaylee, but larger than the queen, placed a bowl of soup before Kaylee. She reached across the table to set a basket of fresh rolls down, sending a shiver through Kaylee as their skin touched. She paused for a moment, then stood straight and moved to return to the kitchen for more food.

"Kaylee, tell me of your life before you changed." Queen Sherr turned slightly to have a better view.

Kaylee blinked and swallowed the spoonful of soup as she regarded the queen before her. She glanced at Asher, but he only looked at her with the same interest as the queen. "I grew up in a small village. My mother died when I was twelve. My father took her death pretty hard. About two years later we discovered I bled blue. He took me from my home and we started traveling around, never really staying in one place very long. Eventually he stopped at the monastery and we stayed there. I don't know if he planned to ever leave, but he died suddenly of a sickness and I had nowhere else to go."

"You lived with the monks?" Queen Sherr asked. "Is that why your hair is so short?"

Kaylee nodded.

"And they never suspected you were a woman?" Queen Sherr asked. She looked at Kaylee closer as if studying her features.

Kaylee shrugged. "We were pretty isolated there. We rarely spoke, and privacy was important to the monks. It never became an issue."

Queen Sherr chuckled. "I suppose when they discovered you, it was quite the shock."

Kaylee nodded. "Master Falon didn't take it very well." Kaylee frowned at the memory. "I think he was disappointed in my deception."

"I'll bet." Queen Sherr laughed. "And then along comes Asher to lead you to your salvation." She turned to better face Asher sitting to her left.

Asher blushed. It was interesting to see the way his skin changed color.

"How many more of us have you taken to the king in the last few years?" Queen Sherr said.

"Two."

"And how exactly do you find them?" Queen Sherr asked.

Asher hesitated a moment. "It's a gift."

"Indeed." Queen Sherr took a bite of her meal. "Will you use that gift for me?"

"What do you plan to do with Blue Bloods?" Asher asked.

"Put an end to King Inwer's tyranny."

"You think him a tyrant?" Asher asked.

"I know him to be one. I helped make him."

Kaylee watched the two as they talked, feeling overwhelmed at the idea of dethroning a king.

Asher shook his head. "What will you do once you've deposed the king?"

Queen Sherr placed both her small hands in front of her. "I will rule the nation. I will give the Blue Bloods the honor and power they deserve. They will no longer be forced to do what one man wants. They will be organized into a ruling body that can benefit the world instead of just lining the pockets of and protecting a selfish man."

Asher crossed his arms over his chest. "From what I've seen, the king has kept his nation from going to war."

Queen Sherr snorted. Kaylee smiled at the disparity of her body language and her sounds. "No one dares to come against him because of his Blue Bloods. And any nation that tried to attack has been wiped out immediately. But, now that I know his weaknesses, I can defeat him."

Asher took a sip of his drink. "He has made peace common throughout the land. The people are free to do as they wish and still have protections. There is law and order. I doubt you'd gain much of a following among the people. If you went in there to attack, you'd be stopped by those you want to rule."

"Once I reveal what the king has done, I'll have the support I need. Who knows better than a Blue Blood who lived through it? I have seen what he's become. I was privy to so many things."

"How did you lose your life?" Asher asked. Kaylee leaned forward, her food forgotten.

"The king himself took it."

"What?" Asher asked.

"The king had a crazy notion that he could become a Blue Blood himself. He tried an experiment and it failed. His failure cost me my life."

Asher bowed his head. "I'm sorry for your loss."

Queen Sherr grimaced. "I suppose I'm luckier than some. I have this second life. It is nowhere near as blessed as the first, but I can say I've enjoyed what I've lived of it."

Kaylee wanted to know more details. Did it hurt when she died? Could she remember everything about it? Kaylee finally settled on a question she thought would be okay to ask. "What was your power as a Blue Blood?"

"I could affect the elements. I brought rain or snow to areas that needed the moisture. I could prevent it from coming to places that needed a little persuasion to do as the king asked." Queen Sherr frowned, her petite nose wrinkling just a little as she did.

"You caused droughts?" Kaylee asked. She'd seen the effects of the lack of rain in many of the places she'd traveled through with her father.

"All in the name of the king. You see now why I want to stop him. Why he needs to be taken from his power." Queen Sherr leaned closer to Kaylee. "And I wasn't even one of the more amazing Blue Bloods. There were others who could do so much more, some on a larger scale than me. Others were more refined in their distance, but their powers were amazing nonetheless."

"Did he use them against the people?" Kaylee asked.

Queen Sherr nodded. "He would send his Blue Bloods who could move the earth to mine for his gold. That would disrupt the people and the livelihood of those who lived in the mountains. He always gave them the option of relocating, but for those who wouldn't move or didn't go fast enough, they were buried under the landslides that resulted from the mining."

Asher choked on his drink. Kaylee had stopped eating as Queen Sherr described the horrors the king imposed on his people.

"I have never heard this."

"Of course not," Queen Sherr said. "Any who may have survived it or seen it have had their memories altered by one of his Blue Bloods, if they were lucky to meet her instead of one of the others sent to silence them."

Kaylee thanked her God she'd been intercepted by Dolf and Zeb.

Asher leaned forward, arms resting on the table. "How do you expect to stop him? You have no power. And Kaylee is just one. Her gift is nothing that will help you stop a king."

"Don't you think she would be able to heal my armies? They could go to war more than once. They would be able to continue fighting when most men would be gone."

"But the cost is too high for Kaylee. She would never be able to withstand the pain."

Queen Sherr turned to Kaylee in surprise. "What is he talking about?"

Shame washed over Kaylee. "I have to feel pain in order to heal. If I'm hurt, my energy comes through my own pain. If someone else is injured, I have to feel something too before the power will take effect. I can see what needs to be done without the pain, but for me to make any difference in someone else, I must feel something comparable."

The queen frowned and looked like she was considering a variety of possibilities. "Perhaps my plan won't work out exactly how I envisioned it, but it is still worth looking into." She turned back to Asher. "As for you, hunter. I want you to find me more Blue Bloods. There have to be some near me that I could recruit. People who could see things my way. I want you to find them."

"I felt no indication of any in this area as we traveled." Asher shook his head. Kaylee wondered again how he could sense them.

"Then maybe you will have to go on a journey to bring me more."

Asher frowned. "I will think on it."

Queen Sherr placed her hand on his. "I can pay you. I have money. It was easy enough to amass my wealth. And it helped to know where the king kept his riches." Kaylee looked at the queen. "I figure it was payment for my death." Queen Sherr winked.

Asher chuckled. Kaylee allowed a smile to cross her lips.

CHAPTER SEVENTEEN

Asher turned his attention to the meal. The next few minutes passed in silence, each one seeming to be lost in their own thoughts. A servant entered the room to clear away the used dishes. Asher sat up straight. Something seemed different. He touched his talisman hanging beneath his shirt. It pulsed gently, indicating there was another Blue Blood present. He had become used to the vibration he got with Kaylee on it, but this was stronger.

Asher stared at the young girl, who took away a plate from Kaylee. He leaned closer over the table trying to see if there were any indication that she was the one. He had never relied only on his talisman to find them. Once they were cut, he could smell the signature scent of Blue Blood. Asher considered pulling out his knife, but didn't think it would be wise with the queen right there. He didn't know how she would react to that, and he wanted to have the leverage needed to get his price before the queen discovered one of her own servants was what she was looking for.

He studied the servant girl until he felt the queen's attention on him. Asher winked at the girl trying to make the queen think that was his only interest in her. The girl blinked and lowered her eyes. He waited for a pink blush to creep up her face, but the color on her skin never changed. He had noticed with many of the other Blue Bloods he had encountered that they rarely flushed. Something about their skin seemed different with the blue blood that flowed through their veins. Asher was almost certain this girl was one. But how had his talisman missed the indication of her before? He hadn't felt even a hint that there would be any around here.

The servant girl kept her head down for the entire time she stayed in the dining hall, not glancing at Asher once. He wasn't actually interested in her, besides the fact she might be a Blue Blood. But rarely was he treated with such control as this girl showed. Asher looked back over at an unhappy looking queen. He turned his attention back to her, hoping to distract her from the serving girl.

"How long have you been here, Sherr?" Asher asked. At her raised eyebrow, he realized he had left off her title.

"It has been over a year since I left the company of the king. I have been at this location for near six months."

Asher nodded. "It looks like you are making efforts to fortify it." Kaylee watched him closely.

"It will be completed soon, or so I'm told."

Kaylee stopped mid-bite and looked over at the queen, surprise evident on her face. Asher watched, waiting for her to comment, but she kept her mouth closed.

"You don't think it seems close, Kaylee?" Asher asked. Queen Sherr turned to Kaylee. Asher waited again to see some indication of embarrassment on her face. Still nothing. Her skin was clear and perfect without any hint the color was changing. A thought occurred to Asher and he wondered what temperature her skin felt. He could only remember it felt soft. Her hands were a little rough, but he couldn't recall anything specific about her temperature. He'd have to make an excuse to touch her and see.

The queen said, "Speak child. I want to know what you think of your new home. Don't you believe it will be a grand fortification soon?"

Kaylee shook her head gently. "It's not that. I only know the structure of the monastery I left. It was built strong to withstand the raiders who used to come into the country hundreds of years ago. The walls were thick and there were no windows larger than the spread of your hand."

Queen Sherr glanced at the large window then back to Kaylee. "Perhaps this window is a bit foolish, but I can't bear to be hidden away in the dark. I want light. But maybe I should think of some way to keep us better protected."

Jayshon entered the room and moved to the queen's side. He whispered in her ear. She glanced at Asher and Kaylee before nodding. "I must see to something. Please finish your meal and then return to your rooms. We will meet again tomorrow." She looked at Asher. "I expect an answer from you."

Asher nodded and stood as she rose to leave. He waited until she slipped out the door before sitting down and turning his attention to Kaylee.

"What are you thinking?"

Kaylee looked at him. She pressed her lips together gently and merely watched him.

"You aren't going to tell me, are you?"

"There's no need."

"Of course there is." Asher leaned back casually. "What do you think of your new home?"

Kaylee took her fork in her hand. "It is not my home." She ate a bite of food and chewed slowly as Asher watched her.

"Do you wish to be elsewhere?"

Kaylee didn't answer.

"It was you who decided to come with Dolf and Zeb to this place instead of to the king."

She nodded.

"So why won't you tell me what you think of this place?"

"Because it isn't important. What is important is knowing what she has planned for me. And for you. And until I know those things, I've formed no solid opinion."

She continued to eat and mostly ignored the questions he asked, frustrating him to no end. He didn't have difficulty with women for the most part, but she was a different story. Not to mention that serving girl. Asher let Kaylee eat in silence as he returned to his meal.

"Would you like me to escort you back to your room?" Asher asked when they'd finished.

"If you'd like." She said it in a way that made him think he was completely unnecessary. He offered his hand, but she ignored it and walked with her hands clasped behind her back.

He didn't think it appropriate to reach for her just to test the temperature of her skin. He'd have to find out another time. And he needed to find out where that serving girl had gone. If she knew she was a Blue Blood, she would have either gone into hiding or told the queen. It wasn't a secret that Queen Sherr was a former Blue Blood.

When they got to the hallway with their rooms, Asher blinked. He had walked back there without being aware of their surroundings. Kaylee led them without fail. She stopped at her room and turned to the door.

Asher had a quick thought and reached before he could talk himself out of it. He took her hand in his and brought it to his lips. He kissed it gently, surprised her temperature felt completely normal. Kaylee's eyes rose and Asher realized what he had done.

He tried to act casual about it. "Thank you for your company this evening. It was a pleasure to dine with you."

Kaylee tilted her head to the side and considered him for a moment. "We dined many times together. What makes this so different?"

Asher stumbled over the words. "Perhaps it's that the surroundings here have added to the experience."

Kaylee glanced at the hallway and looked toward her room as if she couldn't wait to escape him.

Asher bowed slightly and walked away. He didn't look back, but he heard the door to her room close. He shook his head, vowing to not let her get under his skin anymore. He should be immune to any charms she might possess. Not that she had many, having lived among men disguised as a boy, but still.

Asher pulled his talisman out from under his shirt. He held it in his hand and focused on the feeling it gave off. There was definitely a Blue Blood besides Kaylee here. Had she been farther away when they first got here? Or had he just been so distracted by everything when he got here he missed it?

It didn't matter. What mattered now was finding her, determining if she were a Blue Blood, and then taking his discovery to the queen.

Kaylee looked at her hand. Why had Asher kissed it? She couldn't understand why he began treating her so differently. Was it because of the surroundings, as he said? Or was it because of the dress she wore? She was surprised she liked the way it felt, but still wished she could've worn the clothes she'd shown up in. She glanced at them still hanging, damp, near the fireplace. It wasn't lit, but she felt the draft that went up it. It should provide for a good fire when the temperature changed enough to warrant one.

Kaylee moved over to the bed and sat on its corner. She pulled out the book she had tucked under the pillow, hoping it hadn't been touched. She didn't like leaving her things in a strange place, but eventually this room would become as familiar to her as her cell in the monastery. Here she would have servants coming in and out of her room. She would need to find a place to put her things that didn't make anyone want to snoop.

The few small things she had were of no value. The book might be interesting to someone, but it wasn't worth anything monetarily. There was nothing special about it that she could tell. It looked like it had been a book where someone jotted down things without much comprehension. But she loved this book for many reasons. She felt something when she read it, almost like she was being comforted by her father. She found this thought odd, since he forbade her to read it.

She wished she could have asked him about it. What would he think about her reading it now? He'd been very upset the first time he caught her with it. He'd hidden it away from her and scolded her enough that when the monks had brought her his things after he died, she hesitated to even touch it. She hadn't pulled the book out until she'd been forced to leave the monastery.

Kaylee leaned her head against the headboard of the huge bed. She refused to let the tears fall. She had no reason to dwell on her sadness. She'd mourned for her father enough. Through the teachings of the monks, she knew he was in a better place. He was serving God personally now. He would not want her to spend more time missing him, not when she could do something to help the people in the world she lived in.

Kaylee wondered what her reward would be when she died. Well, she knew what one would be. A second life. She would live again without the burden of this new power. If only she could have healed her father. Knowing the way he felt about Blue Bloods, Kaylee doubted he would have let her do anything.

Tears filled her eyes and spilled onto her cheeks. Her father would have been ashamed of her. He would have thought her desire for power an evil she should purge. Though she would use it to help people who were ill or sick or hurt, he would probably have been concerned about her using it.

Kaylee caressed the book's leather cover and wiped the tear away. She sniffed and wiped the back of her hand across her nose then shook her head to clear her thoughts. She would not allow such memories to bring her down. She may be able to see her father in the next life.

Or the one after that. Kaylee chuckled.

Whenever she saw him, she would be sure she had lived her lives and used her power for good. She would be able to stand before him with no shame.

Kylee opened the book to the last page she had read, placing her fingers on the symbol in the corner. It was different from the one on the page before and the one following. They each had similar elements to them, squares, circles, triangles, wavy lines, but each arranged in a different way. *What does it mean?* The words still didn't make any sense when read in order.

She read through the page from top to bottom, then tried bottom to top. Still nothing understandable.

A knock on the door brought Kaylee out of her study. The candle on her desk had burned more than halfway down. She put the book under her pillow again and moved to answer. One of the girls who helped her bathe and dress stood with a handful of clothing. She shifted the bundle and brushed a strand of light red hair off her freckled face.

"Good evening, Miss Kaylee." She bobbed a curtsy, and then she marched into the room, nearly pushing Kaylee to the side. "The queen has sent these to you." She laid the dresses, night clothes, and various other clothing items Kaylee didn't know were even necessary on the bed and stepped back.

"Please give the queen my thanks." Kaylee looked them over.

"Of course." The girl bobbed again. "I'm Lacey. Can I help you undress?" Lacey didn't wait for a response before moving behind Kaylee to undo the buttons.

Kaylee jumped in surprise and turned quickly to grab Lacey's hand. A sensation similar to healing crossed over her as she touched Lacey's skin. "Are you injured?" she asked. She hadn't felt any pain herself, making her doubt it was healing.

Lacey stared at her, unblinking for a moment longer, then blinked rapidly and bobbed her head, looking embarrassed. "I'm sorry, miss. May I help you with your clothes?" She looked down at Kaylee's hand still on hers.

Kaylee allowed Lacey to help her with the buttons since they were in the back and difficult to reach on her own. She soon found herself dressed in the soft night gown. She touched the fabric and rubbed it gently between her fingers.

Kaylee looked up to see Lacey watching her. "Again, please tell the queen I appreciate her gifts."

Lacey nodded and glanced at the mostly dry breeches and shirt before slipping out of the room. Kaylee smiled as she imagined what the serving girls thought of her strange clothes. Once they were dry, she'd pack them away.

CHAPTER EIGHTEEN

Asher woke early the next morning feeling more rested than he had in months. He wondered if that was a good sign, or if it would allow him to get too much at ease. He dressed quickly, bumping his talisman in the process. He placed his hand on it to steady it and realized there was something different about it. It hummed and vibrated, and he felt an additional pulse he had missed before. Was it possible there were two new Blue Bloods here?

He rushed from his room and wandered the hallway. He couldn't tell what direction the Blue Blood might be in. He just knew they were close. Within a mile for sure, but more likely within the immediate area of the castle grounds. He would find her. He had to know what was happening.

He sniffed the air cautiously. He smelled no indication of bleeding. He wished his ability were more refined, but he had limits. He wanted to find the serving girl he'd seen at dinner last night. He would investigate her first. He figured the best place to look for her would be in the kitchens. He didn't know exactly where the kitchens were, but most castles had a similar layout. He'd start with the ground floor, near the outer edges. They'd want to be close to the gardens and have access to the outside.

It didn't take him long to find it. Once he got close enough, he could smell the breads baking along with some hearty meat and something sweet. The stifling heat inside the kitchen made him hesitate to go in. The workers inside sweated, their hair clinging to faces and necks. Sweat stained their backs and under the arms. He had never given much thought to what went into preparing a meal. He would have more respect for the kitchen workers now.

He stepped into the kitchen but a small, feisty woman soon escorted him back out into the hallway. She crossed her arms over her apron covered chest, and shook her head. "You aren't allowed in here, sir."

Asher tried to speak. She held up her hand. "We'll bring you your meal in your room, or you can have a seat in the dining hall." She pointed to the door down the hall. Asher glanced at it. When he turned to look back into the kitchen, he spotted the girl who had served him last night. She met his eyes, and then she quickly looked down and stepped behind a girl scrubbing a pan.

Asher took a step forward, immediately stopped by the woman in front of him.

"I need to see that girl over there." Asher pointed where she had stood. "Where'd she go?"

"Sorry, sir. You cannot come in here and molest my girls. Jenna is too young for you anyway. This is not some pub you can find yourself a play thing. You will not touch a one of them." Her eyes spoke volumes. Asher stopped trying to slip past her.

"I'm sorry if you think that of me." Asher shook his head. "I am not going to bother her. But I must speak to her. You don't want me to go to the queen to get her involved, do you?"

The woman didn't budge. "The queen knows my girls are not to be messed with. If you think what you have to do is so important, you go ahead and get Queen Sherr involved." She emphasized the last word and wrinkled her nose at him.

Asher knew his bluff had been called. He would have to find a way to see her on his own unless he wanted to hand over his one small advantage before he could reach an agreement with the queen.

Asher took a step back and turned down the hallway toward the dining hall. Just before pushing the door open, he looked back to see her still standing at the doorway watching him closely. He entered the dining hall. He smiled when he saw Kaylee, dressed in a simple brown dress. It was loose and flowing, but still more fitting than the robes she would've worn masquerading as a monk. He almost wished he could have seen her wearing her monk's robe. He would have liked to know if she looked as beautiful in it as she did now.

Her hair was still shorter than his, but it shone beautifully in the light coming through the windows. He joined her at the table. "How did you sleep?"

Kaylee lifted one shoulder slightly. "Tolerably."

"Just tolerably?" He grinned. "Did you have an issue with something?"

Kaylee didn't answer as she spread some butter on a roll. Asher picked one up as well and sighed as he took a bite of fluffy heaven on his taste buds. They obviously had a gift when it came to baking. This roll tasted better than any he'd had before.

Asher tried to bring Kaylee into conversation, but she politely declined. When the queen entered the room, Asher stood. Kaylee followed his example. The queen waved them both to sit back down.

"I am not here to eat with you." She reached for a roll anyway and took a bite. "I wanted to know your decision, Asher."

Asher said, "I believe I will be able to find you some Blue Bloods. I don't think it will take too long. But I want your assurance I will have the payment I deserve."

"I will pay you the same bounty you received from King Inwer."

Asher fought the smile that threatened. He hadn't hoped for that much. But he knew she wanted them desperately. "No matter where I find them?"

Queen Sherr allowed a smile to cross her lips. "I would even pay you double if you can convince the ones in his service to join me."

Asher tried to gauge whether she were serious or not. She seemed genuine about her offer.

"I won't need to go that far."

Queen Sherr glanced at Kaylee. "Speaking of bounties, I have not paid you yet for this one. There will be a bag left in your room by this evening."

Asher was surprised about the cold manner she treated Kaylee. She didn't act as if she were important to her anymore.

As soon as he had those thoughts, the queen turned to Kaylee and spoke. "As for you, my dear. I believe you and I should meet soon to figure out how we can best help one another. I want to see what we can learn about your talents in a way that will cause you the least amount of discomfort. No need to use the barbaric methods Zeb tried with you." Queen Sherr shook her head. She moved closer to Kaylee and placed a hand on hers. "I am sorry for his treatment of you. I don't think he will bother you again."

Kaylee nodded to the queen and pulled her hand away from the queen's. "Thank you. He was actually kind enough in most ways."

Queen Sherr looked as if she didn't believe it. "This afternoon we will meet in my study to go over what we can." She gave a parting look to Asher. "I expect you to have fast results. I need to gather my own to me."

Asher nodded. He turned back to Kaylee once they were alone again. Kaylee's wide eyes were sad as she met his.

"What?"

Kaylee didn't respond. Instead, she got up and left the room. Why would she be angry at him? What had he done?

Kaylee couldn't believe Asher. The only thing that mattered to him was money. What about the lives of the women he would change when he brought them to the queen? It didn't matter that this queen had once been a Blue Blood. She would know what to expect of them; she'd know their limits and their abilities. She would more than likely be more tolerable than the tyrant king would have been.

But still, serving any ruler meant asking a woman to give up her entire existence. The more Kaylee thought of it, the more upset she got.

And as far as she could tell, the only thing she would be given in return would be a place to live, clothes to wear, and work to do. Work not of her own choosing. She wanted to use her power to help others. Perhaps the queen would allow her to do that. If they could stop the king from his path, she would be able to go out among the people and do what she could to heal them from their illnesses.

Surely Queen Sherr would understand that. She kept her hopes to herself. She didn't feel like she could talk to anyone here. And though it seemed like Asher had once taken an interest in her, now that she was here and paid for, he wouldn't take any time out of his day to talk to her.

She should be used to it. She'd spent so long not speaking much. It shouldn't be any different for her now. But she enjoyed talking to him on occasion as they traveled. She hadn't seen Dolf since they arrived and he delivered her to the queen. She missed him and wished she could spend time with him. She still had the sling he'd given her in her pack. She could always practice it in her free time.

When she reached her rooms, it wasn't long before one of the serving girls entered. Kaylee realized at once she was the one Asher had been flirting with at dinner last night. She didn't understand the flush of anger that spread through her heart. She stamped down the unkind feelings and turned to the girl. She was surprised to see fear in her eyes.

"What's the matter?" Kaylee asked.

"I . . ."

Kaylee dropped her hands to her side hoping to look less intimidating. "Don't worry, you can talk to me."

The girl held up her hand. Kaylee leaned closer. Nothing looked out of the ordinary at first until she noticed some swelling of a finger. "Oh, did you hurt yourself? I can heal you if you need. Is that why you came?"

The girl shook her head, eyes growing wider.

"Then what?" Kaylee looked closer and saw it. Where it should have been red amongst the swelling, a deep indigo bloomed. A small cut in the corner of her fingernail bled blue. Kaylee gasped in surprise and looked up quickly at the girl.

"You're one, too? How long have you known? Does anyone else know?"

The girl hid her finger in her other hand and glanced at the door. "I smashed my finger as I was helping to move a cart full of potatoes. As soon as I saw this I left and came straight here."

"Have you ever bled blue before?" Kaylee asked.

"No. I even cut myself a couple weeks ago and it was red as anyone else's."

Kaylee held the girls hand in hers.

She looked up into Kaylee's eyes. "Did you do this to me?"

Kaylee blinked. "No. How could I?"

"I don't know, is it contagious? How did you get yours?"

"I have no idea. It came to me one day. Scared my dad, too. He took us away and kept me hidden. Didn't want me to become a servant of the king."

"Do you think a queen will be any better?"

"You know her better than I do," Kaylee said. "From what I've heard, she seems to be all right. She was once treated badly by the king. She wouldn't do the same to us, I'm sure."

"But how can I be a Blue Blood? It never would've happened if you weren't here." Her voice didn't seem to be accusing, but it still stung Kaylee.

"I don't know how it happens. No one seems to know. Not even Asher, who finds people like us."

Her eyes widened. "Is that why he's been following me around?"

Kaylee smiled. "Probably. Have you talked to him at all?"

"No." She shook her head. "I thought he was one of those kinds who think they can have a girl just for asking. I didn't want anything to do with that. I had a friend who got involved with that kind of man. It didn't turn out well for her."

Kaylee nodded. She still held the girl's hand. "Do you want me to heal this . . ." Kaylee paused, waiting for the girl to give her name.

"Jenna."

"Would you like me to fix this, Jenna?"

She nodded slowly, keeping her eyes on Kaylee's. Kaylee led her over to the edge of the bed. Kaylee placed her free hand on the back of her arm and scratched down quickly leaving deep blue marks on her skin. Jenna flinched in surprise, but Kaylee felt enough pain to allow the healing to work. Jenna pulled her healed hand away from Kaylee and held it close to her chest.

"Why did you do that?" Jenna asked.

"It's the way my power works. I have to feel pain to heal."

"You shouldn't have done that for me. If I'd have known, I would have just let it heal on its own. It's not really that bad. The blue caused me the most worry."

"It's done. No need to fuss."

Jenna nodded. "So what should I do?"

Kaylee smiled. "Well, we could either let Asher take you to the queen, or we could deny him his bounty and you can tell her yourself."

Jenna paled. "I don't know if I dare tell the queen. What if she thinks I've been hiding it from her?"

"Have you?" Kaylee asked seriously.

"No. This is the first time I have ever seen my blood that color."

"Then there is no reason to fear her. I believe you. And she will, too. Besides, she needs you. She wants to build up her own army of Blue Bloods if she is going to have a chance to stop the king."

"I don't want to be part of an army."

"I doubt we'll have to fight like they do. And until we know what power you have, it's useless to worry."

"How will I know what my power is?" Jenna asked.

"Mine took years to show up. It happened after I fell from a horse and broke my arm. Asher said something big has to happen to you. Kind of like shocking you into it."

Jenna wrapped herself with her arms. "What will they do to me?"

"I don't know. But I can heal most anything, so don't worry about that. Plus, I doubt they'll want to harm you. The queen will know of ways to bring about the shock. I can't imagine it will be all bad."

Jenna took a while to calm down, but Kaylee eventually convinced her that when she met with the queen this afternoon, Jenna would accompany her.

"For now, you will stay here in my room with me."

"But what about my other chores?" Jenna asked looking to the door. "If Cook finds me in here without having completed my work she'll have me whipped."

"You're a Blue Blood now. Do you really think you'll be doing chores anymore?" Kaylee lifted one eyebrow. Though Kaylee longed to be able to do something useful, she didn't wish for the labors she'd done before. "Besides," Kaylee said. "I need your help in here. I just can't do this by myself."

Jenna looked around. "Do what by yourself?"

"Oh, I don't know. Anything. Apparently I can't even get dressed by myself anymore."

Jenna smiled.

When lunch time came, Kaylee made sure Jenna was busy doing something in her room just in case one of the serving girls who brought the lunch in saw her. The girl who brought it glanced at Jenna as she brushed the boots Kaylee traveled in. As she left the room, Jenna visibly relaxed.

"Here, there is plenty of food for the two of us. Why don't you join me?"

Jenna shook her head as if horrified by the suggestion.

Kaylee sighed. "I know it will take some getting used to. It did for me, but you have to admit you're different now. You will be treated differently. You might as well act like you deserve some special treatment. They will pile it upon you without your permission."

Jenna looked at Kaylee with hope in her eyes.

Kaylee shrugged her shoulders. "Of course, you also lose some of your freedom too. I don't think I'll ever be able to live my life the way I want to now. But I am probably better off here than I would be if I tried to go off somewhere on my own."

Jenna took a small piece of meat, about a third of the cheese, and a tiny section of a roll. She wouldn't accept more no matter how much Kaylee offered.

A knock on the door brought Kaylee's eyes up from her tray. Panic filled Jenna's face. Kaylee waved her hand and motioned for her to get back to working on the boots. When Jenna looked sufficiently busy, Kaylee answered it. Jayshon stood there looking impatient.

"I will take you to the queen now."

Kaylee walked over to Jenna and took her hand. "She's coming with me."

Jayshon narrowed his eyes. "She is not needed."

Kaylee stood tall. "She is. She will come with me."

Jayshon frowned and motioned for them to follow him. Kaylee squeezed Jenna's hand and led her down the hallway.

CHAPTER NINETEEN

Kaylee could almost feel the fear rolling off Jenna as they walked hand in hand to the queen. Kaylee tried to act brave, hoping the queen would be reasonable and accept the news of Jenna's blue blood with composure.

Jayshon opened the door to the queen's study and gave one last look of annoyance to the serving girl with her. Jenna cowered and Kaylee pulled her forward.

Queen Sherr looked up from her desk and a flash of something crossed her eyes before she looked at Kaylee for explanation.

"I have some news for you, Your Majesty." Kaylee approached the queen, pulling Jenna with her. The girl moved with halting steps, but Kaylee placed her other hand on Jenna's arm and she soon calmed enough to walk forward.

Queen Sherr looked between the two expectantly, her eyes finally resting on Kaylee. Kaylee glanced at Jenna and knew she would not speak for herself. Kaylee took a slow breath and smiled. "You wanted to build up your own group of Blue Bloods. Well, now you have two."

Queen Sherr's eyes narrowed in confusion and looked again at Jenna. "Two?"

Jenna looked up and finally met the queen's eyes. She nodded her head quickly, and then looked at the ground as if afraid again.

"You're a Blue Blood as well?" Queen Sherr stood and walked around the table. The control in her voice worried Kaylee. Was she surprised, confused, angry, or just accepting it as easily as if she were told what was for dinner?

Jenna nodded curtly once more.

"How long have you known?" Queen Sherr asked.

Jenna glanced at Kaylee with wide panic filled eyes. Kaylee turned to the queen. "She came to me this morning with a smashed finger. It bled blue."

"Why did you not come to me immediately?" the queen asked.

"We believed you would be very busy. I decided to wait until my appointment with you."

"If there is ever another found, you will come to me immediately. No waiting. Am I understood?"

Kaylee nodded and squeezed Jenna's hand. Jenna nodded quickly, but kept her eyes down.

"So this will change our plans for this meeting." Queen Sherr returned to her chair behind the desk. She motioned for Kaylee and Jenna to come closer and sit across from her. "First things first, we'll need to find out what Jenna's powers will be." Queen Sherr looked at Jenna and gave her a sympathetic smile. "I can't promise it won't be difficult, but I'll be as gentle and humane as possible."

Jenna nodded. Kaylee felt the tension leaving her as the queen's calmness allowed Jenna to relax.

Kaylee left Jenna in the queen's study as she returned to her room. The news of a second Blue Blood in the castle would be out soon enough when Jenna moved from her servant's quarters into her own room in the same wing as Kaylee's. She felt sad for Jenna, knowing that her friends would now be afraid of her.

And it was strange to think that since Kaylee arrived, Jenna's blue blood had manifested. Was it contagious like Jenna suggested? She'd have to ask Asher what he knew of it. The queen didn't think it was but had indicated she would be checking her girls to see if anyone else had changed. Kaylee would be busy tomorrow healing the cuts the Queen would inflict in her search. It would be simple and relatively painless for most of them, just a quick prick in the finger, but the queen wanted Kaylee to heal them to show how useful a Blue Blood could be. The idea of testing all girls in the castle, and the surrounding countryside, made Kaylee nervous.

Kaylee lifted her head when she heard boots running through the hallway. Asher rushed toward her, almost knocking her down before he noticed her.

"Where's the queen?" Asher's breath came heavy, making Kaylee wonder how long he'd been running.

"In her study." Kaylee pointed behind her and Asher rushed past her to the door. He hesitated a moment then knocked.

A muffled voice said, "Enter."

Asher looked back at Kaylee before opening the door. Kaylee wondered what he had to tell the queen. Since the door didn't close behind him, she stepped closer to watch what happened.

"Forgive me, Your Majesty. I have some . . ." His voice trailed off and Kaylee took the chance to peek around the doorway. He seemed surprised to see Jenna in conversation with the queen.

"You have some . . ." Queen Sherr prompted.

Asher cleared his throat and looked back to the open door catching Kaylee watching him. "I have reason to believe there is a Blue Blood here."

"You are correct, Asher." Queen Sherr motioned to Jenna. "May I introduce Jenna? My newest acquisition."

Jenna's head ducked, but then she looked up and met Asher's eyes. Kaylee cheered silently that she was gaining some backbone. Asher must have recognized her as the girl he'd been flirting with because he took a step forward. He looked back at Kaylee as if she'd betrayed him before turning to the queen.

"That is wonderful news, my queen. I also hope to be able to find more since we are so fortunate to have one here now. If you will excuse me, I'll leave you and return to my search."

Asher turned on his heels before the queen could excuse him. He marched out the door. Kaylee stepped back in surprise at the frustration on his face. He reached for her quickly and took her by the arm.

"What happened? Did you know about this?" He jerked his head back to the queen's study.

"Jenna came to me when she cut herself this morning in the kitchens. It was the first time she'd ever bled blue. It just happened to her."

"Just now? This morning?"

Kaylee nodded.

Asher cursed under his breath. "I've been looking for her all morning. I knew something was different about her. But the kitchen matron wouldn't let me in, and then she was gone."

"And now you won't get your bounty for her. Poor Asher. Whatever will you do?"

Asher dropped her arm and narrowed his eyes. "I don't care about the money. I . . ." He shook his head and stomped away. Kaylee was surprised to see him leave. She hesitated a moment and then rushed to catch up.

"What is it then?" Kaylee asked. "If it isn't the money, what is it?"

"Nothing." He continued to sulk as he walked through the hallway.

"Can I ask you something?" Kaylee said.

He turned his head toward her but didn't slow down.

"Where do we come from?"

Asher stopped and Kaylee had to turn to face him.

"What do you mean?"

"Why did I develop blue blood? And why did Jenna? She asked me if I had done it to her. If it was contagious. Is it?"

"No. If it were, there would be so many more Blue Bloods."

"How many have you found?" Kaylee asked.

"I don't know, more than forty."

"How often would you find us?"

"A handful every year at first, but lately it has been much more sporadic."

"And where have you found us?"

Asher shook his head. "I don't know, all over the kingdom. I never knew they would be this far out. Of course I had no idea that anyone lived this far north. Perhaps it's something to do with your family history?"

"I don't know of anyone related to me or to my father that was a Blue Blood."

"I once found two sisters. No one else in the family showed any signs of it. And I didn't find another one in that area of the kingdom again."

"Did you find many in the same area?"

"Yes. But not at the same time. Sometimes years would pass before I found another Blue Blood in the same place. But not every village had another when I returned again. As far as I can tell from all my time searching for them, there has been no pattern or reason for multiple Blue Bloods in the same area." Asher stared at the wall in the hallway, his eyes boring into it as though looking for something hidden behind.

Kaylee watched him for a moment. "Do you think there is another one here now?"

Asher looked at her and then touched a hand to his chest. He dropped it before he touched his shirt and looked back at the wall he'd been staring at. "I'm almost sure of it."

"How?"

Asher looked at her. "How do I know, or how are there more than one here?"

"Both."

"I know because of my medallion. As for why there are two, I have no idea."

CHAPTER TWENTY

Asher couldn't understand it. How could there possibly be two Blue Bloods here, and why hadn't he noticed them when he first arrived? Of course, he'd been preoccupied with whether his offer of service would be accepted by the queen. Discovering she was the fourth Blue Blood he had taken to the king had been even more distracting.

He still wasn't sure if he should offer his service to Sherr. She wanted to kill King Inwer. Would the resulting war and hardships be worth what they would gain by dethroning him?

Kaylee obviously wanted him to explain more about how he found Blue Bloods, but right now, he felt the presence of another one somewhere in the castle. He had to find her before she turned herself in to the queen. He had to prove his worth to Sherr, and maybe in the process he could figure out how they had been hidden for so long. Or how the change had happened. He didn't want to worry Kaylee, but it was very odd that when she showed up, two more Blue Bloods appeared.

Asher bowed. "Please excuse me. I have things to do."

Kaylee blinked. Her mouth dropped open, but she shook her head and closed her mouth. Asher knew he'd upset her, but he didn't have time to try to smooth things over.

He stepped around her and continued down the hallway, turning right when he came to an adjoining hall. He picked up his pace. The Blue Blood was in front of him somewhere, but in the maze of castle walls it was difficult to know exactly where to turn. He found himself back tracking multiple times and still ended up confused and more frustrated than when he started.

Whoever she was, Asher doubted he would find her soon. He would have to wait and see what he could do after dinner. Since Jenna had been a serving girl, he wondered if maybe the other Blue Blood was a servant as well.

Asher watched each woman more closely as they went about their work. More than once, he caught them staring back. Some looked leery of him, while others seemed to be encouraging him to keep watching them. His scrutiny of Jenna had probably panicked the girl and cost him the opportunity to discover her blood. He would have to be more careful of how he observed the women.

Asher turned around and returned to the queen's wing of the castle. He had to let her know another one was close by. If he didn't prove his worth soon, she might send him away to search for others. If he left, he would have no way to ensure they treated Kaylee well.

Though he thought Queen Sherr would be kind to her Blue Bloods, until he saw her in action, he wouldn't trust her to be any different than she claimed King Inwer to be.

Asher's gaze took in the crowd of women. After Asher told Queen Sherr he was sure another Blue Blood worked in her castle, she had gathered all of her serving girls and women into the Grand Ballroom. He looked around the room and thought it was anything but grand. Of course, it was more important to fortify the outer walls than decorate the inside.

The women whispered to each other and looked around in confusion as they waited for the queen to enter. Asher moved through the group, searching for the girl. Unless they bled, it would be just a guess, but Asher was sure there would be some other indication to him who it was. The difference of their complexion was subtle, but he had seen enough Blue Bloods to have an idea of what to look for. Although their blood smelled different to him, he wondered if it were possible for him to identify her before she was cut.

Kaylee sat in a chair to one side of the queen's throne, while Jenna stood behind a chair on the other side. Jenna looked too nervous to sit. While Asher could understand why, he hoped she'd soon get over her fear. She was a Blue Blood now and much would be expected of her.

Asher slowly moved between the women. Some of them watched him. Others stared at the floor. He could smell many different scents on them. Some smelled of yeast and bread flour. Others had a strong aroma of lye and soaps. A couple smelled of dirt, and he supposed they must be in charge of the gardens. Each of them had their own scent, owing to their perspiration. One girl he passed seemed slightly different than the rest. He walked around her a few times. He looked into her eyes and when she finally looked up at him, he winked. She blushed, her face blossoming red. Asher felt disappointed. He doubted she was the Blue Blood. The red behind her cheeks was too obvious.

Asher smiled at her and moved on. He winked and smiled at many more girls, most of them blushing, but a couple keeping a clear face. He moved around those and leaned closer, checking for a difference in smell around them. A shapely girl with lots of freckles and light red hair met his eye and smiled back at him.

"What are you looking for, Master Herst?" she asked.

"I'm just getting a feel for you all."

"That's not the way you get a feel." The girls around her immediately snorted in laughter, but they quickly quieted down as if unsure of their responses.

"Probably true." Asher smiled and rubbed his finger under his nose to keep from grinning too much. "What's your name?"

"Lacey," the girl said.

"Perhaps, Lacey, you could explain the best way to get a feel for this group?"

"Well, sir, if you don't know that by now, there may not be any hope for you. Then again, I'm always up for a challenge."

Asher blushed at the look in her eyes. The women surrounding Lacey laughed again. He nodded his thanks. "I'll be in touch."

Lacey grinned. "I'm looking forward to it." Again the women giggled as Asher moved away. When the door to the room opened, Asher realized he hadn't paid attention to her face to see if she had blushed. And he didn't know if she had a different scent, but as he moved away from Lacey, he was almost sure his talisman reacted. He turned back to her and took her hand in his.

Lacey's flirtatious behavior stopped when the queen entered the room. Asher ignored her attempts to pull her hand free. "It is you."

Lacey stopped pulling her hand and stared at him. "What's me?" she asked. No sign of her easy banter remained.

"Come with me." Asher pulled her with him. The girls surrounding them parted. He made his way to the front of the room and stopped just as the queen reached her throne.

Lacey's hand felt sweaty in his. He could smell her fear, but something different underlined the scent. He was almost certain it was her, but he wouldn't know until she bled.

Asher bowed before the queen but remained standing. Lacey looked around in confusion and tried to slip back into the crowd. He kept a tight hold on her hand. She leaned closer to him and whispered. "Forgive me, my lord, for having been so forward. Please don't punish me." She choked on the last words.

Asher turned to her quickly, surprised at her fear.

Lacey hunched over and tried to slip away again. "I meant no disrespect. Please, please, forgive me."

Asher took her by the shoulder and stood her up straight. "You won't be punished."

The relief in her eyes concerned Asher. Had he terrified her that much? He hadn't meant to. He just wanted to show the queen that he could find the Blue Blood. He spoke softly. "Do not move from here. I am going to let go and you will stay here. Understand?"

Lacey nodded and Asher stepped back just a bit. When he was sure she wouldn't bolt, he turned his attention to the queen. "I believe this is the one you are looking for."

Queen Sherr looked at him with amusement in her eyes. "Worried I couldn't find her on my own?"

Lacey let out a little squeak and Asher glanced at her. He realized right then that the girl had no idea what they were talking about and probably none of the other girls did either. He looked behind him and saw the rest of the women staring at Lacey's back. Most feared for her. Others looked worried they might be next.

When had Asher lost his compassion and his ability to read people? He was so worried about his own needs that he had stopped caring about others. Maybe Kaylee was right. Maybe the money *was* the most important thing to him. Or maybe just the praise he would get from being able to find them. Or maybe he just didn't want to be expendable.

Asher looked back to the queen. "No, Your Majesty. I am sure you could find what you were looking for, but I thought I could make it easier on you and all of them. This way you will only have to test a few instead of going one by one through each of them."

Kaylee seemed to approve of his idea. It would save her a lot of effort to not have to heal each woman after they cut her. Asher looked to Lacey again. Queen Sherr motioned for her to join them on the raised platform. He put his hand to her back and motioned her to move forward. Lacey took a faltering step. Asher placed his other hand on her elbow. He leaned closer. "It will be all right. She just wants to see if you're a Blue Blood."

Though she hadn't blushed earlier, it was obvious that the color drained from her face. "I'm not. I would have told you if I was. I swear it, I'm not." Lacey looked to the queen with pleading eyes.

"The change happens suddenly. You weren't one before, but perhaps you are now." She pulled a small knife out of a sheath at her waist. "Hold out your hand, Lacey."

Lacey trembled under Asher's touch but she reached her hand forward to the queen. Her courage impressed Asher.

"It'll be practically painless." Queen Sherr pressed the knife to the side of Lacey's finger. She made a quick poke and pulled the knife away. Asher smelled the blood immediately. Lacey gasped and pulled her hand back, staring at the indigo color staining her hand. Kaylee stood and moved closer but the queen motioned her back.

"Lacey, you are now a Blue Blood. I trust you did not know this before, but now you do. I charge you with becoming mine and ask you to serve me with your powers."

Asher was surprised she had asked for her service. Had she formally asked Kaylee and Jenna? He could see the wisdom in asking them instead of demanding it. If the Blue Bloods felt valuable, they would serve her much better than if they felt like slaves. Perhaps Queen Sherr had a lot more going for her than King Inwer did.

Lacey tore her eyes away from her bleeding hand long enough to nod. "Yes, my queen. I will be yours."

Queen Sherr motioned for Kaylee and Jenna to approach. She turned to them. "I also charge you with becoming mine and ask you to serve me with your powers." Jenna immediately nodded and agreed.

Asher watched as Kaylee looked from the queen, to him, to the women in the room, and then to the other Blue Bloods. She seemed to think for a moment before saying, "Yes."

Queen Sherr smiled. She placed her hands on Lacey's head and pressed a kiss to her forehead. "Then I mark you mine. I will be good to you, and you will be good to me. And together we will change the world for the better." She repeated the oath to the other two and stepped back to her throne.

"My ladies, it is possible that some day you may become a Blue Blood as well. I have been one. I know what your trials and struggles will be, but I also know how to help you reach your potential. I ask that if any of you discover you have been changed, you will come to me. I will treat you well. I will give you responsibilities. I can't promise things will be easy for you, or even safe, but I do promise that I will make this world a better place. And I will put an end to a tyrant who would use you for his personal gain."

She paused and looked at the women staring at her in awe. "You have been treated well here. I ask that you decide now if you will serve me without hesitation. If you feel you'd be better off somewhere else, I give you leave to go. But make that choice now. For by staying in my kingdom and knowing my plans, I expect complete loyalty from you. Do you accept my terms?"

The women burst into ayes and yesses, eagerly proclaiming their devotion to her. Asher was amazed at the support this small woman could gain. When they quieted down, the queen looked to Asher.

She stood one more time and approached him. "Master Herst, I ask you to serve me and only me from this point on. Any Blue Blood you find will be brought to me. Not for payment, but for the greater good. We need to stop the king from spreading his evil the way he wants. I will provide for you and you will be my faithful servant. Do you accept?"

Asher could see the nervousness she kept hidden behind her sharp eyes. She worried he would refuse her and he knew he was free to go if he desired. There was no way she could force him to stay and keep the respect of her people. By staying, he promised to follow her always. Could he do that? Could he give up the opportunity for gain? She wouldn't pay him any more than what he already received for Kaylee. He didn't need money now that he was in her service, but he would no longer be his own man. He looked at the women who watched him. He studied Lacey and Jenna, who still looked uncertain of their duties but sure of their queen. He looked at Kaylee. When their eyes met, he knew he could never leave this kingdom. He was bound to it already. Kaylee was here.

Asher met the queen's eyes and said, "Yes. I agree to be your faithful servant. I will serve you as long as you maintain your cause. I will help you make a better world."

Queen Sherr didn't change visibly, but he knew she was relieved he agreed. She stepped forward and he knelt in front of her so she could kiss his forehead. "I mark you mine."

The room burst into more cheers as Asher stood and bowed his head to the queen.

"Now, let us determine to do good. Encourage all you meet to decide what side they are on, because before the summer ends we will go to battle against the king. He has ruled long enough. It is time to put his tyranny to an end."

CHAPTER TWENTY-ONE

Kaylee wandered the dimly lit hallway as she returned to her room. It had been days since Asher pointed out Lacey was a Blue Blood. No more had been found since. Kaylee wondered how it happened, sure it had something to do with her. Both of those girls had interacted with her one on one. Kaylee paid close attention to every woman she had any contact with. She knew something had happened to them and wondered if that girl Melina, back at one of those first inns, had been infected or changed as well.

Kaylee watched the smooth stone floor as she walked. The coolness of the stone wasn't enough to seep into her leather soled shoes, but she could feel an ache in her ankles. It would be easy enough to reach down and heal herself, but to what purpose? She didn't want to miss out on experiencing life by over-using her power.

Besides, her soul ached more than her feet. She still felt alone. Jenna and Lacey were with her physically for most of each day as they studied with the queen and tried to learn everything she knew about Blue Bloods. But they were more at ease with each other than with Kaylee. She was sure it was because her powers had already manifested.

They also seemed to worry that each time they were with her, the queen would revert to hurting them to force the snap. The stories Queen Sherr told them of the barbaric ways the king used to force his Blue Bloods to change made even Kaylee nervous. And when she had described how she had been thrown from the horse and broken her arm as well as hit her head, it seemed to make Queen Sherr believe pain would be the only way to make the change.

Kaylee flexed her hands to ease the stiffness that remained. Writing down all the queen knew about Blue Bloods had been Kaylee's idea. She'd taken notes in hopes of compiling some information that would allow them to puzzle things out. They knew the king's Blue Bloods had at least ten different abilities.

Healing was something she could study. Manipulating the elements involved so many different things—affecting the weather patterns, conjuring fire, throwing wind. Some of the king's Blue Bloods were able to imbue objects with special powers, though that was something Kaylee might have to ask Asher about. She was sure that was how he got the talisman that helped him identify Blue Bloods.

Some of the powers Blue Bloods demonstrated in the past were scary and made Kaylee nervous just thinking about them, like being able to take someone's life by touching them. It seemed so evil. Kaylee hoped it would not be the skill Jenna or Lacey developed.

According to the histories Queen Sherr could remember, Blue Bloods had many more abilities, but some were very rare and hadn't been seen in ages. The king had more than thirty Blue Bloods when Queen Sherr was there. She didn't know if he had more or less, but trained Blue Bloods awaited them. Kaylee couldn't fathom how Queen Sherr thought she'd be successful in her attempts to overthrow the king.

Kaylee could heal the soldiers during the inevitable battle, but for how long? And would she be able to repeatedly stand the pain necessary to heal the kinds of wounds that a battle would bring? She didn't know the limits to her healing. Would she be able to maintain her strength and ability to heal hour after hour, day after day?

She would have to practice, but where? And how? It wasn't like she could tell the men to fight each other so she could heal them. Perhaps she could stay close during their training and drills. Plus, others in the countryside must need a healer. Perhaps she could convince the queen to let her go out among the peasants and heal them of their sicknesses and any injuries they might have.

Although she hated to think that Jenna and Lacey would be abused, she realized the only way to have them break through their power would be through pain.

They tried for days to surprise them or make them physically exhausted or even angry enough for them to snap. They saw no change. Kaylee looked out the window at the setting sun. They only had until sunrise tomorrow before Queen Sherr would insist on them trying it her way. Kaylee sighed deeply. At least it would give her more practice.

When she reached her room, Kaylee wanted nothing more than to climb into her bed and sleep, but she wondered if there was something she had missed during her discussions with Queen Sherr. The papers were in the queen's office, but Kaylee's memory was good enough she was sure she could jot down some notes about their potential powers. Had Kaylee's gift developed because of her injuries? Would she have developed a different power if she hadn't had to heal herself right off?

What about the gift of fire throwing? Had the Blue Bloods who developed those been burned? It was possible, but how would the ability to manipulate elements, or the one to stop a life have started. Maybe the woman who could kill by touch had needed to protect herself from an attacker.

Queen Sherr hadn't known the history of any other Blue Blood, but she had snapped after a near drowning.

Perhaps her ability to affect the weather was related to her experience with water. She'd grown up in an area that had a nearly perfect climate. Not too much rain, and never any drought. Did the environment determine how these gifts manifested?

Kaylee scrubbed her face in frustration. She'd never had a reason to heal herself before being thrown from the horse, yet her blood had been blue for years before she snapped. With Queen Sherr rushing them, they had no time to allow the change to happen gradually for Jenna or Lacey. It would be as she said. In the morning, Queen Sherr would hurt them in order to force the change. And Kaylee would have to be there to make it all right.

Asher knew it was important to see what their power would be, but he couldn't understand how Queen Sherr could do the same to them as had been done to her. They had only spent a few days trying to discover the new Blue Bloods' abilities. He never knew exactly what the king did to the ones who hadn't snapped before Asher delivered them, but from Sherr's comments, he knew it wasn't pleasant.

His cousin Fran had already snapped before he took her to the king. She came down with the scarlet fever that wiped out half of his village. When they thought she was not going to make it through the night, she suddenly started clutching her chest and screaming. She pulled fire away from herself, the flames dancing in her hands. Fran's mother fainted from the shock.

Fran had been so surprised she had insisted Asher take her to the king the next morning, all signs of her illness gone. Perhaps they needed to be close to death. Asher looked at Kaylee, relieved she was at hand to heal them if it became too much. But what about the pain Kaylee would experience? She didn't look nervous. Just determined. Her courage always made him want to try a little harder.

Jenna and Lacey were nearly opposites. Jenna paced the room, her thunderous scowl enough to make Asher glad she hadn't found her power yet. She seemed to have her temper just barely under control. He expected Lacey to move around, but she stared straight ahead, not looking at anything in particular. They both looked so young before they learned they were Blue Bloods. Now they walked with an air of authority he wouldn't expect from someone their age.

He'd already tried talking to both of them. They ignored him or brushed him off. For the third time that morning, Asher found himself wondering why the queen requested his presence. Did she think he knew more about the Blue Bloods that could help? It was true he was more familiar with them than any other man in the castle, but he doubted he knew more than the queen herself did.

As he watched the two women await their fate, he turned his attention to Kaylee. She seemed to be studying them as well. He detected no sign of nervousness in her eyes, but he couldn't tell if the depth held compassion or resignation. It would be a terrifying thing to discover you had powers you didn't know what to do with. Kaylee managed to handle herself amazingly well.

Blue Bloods had the potential to do so much good. Asher could only pray they never turned against him. He wondered if the king had somehow been able to control them. He had treated them well, giving them all the wealth and riches they could want, but he also demanded so much of them.

Queen Sherr hadn't gone into much detail about how the king took her first life. She seemed angry every time the subject arose so he stayed away from it, waiting to see if she would share more later.

She didn't have much time for him. Ruling a budding nation of misfits and peasants looking for something better and planning to overcome an opposing kingdom took a lot of time. She also kept Kaylee and the other Blue Bloods occupied so he couldn't even study them. Asher looked at the intricate gilded clock on the mantel. She told them to be here more than twenty minutes ago. He wasn't going to complain. He was fascinated watching these women, but he could see their nerves increase with each minute that passed.

Asher glanced at Kaylee. She met his eyes and immediately turned away from him. He had to make things right with her. There was no reason for animosity with each other. Would Queen Sherr allow him to be friends with one of her Blue Bloods? He knew they would have to stay focused on what lay ahead, but what harm would come from talking to each other?

Asher took a step toward Kaylee as the door opened. Jenna stopped pacing. Lacey turned expectantly. Queen Sherr strode purposefully to the women. She held her hand out and beckoned them to join her in the center. Jenna moved immediately, but Lacey hesitated. She looked at Asher, and then at Kaylee. When Kaylee smiled encouragingly, Lacey joined the queen as well.

"Do you have a preference for the source of your pain?" Queen Sherr asked quietly.

Lacey shook her head. Jenna took a quick breath. "What are our options again?"

"Fire. Blades. Or fists, to begin with." Queen Sherr said quietly.

"Fire," Jenna said.

"But the blades would probably be quicker," Lacey said.

"Exactly, and maybe less painful. I want to do it as quick as possible and get this thing to snap. I don't want to have to do it multiple times." Jenna frowned.

Lacey nodded and in a small voice said, "Fire."

Queen Sherr moved over to the hearth and placed a poker in it, burying it deeply in the coals. She stood and met Asher's eyes for a short moment before looking away. She had to hope this would work. Branding someone with hot iron was harsh, even for the king.

Lacey and Jenna stared at the fire for a moment. Jenna took a deep breath and said. "Might as well get started." She moved quickly and bent down in front of the fire. She looked up at the queen. "You might need to help me."

She thrust her hand into the center of the flames before Asher realized what she was doing. She screamed in pain. "I can't do it. Help me!"

Queen Sherr knelt down beside her. Wrapping her arm around Jenna's shoulder, she gripped the hand and forced it back into the flames. The queen's shoulders shook with her sobbing and the strain of keeping Jenna's hand from pulling back.

Asher stared in horror.

Kaylee moved forward quickly, fear in her eyes. He knew she would have to endure too much to heal Jenna.

Lacey stared without moving. The horrid smell of burnt flesh made Asher want to gag. It snapped him out of his stupor. He moved to the queen and pushed her to the side. He took Jenna by the shoulder and pulled her from the hearth. Her hand was black beyond recognition. How could she have endured it? And how could Kaylee possibly hope to heal her without feeling the same thing?

Lacey took one look at the charred hand and bolted.

"Stop her!" Queen Sherr shouted.

Tige stepped out of the shadow of the door and drew his sword. Lacey screamed and dodged him.

"Don't kill her!"

The guard shoved his blade back into its sheath and grabbed for her. She struggled against him and nearly broke free. She screamed and clawed, leaving bleeding scratches down his face. He nearly lost his hold on her, but grabbed her from behind and held her arms against her body. She kicked and rocked her head back, slamming it into his face, breaking his nose, and knocking herself unconscious. He staggered for a moment then shook his head and gripped her tighter. She slumped forward and he eased her to the floor.

"I said don't kill her!" Queen Sherr ran to Lacey as Kaylee bent over Jenna. Asher held Jenna as she sobbed and moaned against him, her charred hand cradled in her good one.

"What have I done?" Jenna whimpered.

Asher shook his head.

Kaylee took Jenna's face in her hands. "Did it work?"

Jenna stared blankly for a moment and then looked down at her own body. "I don't know."

"Ignore the pain as much as you can. Do you feel anything different?" Kaylee asked.

"I . . ." Jenna took a deep breath. "I think." She shook her head and sighed. "I don't know."

"Do you want me to heal you?" Kaylee asked.

Jenna only nodded.

Asher held Jenna tightly knowing if he let go of her, he would stop Kaylee from hurting herself in order to heal Jenna. He closed his eyes, not wanting to see what Kaylee did. Jenna lurched forward and his eyes snapped open. Jenna was trying to stop Kaylee from grabbing the iron poker from the coals.

She placed it against the skin on the back of her hand. The hiss of the iron on her flesh made Asher's stomach lurch in disgust. There had to be a different way for the change to happen. He couldn't allow this to continue.

Kaylee pulled back from Jenna when she grabbed the poker, but after setting it down, Kaylee scooted closer to the huddled woman in Asher's arms and spoke through clenched teeth. "It will be fine. Just breathe."

Asher felt the flow of power as it left Kaylee's body and entered Jenna. Nothing in him needed healing, but he felt better anyway. Kaylee took her hand off Jenna's once blackened hand. Asher was stunned to see the perfection before him. Jenna held it up, turning it back and forth.

"I . . ." Jenna stopped and looked up at Kaylee. "How?"

Kaylee smiled, though it looked forced. "I don't know."

Asher stared at her. That she was still in pain was obvious. He looked at the back of her burned hand to see the blistered and charred flesh still there. She must've seen the focus of his gaze because she stood up and hid the hand in the folds of her skirt. As Kaylee looked at something behind him, Asher remembered the queen and Lacey. He helped Jenna to her feet and then moved to the other two and the guard. Kaylee placed her hand on the guard's face without asking. His scratches and broken nose healed at her touch.

"Thank you."

Kaylee just nodded then bent down to Lacey. "How is she?"

Queen Sherr shook her head. "I don't know. She hasn't moved since hitting her head against Tige's face." She placed a slender finger on Lacey's brow.

"Is she alive?" Kaylee asked.

226

"Yes." Tige's short answer filled them with relief. Asher smiled at the glare Queen Sherr gave him before turning back to Kaylee.

"Can you check her mental state without healing immediately?" Queen Sherr stroked Lacey's hair off her face.

"I can." Kaylee placed one hand on Lacey's face and lightly touched her closed eyelids. "I can see no permanent damage. She should wake from this with no serious effects."

Behind him, Asher heard Tige breathe a sigh of relief.

"Does she need to be healed at all?" Queen Sherr asked.

"I don't know how much pain she will feel when she wakes, but there will be some."

Queen Sherr took Kaylee's injured hand in her own. "Then heal yourself." Her voice was full of compassion. Kaylee placed her palm over the burn and when she removed it, the injury was gone, replaced with perfect skin again. Queen Sherr touched Kaylee's cheek. "Thank you."

Kaylee blinked and looked away, meeting Asher's eyes. He could tell she was touched by the Queen's words as much as he was. Queen Sherr stood up easily as if having been on the floor leaning over Lacey were perfectly acceptable.

"Jenna, are you well?"

Jenna nodded.

Queen Sherr wrapped Jenna in an embrace. Although she stood a head shorter than Jenna, it was obvious who was in control. "Why did you do that?" Queen Sherr asked, concern in her voice as she stepped back.

"I wanted to get it over with."

"Did you snap?"

"I don't know for sure." Jenna placed her hands on her middle. "I feel different than before, but I don't know if that is due to Kaylee's healing, or if it is my own."

"We should know soon. The pain you chose was so much more than what I would have done. I can't imagine we need to try again."

Jenna nodded and looked down at Lacey. "Will she be all right?"

Kaylee smiled. "Yes. But we'll let her have some time to just rest. I'm sure she'll wake soon."

"Tige," Queen Sherr said as she turned to him. "Thank you for your service. I expect you to be more careful in the future. My girls are precious to me."

Tige nodded.

"You may go."

Tige left quickly and Asher thought he was probably relieved to be gone.

Queen Sherr looked down at Lacey again and then around the room. Asher examined the room as well and decided there really wasn't any better place to put Lacey than where she currently lay. The queen took Jenna by the hand and examined her once burned flesh.

"Amazing."

Jenna nodded. Kaylee smiled softly at the praise.

"It pains me to know you had to suffer as well." Queen Sherr looked at Kaylee. "Your courage astounds me."

Kaylee didn't say a word. Asher could see she felt uncomfortable. He stood as well and addressed Jenna. "Can you describe how you feel different?"

Jenna paused for a moment as if trying to decide for herself. "I feel like there is a connection to something out there that wasn't there before. Lots of little things seem to be just out of my reach or sight. I feel like I should know so much more than I do. Almost like I've forgotten something that is rather important. But for the life of me, I don't know what it is."

"Reach for it gently. See if it comes to you," Queen Sherr said.

Jenna frowned in concentration. Asher waited eagerly to see if there would be a change in her. He wasn't worried about her being dangerous, even though some Blue Bloods could be. It didn't seem to be anything like what his cousin Fran or any of the other Blue Bloods who snapped had described their powers.

Jenna leaned forward as if longing to move toward something else. Asher stepped back, allowing her free movement if she desired. The Queen and Kaylee also parted. Kaylee brushed against him as she took a place next to him. Her personal scent was intoxicating. He tried to ignore the tightness in his chest, focusing instead on Jenna, who closed her eyes and walked slowly. Her movements were halting at first, but she soon walked with confidence toward a tapestry that covered a small, opaque window. She looked out the window and frowned.

"Whatever it is, it's out there. At least the strongest pull is. There are much smaller pulls from all around me, but there is something larger outside."

"Can you pull it to you? Or is it just beckoning you to come to it?"

Jenna closed her eyes again and stood still. A thump on the glass made her turn around quickly. Asher saw the outline of something small slide down the window. It must have hit the castle. Jenna whipped around and shook her head. "It can't be."

"What?" Asher asked.

"Whatever it was, just hit the window and now it's gone. I don't feel anything from it anymore."

"You called a bird to you?" Kaylee asked.

Jenna shrugged. "I don't know. I tried to bring whatever it was to me, but then it's gone. Just after that noise."

"You can call animals to you?" Queen Sherr asked. She looked around the room as if trying to find some animal. "You feel other things close by?"

Jenna nodded slowly. "Very small."

"Rats?" Asher asked.

Queen Sherr shook her head. "I do not have rats in my castle."

Asher smiled. "Every castle has its vermin."

The queen crossed her arms over her chest and scowled at him. He would have laughed if the sound of screaming in the hallway hadn't distracted him. He put his hand on his sword, ready to pull it out in defense of the women with him. Instead of the door opening, mice, rats, and insects scurried into the room through the crack between the floor and door. They crawled over each other and even over the top of Lacey still lying on the floor.

Jenna gasped in horror at the mass of animals crowding around her. Queen Sherr moved closer to Jenna. Kaylee stood her ground, leaning forward with her head tilted to the side. Jenna reached for the queen and held onto her arm like she'd forgotten who she was touching. Asher watched the rats with caution, but they didn't seem to be interested in him. They watched Jenna with unwavering, beady little eyes.

Jenna turned around slowly to see herself surrounded completely by a sea of rodents. "What is happening?" She trained her terrified eyes on Queen Sherr, and then to him and Kaylee.

"I think you must have called them to you," Kaylee said. Asher couldn't tell if she were trying to suppress a laugh or if she were concerned. The small twitch at the corner of her mouth made him sure it was the first.

"No." Jenna shook her head. "I do not command vermin."

"Tell them to go away," the queen said.

"Shoo!" Jenna stomped her feet and feinted to the left. The rodents scattered and moved toward the walls. Jenna frowned. "Go away. Leave this room."

The critters turned around and scampered back out as quickly as they had come, once again crawling over the top of Lacey who lay in their path.

"I can't have the power over animals." Jenna sagged to her knees.

Kaylee smiled kindly. "It appears you do."

"What good will that be?" Jenna asked completely defeated.

Queen Sherr knelt down next to her. "Perhaps King Inwer is afraid of rats?" She smiled, and one corner of Jenna's lip lifted.

CHAPTER TWENTY-TWO

Rats. Kaylee shook her head. It was so strange that Jenna would have power over rats. And, more than likely, birds. It would be interesting to see what other kinds of animals she could control, but what good would it do? Queen Sherr's comment about using them against the king didn't sound very realistic. Perhaps if she could control larger animals, it might work.

Jenna looked upset about the pain she'd gone through in order to have such a small power. Queen Sherr never mentioned a power like that. But who knew what was out there, and how it all worked anyway?

Jenna and Queen Sherr had moved over to the table, deep in discussion. Kaylee and Asher had been assigned to watch over Lacey. She wasn't in any danger, but Queen Sherr wanted to allow the change to happen as naturally as possible. If it had been traumatic enough for her, she should've snapped. If not, they would need to convince her to attempt the change through pain.

Kaylee looked back at Asher. He'd been watching her off and on over the last half hour when he wasn't watching Jenna and Queen Sherr. Kaylee wasn't sure what to think of his constant observance. He hadn't spoken to her much. She missed the easy conversation she enjoyed with him on her travels. Even after Zeb and Dolf had taken her, Asher came back. He always made some excuse to talk to her.

Kaylee looked at the queen. She realized he had someone so much better to talk with, someone wise and powerful. Even if she no longer had her Blue Power, she still carried herself with more authority than Kaylee could dream of having on her own.

Kaylee was tired of sitting on the chair against the wall. She stood and moved closer to Lacey. Asher got up and moved with her.

"I've never spent much time with people who got knocked out."

Asher smiled. "I've seen it a few times."

"She didn't seem to be damaged the same way Zeb was."

"How do you know what damage is done?" Asher took her hand in his, sending a different sort of shiver up her arm. "What does it feel like?"

Kaylee liked how nice his hand felt as it held hers. She knew she should pull her hand from his, wishing she had a reason to let him hold it still. He turned one hand over and looked at her fingers and palm.

"Do you feel it through your hands, or is it somewhere else?"

Kaylee focused on the tips of her fingers as Asher gently touched the pad of each one. "I can feel it when I have contact. I've never thought about how it happens." Kaylee swallowed and curled her fingers around his. When she realized what she was doing, she pulled her hand away from him and rubbed her still tingling fingers with her other hand. She looked up at him and couldn't understand the glimmer in his eyes.

He looked amused, but kept his face serious. Was she mistaken about him? Oh, how she wished she could understand a man. Living as one had never prepared her to know them.

"How do you know what damage was done?" Asher asked again.

Kaylee knelt down by Lacey and placed her hand on Lacey's forehead. Her temperature felt perfect. Her mind seemed at ease beneath the layers of skin and bones. Kaylee listened to her breathe. It was slow and steady, making Kaylee think Lacey could easily have been sleeping.

"I think by having contact with someone, it allows my powers to flow. To heal, I have to have a surge of power, but to feel what's wrong, I just need to touch."

Asher knelt down as well and touched Jenna's forehead. "I just feel her temperature and the smoothness of her skin." He looked up at Kaylee and she blinked at the closeness. Her face was inches from his. Kaylee looked back down, sliding away just a little.

"I can feel those too, but underneath, I feel a sort of blockage. Like her flow of energy and life force is resting."

"But what does that tell you?"

Kaylee glanced at him from the corner of her eye. She didn't want to look at him full on, thinking she'd probably stumble over the words, but she wished to see his face. The strong jawline had a day's worth of beard. His lips were cast downward in almost a frown, but more like one of relaxation, not distress or annoyance.

Kaylee cleared her throat and looked back at Lacey's calm face. "When I examined Zeb's injury, it felt more like something was out of place. A stronger blockage. Like there was no way for things to flow smoothly unless I removed the blockage. Lacey is different. It's like things have slowed down, but not stopped."

"Will she wake up on her own?"

Kaylee nodded.

"Do you think she'll have snapped?" Asher asked.

"I don't know. Queen Sherr said emotional trauma can be as strong as physical. If she was distressed enough seeing what Jenna did, she could've panicked herself into a breakthrough."

Asher glanced back at the fireplace and then to Kaylee's hand still resting on Lacey's head. He put his hand on hers and said, "For both your sakes, I hope that's true."

Kaylee smiled and pulled her hand back. She didn't know what to make of Asher's words or the fact that he kept touching her. It pleased and disturbed her equally. She knew he didn't like to see her get hurt, but why should it matter to him? It wasn't like she was in constant danger. She could heal herself.

Asher stood up and looked down at Lacey. Kaylee stood as well. He offered his hand to help her up, but she didn't dare touch him again. Contact with him made her nervous and sent an odd sensation down her back.

"What do you think her power will be?" Asher asked. Kaylee shrugged.

They stood in silence. Kaylee allowed her mind to wander. The potential for power was endless. If only there was a way to indicate what kinds of powers a person would have. Or a way to know who would turn into a Blue Blood. There had to be something in common with these other girls and herself.

Both Jenna and Lacey had been in the service of the queen for months, with no idea they were possible Blue Bloods. Both of them had sworn that they had bled red in one way or another over the course of their labors. Once Kaylee got there, they both changed. And both of them had been in contact with her. They must've somehow caught it from her. But how? And if she were contagious, should she go out into the village and pass the power on to others, or stay away from all women so there wouldn't be a chance another would catch it?

Kaylee looked at the queen, still in quiet conversation with Jenna. Kaylee listened to the kindness in her manner. Jenna's expression had gone from anger and annoyance to something that looked like hope. Queen Sherr needed more Blue Bloods. What about the women whose lives would change forever? Did she have that right to change them?

What if she could ask for volunteers? Would that bring women of quality, or would they end up with some who just wanted power for power's sake? The ramifications of a Blue Blood army would be far reaching. How was she to decide? And what did she dare tell the queen of her musings?

Asher moved away, returning to the fireplace. He stared into the flames and Kaylee wondered what he was thinking. A movement from Lacey made Kaylee bend down. She placed her hand on Lacey's forehead again. The difference in her mind eased and Kaylee knew Lacey would wake soon.

Lacey twitched again under Kaylee's hand. She rose onto her knees and placed her hand on Lacey's arm, running it down until she rested her fingers on Lacey's open palm. Lacey's hand contracted and seemed to almost grab Kaylee's fingers before she went still again.

Kaylee turned to the queen, ready to call her over, when the air around her thickened. She struggled to take a breath, but nothing came in. Kaylee yanked her hands back from Lacey and placed her palm on her own chest. The air still felt thick, but breathable. Kaylee looked down at Lacey to see if she struggled with her breathing. She seemed just the same as before. Slow, steady breaths. Kaylee reached for a pulse in Lacey's neck, but as soon as she touched her skin, the tightness of breath came again. When she pulled back quickly, the air was fine.

"Queen Sherr," Kaylee called. "I think you need to come see this."

The queen, Asher, and Jenna rushed over to Lacey and bent over her. Queen Sherr knelt down with no care for her dress. She placed her hand on Lacey before Kaylee had a chance to warn her.

Kaylee watched in fascination as the queen's eyes widened. She pulled her hand back, just as Kaylee had, and placed it on her own chest. "What was that?"

"I don't know. It did the same to me," Kaylee said.

Asher looked at the two of them. "What happened?"

"When I touched her, I couldn't breathe."

Kaylee watched as Asher reached his hand out and touched Lacey as well. He obviously struggled to breathe, but some air still managed to make it inside. He broke contact with Lacey and sucked in the air. "Amazing."

Jenna frowned. "What does that mean? Does she have a power? She's going to be able to stop people from breathing?" She looked up with wide eyes and then placed her hand on Lacey as well. She shook her head and jumped up, gasping as she did.

"It isn't fair." She walked away and stopped in front of the fireplace.

Kaylee could understand her frustration. Lacey hadn't endured nearly as much pain as Jenna had, yet the power did seem to be stronger with the potential to do so much more in battle. Jenna's ability would still be useful. Just different. Lacey, on the other hand . . . it would be a power to watch. Would she affect everyone she touched, or was that just something that happened now? Would her power be controllable? Would Lacey have the strength to handle it? And how on earth could they test it? It wasn't like they should ask her to stop people from breathing. What if she couldn't control it? What if she took someone's breath without meaning to and killed them? Kaylee didn't know Lacey enough to know how she'd handle this new power.

The magnitude of what they could do scared her. If it were up to Kaylee, she'd make sure she didn't pass any power on to another person. But would Lacey and Jenna also be contagious?

"Queen Sherr?" Kaylee spoke softly.

"Yes?"

"Were there very many Blue Bloods that showed up in King Inwer's castle?"

"Asher brought one or two a year."

"I mean, did any of the servants change?"

Queen Sherr thought for a moment. Eventually she shook her head. "I don't recall anyone in the castle or even in Inshansi becoming one."

Kaylee shook her head. It didn't make sense.

"Why do you ask?"

"I can't help wondering why there were two in your castle that have changed in such a short time. Why did they become Blue Bloods after I got here?"

"I don't know," Queen Sherr said. "But I know it isn't contagious."

Kaylee sighed in frustration. She knew deep down that Jenna's and Lacey's change was directly related to her. It may take some time, but she was determined to figure it out.

"She's moving," Asher said.

Everyone leaned back, worried her power might manifest itself much stronger as Lacey regained consciousness. Jenna had come about half the distance back from the fireplace. Kaylee watched as Lacey groaned and lifted her hand to her forehead. She wondered what kind of pain Lacey would feel from the blow to the head.

Lacey's eyes fluttered for a moment and went still. The four of them watched her. After a few moments they came closer again. Kaylee touched Lacey's hand once more to see if the air did the same thing as before.

When her skin made contact with Lacey, the air thickened again, but when Kaylee tried to pull her hand back, Lacey gripped her wrist and sat up, clinging to her. Kaylee tried to pull back. The lack of oxygen seemed to be only a part of it. The whole area surrounding them thickened. Lacey's grip tightened on Kaylee as if she were afraid of what was happening. Kaylee tried to speak, to convince her to let go, but no air moved across her vocal cords. Sound wasn't possible. She tried to slap at Lacey to get her to let go, but Kaylee couldn't even move. Lacey pulled on Kaylee harder.

"What's wrong?" Lacey shouted to Asher and the queen.

They couldn't speak either. They appeared to struggle. Both collapsed forward, sprawled across Lacey's legs.

Kaylee saw Jenna run up to them as if to help but was stopped by something a few feet away. "Let go of them!" Jenna shouted.

Lacey turned her head to Jenna, and then looked back at Kaylee and the others. She let go of Kaylee's arm and struggled back as far as she could with the queen and Asher lying across her legs. Lacey kicked at them, screaming in terror. Fresh air finally made it through to Kaylee's lungs, which she gulped hungrily. She crawled forward, wondering if by touching Asher and the queen the power would affect her as well since they were touching Lacey.

It didn't matter. It had to be done. They couldn't last much longer without air. The piercing screams coming from Lacey indicated she was too upset to save them herself.

Kaylee forced her way through the thick air and only caught up to Lacey when she hit the wall with her back. Lacey covered her face with her hands and sobbed. A forceful kick of Lacey's legs shifted the queen enough Kaylee felt sure she could get ahold of her ankle and pull her away.

The severed contact between the queen and Lacey became obvious when Queen Sherr took a ragged breath. Kaylee pulled once more to move the queen even further from Lacey and to get a better angle to reach Asher. He was closer to Lacey's thighs than the queen had been. His skin was tinged blue, mostly around his lips. His eyes were wide and full of terror. Lacey tried to push him away but her sobs made her mostly ineffective.

The air thinned as Lacey's screams turned to sobs. Kaylee could move much easier than before. She gripped Asher's boot and pulled. Lacey noticed and pushed as well, the sobs slowing even more. Asher gasped in the air as he struggled to push himself up. His arms collapsed under him at the same time Kaylee yanked again, forcing his face to smack into the floor. He groaned. Kaylee pulled again and again until she was sure he was far enough away from Lacey to be out of range of her power. She then turned to the queen to help but stopped when she saw Jenna had helped her to her feet and led her away to the other side of the room.

"What happened to me?" Lacey's throat sounded raw.

"You've snapped." Jenna's voice sounded bitter.

CHAPTER TWENTY-THREE

The air was the best Asher had tasted in his entire life. He'd never been so afraid of dying as he had been before Kaylee pulled him away. The air closing in on him exerted immense pressure as Lacey reacted to her new power. Asher rolled onto his back, drinking in the air and trying to focus above him. Kaylee's worried face leaned over him. He wished he could take away her fears and concern.

"Are you all right?" Kaylee asked.

Asher tried to speak but could only nod.

"Can I heal you?" Kaylee bent down and reached out to him.

"No!" Asher croaked as he tried to roll over and get away from her touch. He wouldn't let her injure herself for him. "I'm fine. I just need to breathe." He finally managed.

"What about your face?"

Asher reached a hand to his face, feeling the sticky blood that had begun to dry. "It's nothing. I don't feel a thing."

Kaylee looked at him as if he were crazy.

"I'm fine," he said more forcefully.

Kaylee pulled back quickly and turned her face away from him. He didn't want her to feel any more pain. Why was interacting with her so hard? He touched his face once more, gently probing his cheekbone. He touched a slight cut, but he was sure it would heal quickly on its own. And the bruise wouldn't be too bad.

"Thank you for being willing, Kaylee, but honestly, I think it will be fine. And thank you for saving me from . . ." Asher looked over at Lacey, who had buried her head into her knees as she hunched over them. Small sobs and hiccupping breaths were all he heard from her. He looked up to see the queen and Jenna watching him. Asher got onto his hands and knees and slowly stood. He felt a little wobbly at first, but soon gained his equilibrium. He held his hand out to Kaylee as an offer of peace. She hesitantly took his hand in hers. He immediately felt better. The air flowed easier and his lightheadedness disappeared.

"Are you all right?" He looked deep into her eyes.

"I'll be fine soon."

"You've been holding the pain until you were sure your healing wasn't needed?" Asher touched his face, knowing the bruising had eased and the bleeding had stopped. It wasn't completely healed, but he was much better than a moment ago.

She didn't answer. The look of surprise in her face was enough.

"You can't do this to yourself. You need to be more careful." Asher knew she heard him, but she ignored him.

She let go of his hand and walked over to the queen and Jenna. "Are you well?"

The two women nodded.

"May I examine you?" Kaylee asked the queen.

Queen Sherr's eyes opened in surprise. "Do you think there is something wrong?"

"I don't know for sure. Something feels different in my own center and something was different with Asher at first. May I?" Her words sounded tight. The strain she felt must still dwell inside her.

Queen Sherr nodded. Kaylee placed her hand on the queen's hand. The sigh that escaped the queen's lips made Asher sure she was completely whole now.

"Heal yourself," Asher said.

Kaylee ignored him and turned to Jenna. "Do you feel different at all? You weren't in contact with Lacey, but how do you feel?"

"I think I'm well."

"May I see?"

When Jenna nodded, Kaylee placed her hand on Jenna the same way as before. Jenna didn't react.

Asher raised his voice. "Heal yourself now."

Kaylee glanced at him, but walked over to Lacey.

Asher rushed to her and pulled her back. "Don't."

"I have to see if she's okay."

"You can't touch her. She'll stop your breath." Asher turned to the queen. "Forbid her. Tell her to stop."

Kaylee shook her head. "I will be fine. I know my limits. And I need to know how Lacey is."

Queen Sherr frowned. "Be careful."

Asher scowled at the queen but turned his attention back to Kaylee as she approached Lacey. She seemed to be fine as she got closer and closer. Kaylee took one step at a time and breathed in deeply with each step. At least she could still move and breathe. He looked at Lacey, still hunched over and shaking slightly. Her sobs eased and she was no longer out of control.

Kaylee's soft voice broke the tension. "Lacey?"

Lacey lifted her head. Her eyes were swollen with tears. Her pale skin flushed. It wasn't red, nor was it blue, but an interesting shade of light purple. He had never seen a Blue Blood cry before, so the blotchy skin looked strange.

"Are you well?" Kaylee asked.

Lacey shook her head. "I don't know," she whispered. "What happened? What did I do?"

"It seems you have some control over the air. When you touched us we couldn't breathe or move. The air seemed to solidify."

"But I wasn't trying to. It just happened."

"I know. No one blames you. It will take some time for you to figure it out, but we are here to help you."

"How can you help?"

"We'll do what we can and see what works."

Lacey nodded slowly.

"Are you hurt anywhere?"

Lacey considered the question for a moment before answering. "My head hurts a little in the back." She placed a hand on her head and winced.

"Would you like me to try to heal you?"

"Can you even touch me?"

"I don't know," Kaylee answered. "But if you are calm enough, I am willing to give it a try."

"You'd help me even if it might kill you?"

"I doubt you'll kill me. If I have trouble breathing, I should be able to let go. As long as you don't grab onto me, I think I'll be fine."

Lacey threaded the fingers of her hands together and tucked them into her lap. "I'll try not to hurt you."

"Just relax and stay calm." Kaylee spoke in a soothing voice. Asher stood ready to pull her away if it looked like she was in danger. She reached her hand out slowly and placed it on the back of Lacey's head. She took slow, deep breaths. Nothing seemed to change. She smiled and said, "Things are fine. You have some swelling there, but I don't think there's anything wrong deep inside."

Lacey's face relaxed even more. The tightness left her eyes as Kaylee healed her. She took a deep breath and sighed. "That feels amazing."

Kaylee smiled and stood up.

"Now will you heal yourself?" Asher asked.

Kaylee frowned at him and moved away to the side of the room. She lowered herself into a chair and closed her eyes. He expected her to open them immediately, but after a few moments he approached her. Kaylee's breathing had slowed down and her face had gone soft.

He leaned over her, worried at first something was wrong. When he realized what had happened, he turned to the queen, who had joined him. "I don't believe it. She's asleep."

"You have feelings for her." Queen Sherr spoke it plainly, but soft enough the others in the room couldn't hear.

Asher glanced at the queen. Did he dare deny it? Queen Sherr turned her attention back on Kaylee but spoke softly to him. "She won't age."

Asher looked at the queen more fully. He already knew that.

"You will," Queen Sherr said. Asher looked at her as she wiped away a tear. "It will be torture for her to watch you grow old and die in front of her." She met his eye.

Asher realized the queen was right. There was no hope for them. He could never cause her pain, and the only way to ever be with Kaylee would be for her to die. And that he could never allow.

CHAPTER TWENTY-FOUR

Kaylee's days were filled with practice and study and waiting and wondering. There was only so much she could do to practice her abilities at healing. She learned that if the injury were minor, she no longer needed to hurt herself. She could feel what the injured needed and imagine how the pain felt enough that her powers would flow. Anything more severe than a bruise, a small cut, or indigestion, still required equal pain.

Finding out what was wrong took no pain at all. Occasionally when Kaylee saw the pain in another's eyes, it would allow her healing to flow enough to ease their pain, but not heal it completely.

Kaylee couldn't understand why Asher worried about her practicing. He didn't seem to be as concerned about Jenna or Lacey. Both of them had made leaps and bounds in their abilities. Jenna could control the horses in the stables and call birds from the sky. She even asked for permission to go on a trip into the forest looking for a wild beast to practice on.

As soon as Queen Sherr's hunters returned from their search for wild game, Jenna and a few soldiers would go back out with them. Kaylee volunteered to go as well, but after Asher whispered to the queen, she'd been denied.

She refused to speak to him for days after that, but it didn't seem to bother Asher. He never got close enough for her to give him the silent treatment.

At least she'd been able to practice with the sling Dolf had given her. Dolf had been training with the other soldiers lately, but he slipped away every once in a while to come talk to her. The other soldiers seemed to be curious as well and would watch as she slung rocks at the target Dolf and his brother Tige set up.

She smiled at the antics the soldiers got into. They tried to outdo each other, often teasing Kaylee about how they could hit the target better than she. The teasing motivated her to practice harder, and she soon found herself able to hit the small circle in the center of the target more often than not. Dolf started to add more targets, placing them at different heights. It took a little effort, but she soon managed to get the stone to strike where she wanted.

Kaylee saw Asher watching her once, but when Queen Sherr caught him studying Kaylee, she took him with her and he never returned during practice time. Kaylee wondered if Queen Sherr had feelings for Asher.

She never saw any definitive signs, but she knew they were becoming closer as they discussed options on how to attack King Inwer.

As the days progressed, Kaylee found herself with less time to practice her sling, but more chances to heal the minor injuries that resulted in the soldiers training with their practice swords. If they got this roughed up practicing, what would happen when they actually went to war and fought against someone who truly wanted to kill them?

Kaylee wandered the deserted hallway on her way back to her room, looking forward to a rest. She had been busy lately helping Jenna and Lacey test their limits, not to mention healing the cuts of the other servants in the queen's pay when they were tested daily for signs of new Blue Bloods. Tomorrow, Queen Sherr wanted to go into the surrounding village to see if any of the women there had the gift. She'd sent a proclamation throughout her realm asking for those willing to be tested to come forth. The offer of riches and power would draw many. Kaylee feared for them.

Jenna and Lacey seemed to handle it well on the outside, but the strain in their eyes was obvious. Kaylee was sure the queen had been hoping for more power from them. And unless they could find more Blue Bloods to add to the ranks, they would march against the king with only the force of her men and three Blue Bloods.

Kaylee closed her eyes in frustration. The task was impossible. Asher tried to convince Queen Sherr she didn't have sufficient strength to go against him yet, but she was adamant that he be stopped. She never gave specifics, but Kaylee was sure he spent time researching and experimenting on Blue Bloods. The idea of him trying to extend his life indefinitely worried her.

Kaylee opened the door to her room. It had been days since she'd had some time to herself, and she longed to just relax. Kaylee lit a candle with a stick from the small fire in her hearth and placed it on her writing table.

She pulled out her notebook to write down some of her thoughts and a couple of the newer discoveries of Lacey and Jenna. The animals weren't able to do anything their physical bodies were unable to perform, but Jenna had the rats eating through ropes, and the birds bringing small objects and dropping them from heights. It wasn't deadly, but uncomfortable enough to be underneath them. They hadn't tested the soldiers' horses, but Jenna worked with the cats, dogs, pigs, cows, and wild animals close enough to feel her pull.

Lacey, on the other hand, tested her distance. She at first struggled to control her power, affecting anyone who touched her. When she was able to remain calm and focused, she soon specified who she wanted to stop breathing. It was hard to find volunteers and eventually

Jenna had to gather animals for Lacey to practice on. Jenna wasn't happy about it either, especially when Lacey didn't stop soon enough and suffocated the critters.

Once she gained control of her ability to affect breathing, she began manipulating the air. She started practicing by stopping people from moving and eventually managed to hold them still without suffocating them.

Kaylee put the notebook down once she had filled it with everything new they'd discovered over the last few days. Her notes might help future generations of Blue Bloods. She shook her head in defeat. It wasn't a horrible life, but it wasn't really her own. And any woman who eventually developed into a Blue Blood would never be able to live by her own rules. Those in higher positions would seek them out. And though Kaylee could probably survive on her own, she wouldn't be free to practice her healing on anyone. They would turn her in for the reward.

Kaylee put the book back in the small trunk she kept hidden inside a larger trunk with her personal belongings, and pulled out her father's old leather-bound book. She opened it again and ran her fingers over the faded blue ink.

Kaylee placed the book on the small writing table in front of her and flipped through page after page.

Each section bore the same symbol in the corner, but every new section was different from the last by at least an extra line, circle, or squiggle. She counted more than twenty five different symbols. Some sections were longer than others and Kaylee knew there had to be some pattern. Maybe even a code that would help reveal the meaning behind the words. She tried reading every other word out loud, then every third. She tried taking the words on each line and reordering them, yet they still confused her.

Kaylee glanced at the candle with gritty eyes. It had burned down to almost a nub. She leaned back and felt her spine popping as she stretched. The book would continue to withhold its answers for another day. She could find nothing that would help her now.

Kaylee walked between Jenna and Lacey as they followed Queen Sherr and Asher through the village. The women lining the road watched in awe at the procession. The adoration on the women's faces embarrassed Kaylee. They really weren't any different from these women, but by some quirk of fate, they had developed Blue Blood. And with it, strange powers.

Kaylee studied their expressions and soon realized not all of the women looked eager to be there. Some looked scared, while others seemed angry. Had they been forced to come? Kaylee looked at Queen Sherr's head as she walked regally in front of them. She knew the queen wanted as many Blue Bloods to join her cause as possible but it seemed like they were rushing it.

Asher held his talisman in one hand and scanned the faces of the women. Was he able to sense any of them? His breathing was slow and steady and Kaylee knew he was trying to detect any hint that a Blue Blood was near. Kaylee looked at each woman with more interest. Would she be able to detect a difference in them? Could it have something to do with their health or wellbeing? She wished she would've thought earlier to check Lacey and Jenna for something different in their basic constitution, but how was she to guess there would be other Blue Bloods in the castle?

Kaylee sighed in frustration. There was no good way to go about it. All they could do was hope and watch. Asher seemed confident that they would find one. He said his medallion indicated there was potential out there. He had already gathered all of the servants in the castle to be tested early that morning. Kaylee had actually been left to dress on her own. It was fortunate her dress wasn't a fancy one or she would never have been able to get it buttoned up. And her hair was just getting long enough she only needed a comb to ease the fly-a-ways.

They'd all been poked with a small needle. Each still bled red so Kaylee didn't need to heal anyone. So, the search had gone out into the village. Asher seemed so sure he would find one, but after walking past the lined up women he still didn't seem to know which one was it.

"There is nothing else to do than test them," Queen Sherr said. She motioned for Asher to begin the test. He pulled out a small leather strip and unfolded it. Inside rested a needle similar to what Kaylee used to mend clothes. He approached the first woman in line and said gently. "It will not hurt much. We merely need to see the color of your blood."

The woman nodded quickly and allowed him to take her hand. He jabbed in a quick motion and pulled the needle away. The woman leaned over her hand with as much curiosity as Asher showed. When he saw that it was red, he thanked her and moved to the next woman.

Kaylee knew she wouldn't be allowed to heal any of the women, nor would anyone really need it, so she remained where she stood. Asher moved through the line at a steady pace, each woman relaxing once she'd been tested and found red.

As Asher reached the end of the line he looked more and more confused. He glanced back toward the center in the area directly in front of Kaylee. Did his medallion indicate the power was somewhere in front of her? Kaylee couldn't help herself. She wanted to know more about the women in front there. What if one of them had the potential to become a Blue Blood, but it just hadn't happened yet? What did it take to make them change?

She moved slowly and watched each woman closely. None of them looked to be ill, but something about their eyes drew her. Nerves? Anxiety? Concern? She couldn't really heal them of those, but perhaps she could give them comfort. She wished she could do more than just watch as they waited to see if their lives would change.

An older woman rubbed her hip as she stood in formation. Kaylee could tell she was uncomfortable. And since she felt so helpless, she decided to do the best she could.

"Will you tell me about your ache?" Kaylee asked quietly as she neared the woman.

The peppered gray head bowed low. "It don't pain me often, just when I have to walk long distances like today."

"I'm sorry. Thank you for your obedience to the queen. May I heal you?" Kaylee asked.

"That isn't necessary," the woman said.

"It would please me to be able to help you." Kaylee smiled at the woman. She reached for a bony hand, surprised at the shiver that went through her as they touched. The woman obviously was startled as well and stepped back quickly, losing her balance and falling to the ground. She tried to catch herself by gripping onto the arm of another girl, but only managed to take her down with her. A scream of pain erupted from the old woman.

"I am so sorry. Are you all right?" Kaylee asked. She knelt down next to the woman and tried to help the other girl stand back up.

The girl ignored Kaylee's offer of help and instead said, "Gran-mama. Are you hurt?"

"My hip." The woman gasped.

Kaylee placed her hand on the woman's hip and felt where the bone had cracked. She cringed in horror at what she had caused.

"I am so sorry. I will fix this." Kaylee pulled out her knife. She hiked her skirt up, revealing her thigh and stabbed her leg. It was so much quicker than trying to find something to break a bone with. The flash of pain in her leg shot power to her hands and into the old woman's hip.

When she was healed, the old woman gasped in surprise. "How did you do that?"

Her granddaughter looked at her in concern. "Gran-mama?"

"Don't worry dear. The pain is gone." She moved her leg to test her words and then accepted help up. "All my pains are gone," she whispered in awe.

Embarrassment flooded Kaylee about the commotion she'd caused. The girls and women surrounding them had all leaned over to help.

Only the words of the queen raised above the chattering finally broke the circle. "What happened?" Queen Sherr asked.

"I must have surprised her when I touched her to heal her. She fell."

"She healed me, Your Majesty. Thank you for allowing it to happen. Thank you for sharing your Blue Blood with me."

"She is not mine to own. I am pleased she was able to help you."

Asher pushed his way through the crowd. "Where is she?" he asked.

"Who?"

"The Blue Blood." Asher held up his clenched fist gripping his medallion. "I feel it strongly here."

Everyone stared at each other in confusion.

"She's here," he insisted.

"But you just tested them all," Queen Sherr said.

"Didn't they all bleed red?" Jenna asked.

"Yes," Asher said, shaking his head as if that didn't matter. "Something has changed. I feel it strongly."

"Test them again?" Lacey said.

Each woman stepped back from Asher.

"Not everyone. Give me a moment." Asher stepped around the group. He looked closely at each woman, smelling some of them, pinching others. The women looked flustered, confused, or offended, but most responses made him push them to the side. He kept his medallion tight in his hand. After gathering about seven women, he said "These."

Lacey took the needle from him and proceeded to press it into the skin of each woman's finger. When she had reached the grandmother Kaylee had caused to fall, Kaylee's heart hammered in her chest.

The needle went in quickly and came out smooth. A tiny bead of blue blood welled up on the old woman's finger. She fell to the ground once more. This time in a faint.

CHAPTER TWENTY-FIVE

Kaylee stood in front of the queen inside the castle with her hands clasped. "I touched her to check what caused the pain in her hip. She'd been rubbing it as if it bothered her. When I touched her, she shivered and fell. By the time I healed her you were back, and you know the rest."

"So healing her made her turn into a Blue Blood?" Queen Sherr asked again.

"I don't know. I've healed other women and they haven't changed. I don't know what did it this time."

"Did you heal either Lacey or Jenna?" Asher asked.

Jenna shook her head. "No, but when I served her dinner that first night, I felt something odd when I brushed against her."

"And I as well, while helping her dress," Lacey said.

Queen Sherr paced in front of the fireplace in her study. "It has to be something about you, Kaylee. Perhaps you have a second power."

Kaylee shook her head. "How is that possible?"

"How is any of this possible?" Jenna said.

"How long had you been a Blue Blood before I found you?" Asher moved closer to Kaylee, making her catch her breath. It was the first time in days he had approached her.

She shook her head to clear it. "Four or five years. My father took me away from our village as soon as he realized what I was."

"Yet you never snapped in all those years?" Queen Sherr asked.

"No. The monastery was a peaceful place. No threat or even major sickness in all that time."

"How did you manage to hide your blood?" Queen Sherr asked.

"I was never injured. Not much chance of it, given the scribe work I did. And I never got the monthly women's courses." Kaylee stared straight ahead at the queen, refusing to look at Asher.

"You never even nicked your scalp while shaving?" Asher asked.

"The monks had an herb that they made into a paste. It caused the hair to fall out. We used that weekly."

Asher rubbed his hand over his jawline as if contemplating the possibilities.

"So do you think her ability to pass on the Blue Blood gift is because she had it so long before snapping?" Lacey asked.

"It's possible, but I don't know for sure."

Asher shook his head. "There were other women I found who had known they were Blue Bloods for nearly a year before they snapped. Some didn't snap until King Inwer had them. It's possible those women passed this on."

"Well, we will have to observe and see what else happens. But it is obvious that Kaylee is spreading it somehow."

Kaylee looked at Lacey and Jenna. They both smiled at her, but Kaylee couldn't help thinking she'd hurt them. "I am sorry."

"Don't be," Jenna said. "This is one of the best things that's ever happened to me. I thought it was creepy at first, but I love being able to communicate with animals."

Lacey nodded in agreement. "I can hold the air with my mind. Nothing compares to that."

"But your lives will never be the same," Kaylee said.

Lacey snorted. "Thank goodness." She blushed and glanced at the queen. "No offense, Your Majesty, but I would much rather serve you this way than in your kitchens."

Queen Sherr smiled. Asher laughed. Lacey gathered Kaylee in a hug. She stiffened for a moment before remembering Lacey had gained control enough of her power that it wouldn't affect her breath. The acceptance of these people meant more to her than she realized.

Asher moved back to the fireplace and looked into its embers. Kaylee frowned at his back. Why did he always move away? "So what do you want to do with Minla, the old woman?" he asked.

"We'll have to see if we can make her snap without too much damage. She is so much older than I would've preferred, but I suppose I can't be too picky." Queen Sherr looked over at Kaylee. "Unless of course you can be more selective in who you change."

"I don't know how it works and why it happens to some women I touch and not others."

Asher grinned and the smile made Kaylee relax a little. "Every one of those women were scared to death when you touched them again."

Kaylee sighed. "I will never be able to interact with anyone without making them nervous."

Asher looked Kaylee over from top to bottom, making her wish he'd come closer. He turned away quickly. Her face flushed in anger. She turned away from him and, facing the queen, Kaylee bowed. "I'll be careful, and if I feel there is potential in anyone I will do my best to assure they are fit to serve."

"Oh, my dearest child. You are so good to me. Let it happen as it will and we'll make the best of it, no matter what."

Kaylee sighed, relieved to know she wouldn't be expected to find the perfect candidate for becoming a Blue Blood. She needed to figure out how it happened in the first place.

Jenna moved closer to Kaylee. "Do you feel anything specific before you pass it on?"

"Not that I recall."

"What happened with Minla?" Lacey asked. "Why did you pass it to her?"

Kaylee looked at Asher still by the fireplace. "I had been watching Asher as he looked back at the middle group. I figured one of them might have the potential, but hadn't transformed yet."

Asher shook his head. "I kept looking back to see how many I had passed without finding the one. I had less than a dozen to still examine when I heard the commotion with Minla."

"So you hadn't been thinking you missed her somehow?" Kaylee asked.

Asher paced the floor. Kaylee wondered why he looked so nervous. He didn't look at Kaylee as he passed her, turning his attention to the queen instead. "I didn't know what direction she was in until I turned to see her on the ground. I knew the Blue Blood was there somehow, but until that time, I could not feel the direction. Just the potential."

"But how did Kaylee touching Minla change the potential to power?" Jenna asked.

"I don't know." Asher shook his head. "And perhaps the two of you, or three now, will also be able to pass it on to someone. It has just been Kaylee so far, but I don't think we should rule out the possibility you may also have the ability."

Queen Sherr looked at her Blue Bloods. "Then we will test every willing woman in my palace and village each day, and have them interact with each of you. We must find as many Blue Bloods as we can." A knock on the door made everyone turn. "Enter," Queen Sherr said.

"Forgive me, Your Majesty, but I believe you will want to see Mistress Minla now." Jayshon waited for Queen Sherr to nod her agreement before opening the door enough for Minla to enter.

"Show her what you can do," Jayshon said.

Minla's eyes flitted between the Queen and Kaylee. The woman took in the three others in the room and widened even further. She glanced back at Jayshon. He nodded and motioned her forward.

Minla glanced around the room until her gaze stopped on a chair near the wall. She closed her eyes and took a slow, deep breath. Kaylee felt sorry for her.

She doubted her hip still pained her, but she was an old woman. She was probably nervous knowing she would be tested and encouraged to break through her barrier. Asher and Jenna had explained how it worked once she woke up from her faint.

Minla's eyes remained closed, but the sound of a chair scraping across the floor brought Kaylee's attention to the wall. The chair moved on its own. The others in the room all gasped and turned around, looking at each other. Queen Sherr recovered first and quickly crossed the room to stand in front of Minla. When she took her by the hand, Minla's eyes flew open.

"You are telekinetic?" Queen Sherr asked.

Minla spoke so softly, Kaylee almost couldn't hear her. "I don't know what that means."

"You can move things with your will. With your thoughts."

Minla nodded.

"How wonderful." Queen Sherr smiled widely. She turned to the others and mouthed "thank you" to Kaylee. She took both of Minla's hands in hers and asked, "Will you serve me?"

Minla nodded quickly.

"Will you perform your magic and abilities on my behalf and for the greater good of my kingdom?"

Minla nodded again.

"Then I mark you mine." Queen Sherr pressed her lips to Minla's wrinkled brow to seal it with a kiss.

"How did you snap?" Jenna asked. "What happened to make your power manifest so quickly?"

Minla shook her head. "I don't know, Miss." She turned to the queen. "I had been in the room you showed me to and felt an oddness behind my eyes. I looked around the room, wondering if maybe it was the change of lighting in the castle. Since it's different than in my little cottage, it caused my eyes to hurt. I focused on the wash basin on the counter and felt it jiggle in my mind. I looked at it more closely and sure enough, it started to move."

Jenna huffed. "It is not fair."

Lacey smiled. "It isn't her fault she's not as brave as you, to place her hand in the fire. Maybe when she fainted and fell, it snapped."

"Or possibly when she fell and broke her hip just after I touched her the first time." Kaylee rubbed her hip as she thought of the injury. "That pain was immense."

"That's better then," Jenna said. She turned to Minla. "I don't mean to make light of your pain, but I'm glad you did suffer something."

Minla blinked a few times at Jenna and Lacey laughed. "Oh, don't mind her. I think she'll always be comparing how any of us snap."

Asher watched Kaylee closely all morning, seeing no indication she would pass on her ability. For the fourth day in a row they found no new Blue Bloods. The women relaxed again and the testing began to run smoothly.

His medallion remained inert and still. Asher tried to figure out a pattern. Did there need to be a few days in between to recharge Kaylee? He cringed when he realized he was thinking of her as a magical object instead of as a person.

He jotted down as much as he could remember about when Jenna and Lacey showed signs relatively close together. The huge gap in time between Lacey and Minla indicated it wasn't timing. But how did she pass it on?

He should go to her and talk about it, but he knew the idea of passing the condition to others bothered her. Jenna, Lacey, and Minla were all happy to have these new abilities, but Kaylee apologized to them often. When she interacted with each of the women during the testing, she looked immensely uncomfortable.

Perhaps if he could get her to go out into the village and allow her to heal the people there, she would begin to see the truly miraculous power she held. It didn't have to be anything serious. Nothing that would cause her too much pain, but something that would allow her to feel of worth and know she could make a difference.

The queen was willing to let her heal them, but on his recommendation she'd kept her in the castle. Asher worried about Kaylee. He promised the queen that he would stay away from her if the queen assured him she didn't feel more pain than she had to. But Asher knew Kaylee wanted to go among the villagers and do what she could to ease any maladies. As long as he made sure she didn't overdo it, all would be well. He wanted a chance to study her more and see if he could discover how she passed on the Blue Blood.

He picked up his pace and found himself running with the eagerness of a boy. He forced himself to slow down, not wanting to make Kaylee wonder what he was up to. Despite his attempt at control, when he saw her in the practice yard with her sling, he rushed forward again.

Now if he could figure out how to word it just right.

"Kaylee," Asher called.

She tucked her sling in her belt, waiting for him to reach her.

"Would you join me on a walk down to the village?" Asher offered her his arm, but she didn't take it. Instead she looked in his eyes as if searching for his reason. "Queen Sherr would like a better idea of the state of her subjects. I offered to go and thought perhaps you would like to come as well. I'm sure you're tired of just practicing here and searching for new Blue Bloods each day. A change of scenery could be just what you need."

She didn't move. Asher tried again. "You could offer to heal anyone who is sick."

"Why now?" Kaylee asked.

Asher cursed himself for thinking he could switch tactics so quickly. "If the people see the good you can do, they won't be as nervous to come to the testing."

Her eyes softened. "That would be wonderful."

He offered his arm once more. Kaylee took it as if not sure what to do. When her small hand brushed the underside of his triceps as she threaded her arm through his, a shiver that had nothing to do with her healing power rippled across his skin. She held a completely different power over him. Maybe this wouldn't be such a good idea. He didn't take his arm back, but he didn't pull her as close as he wanted to. She kept her hand on his forearm. He held his arm out stiffly to keep her from getting too close.

It was torture to walk with her, but he couldn't help himself. If this was the only interaction he could have, it was better than nothing.

They walked in awkward silence for a few minutes. He glanced at her, but she was completely absorbed with the view. They walked out of the main castle gates and into the market area of the village without seeing anything but her. He scolded himself for being so distracted. If there had been any danger, he would've been no protection to her whatsoever.

With the pretense of inspecting one of the booths, he removed her arm from his and approached the merchant. "How are you, my fine sir?"

The man glanced around him to see if Asher were truly addressing him. He cleared his throat. "I'm fine, your grace."

"Good. Her Majesty is interested in how things fare in her kingdom. Is there anything you wish for me to tell her?"

The man ducked his head and blushed deeply. He cleared his throat. "No, sir. We are rightly pleased with her rule. She is a might better than the blasted king. Starting fresh here wasn't easy, but I have more opportunities than under Inwer." He offered a beautifully formed piece of pottery to Kaylee. She smiled and shook her head.

"It is free to you, Mistress."

"I appreciate the offer, but I cannot accept."

The merchant's face fell. Kaylee shifted on her feet. "Can I offer healing to anyone in your family?"

"You're the healer?" The man's eyes lit up and he nodded quickly, nearly bending in half. "Thank you. I'll be back right away." He pushed the cup to the edge of his table and rushed away. Asher heard him calling, "Hurry quick and bring Brio."

A tired looking woman came forward carrying a small boy. The merchant grabbed the boy and hurried back to Kaylee. The boy couldn't be older than four. His arm looked misshapen, as if he had broken it and it'd never been set.

The severity of it made Asher's stomach clench. If she attempted to heal that, would she have to break her arm as well? Did he dare stop her if she tried? Asher needed to let her feel comfortable among the people. She needed to see the value of her powers. If he stopped her from performing her magic, she would still feel worthless.

Asher watched Kaylee closely. She didn't even flinch at the sight. She smiled at the boy and reached for him. He looked to his mother. When she nodded, he allowed Kaylee to take him from his father's arms.

"What's your name?" she asked as she squatted down and sat in the dirt right in front of the merchant's booth.

"Brio."

"What happened to your arm?" She placed her hand gently on his elbow and slid her hand up to his shoulder slowly enough that Asher felt sure she was examining the extent of his injury.

"I fell out of a tree." He ducked his head, refusing to look at his parents.

Asher addressed the boy's mother. "Was it ever set?"

She shook her head. "We were on our way here after leaving our village that had been attacked by bandits. There were no others with us and we didn't know what to do for him."

Asher turned his attention back to Kaylee. She smiled up at the woman, the sympathy apparent on her face. "I'm sure you did the best you could. It was a bad break. I'm surprised it didn't break through his skin."

The woman's face paled as she brought her hands to her chest over her heart. "Thank goodness. Is there anything you can do for him?" Her hope seemed palpable.

"I can't promise anything, but I will do what I can."

"He isn't able to use it at all. We worry he'll never be able to get any kind of employment or be able to care for himself as an adult." Brio's father swallowed hard and cleared his throat. "We appreciate anything you can do."

Kaylee closed her eyes, rubbing her hand over Brio's arm. Asher watched her closely to see if she would attempt to heal him. She frowned and returned her hand to one particular place about one quarter of the distance between elbow and shoulder. She lifted her head but kept her hand still.

"In order to fix this bone, I am afraid it will have to be broken again. I can't do anything to it as it is now other than take away his pain for a short time. For him to have any sort of use of this arm, we need to place it in proper alignment."

Brio's mother sat down on the ground next to the table with her husband's wares. "How will you do that?"

"I don't know for sure, but I can heal it again immediately. He will only feel pain for a short time."

Asher watched as the parents looked at each other. They didn't say a word, but volumes were spoken in that brief moment. Brio's father turned to Kaylee and said, "Do it, please."

Kaylee lifted her eyes to Asher. He felt sick thinking of breaking that boy's arm, but knew it needed to happen. The boy had no hope if he lived as a cripple. It was hard enough to survive with two good arms.

Brio's face held fear, yet he never spoke. He looked at his parents for assurance. His mother gathered him in her arms. Kaylee stood up and leaned close to Asher. She smelled fresh and wholesome, much different than the crowd beginning to gather around them. He tried to distract himself from the thoughts her scent gave him.

He looked instead at her newly grown hair, still shorter than his own. It was a dark brown, but not black. As she turned her head to look at Brio, red highlights appeared.

"Can you break it in just the spot I tell you to?" Kaylee asked.

"I don't know. I've never purposely broken someone's bones, let alone a child's."

"It has to be done with just the right amount of force. I could feel what it would take to snap the bone where it had knitted together wrong. I don't think I have the force necessary to do it. You must do it."

Asher closed his eyes and nodded. "Tell me what to do."

Kaylee moved over to the merchant's small table and examined the area. The table looked strong enough to support the boy, but he wondered what Kaylee was looking for. She placed both hands on the table and jiggled it around. It held firm, but she didn't seem satisfied. She moved a couple of items out of the way and lifted the cloth draped over the table. She examined the legs. Asher bent over to see the kind of table legs they could remove for transport.

"Remove these and place the table on the ground." Kaylee looked around at the growing crowd. "I'll be right back."

Asher helped dismantle the table. When the legs were gone, he placed the table on the ground. He stood up to follow after Kaylee just as she returned with a wooden mallet. He eyed the tool with a cringe. Kaylee placed it in his hand. He wanted to drop it on the ground or throw it far away, but he had agreed. Asher shook his head. He would never willingly bring her out into the village again. This had been a stupid idea.

Kaylee took the little boy by the hand and led him to the table. She instructed him on how to lie next to it and where to place his arm in the table. She turned to the boy's father. "You must hold him there. Cradle him against yourself to show him comfort, but his arm must not move when we begin." She looked deep into his eyes. "Do you understand me?"

He nodded but didn't speak. He got down on his knees next to the boy and stroked his hair back off his forehead. Asher heard whispering, too low to make out. Kaylee found another man in the crowd and instructed him to hold the boy's arm. The boy's mother wrapped her arms around her stomach. Kaylee motioned for some woman close by to help her. The stranger moved over and placed her arm around the young mother's shoulders.

Kaylee returned to Asher. She spoke low. "I will mark the place on his arm. You need to hit it with about the same force you would drive a nail. As soon as you strike his arm, you must do the same to mine. With more force."

Asher dropped the mallet. "No."

"You must."

Asher's throat tightened. "I can't do that. I won't hurt this boy, and I certainly won't break your arm."

Kaylee looked into his eyes and he could see the confusion in her gaze. "Why would you punish this boy because of me?"

Asher shook his head. "I'm saving him and you from more pain. You don't have to do this. The boy can learn a trade that only needs one hand."

Kaylee snorted and managed to still sound tender. "There is nothing for him in his current state. He needs to be whole. I can do this for him." She reached down and picked up the mallet, pressing into his hands.

Asher shook his head but didn't drop the mallet again.

"Do you understand what you need to do?"

He nodded, but couldn't look at her.

"My arm immediately after his. I don't want him to suffer longer than he has to."

"I know!" Asher snapped. He couldn't believe he was doing this. He looked at the little boy, lying next to the table with his father behind him.

Kaylee showed the other man where to hold the boy's hand and stretched it across the table. "Right here. Do not let him move it."

The man nodded. Kaylee pulled a small piece of charcoal out of her pocket. She drew a circle on the boys arm. Asher shuddered at his target.

Kaylee positioned herself on the ground and placed her hand across the table. She drew a circle on her arm in the same spot. Asher closed his eyes and cursed silently for his part in this. He moved closer to Brio, kneeling on one knee, and lifted the mallet.

CHAPTER TWENTY-SIX

Kaylee tried to block out the pain she knew would come, but when Asher brought the mallet down on Brio's arm and he screamed in agony her heart felt as if it were torn from her chest. She clenched her eyes tight, waiting for the mallet to strike her arm. Brio continued to wail but Asher still hadn't done hers. She opened her eyes and met Asher's tortured eyes.

"Please," she whispered.

Asher gritted his teeth and focused on her arm. She watched as he struggled to overcome his hesitance. How could she not have realized how much this would pain him? She should have asked someone else in the crowd.

"Don't let him suffer any longer," she said over Brio's screams of pain, hoping to spur him to action.

Asher swore and raised the mallet again. She watched in detached fascination as he stared at her arm up to the moment the mallet hit. He clenched his eyes tight and threw the mallet to the side the moment it bounced off her arm.

She was so immersed in Asher she didn't register the pain at first. A small portion of her subconscious mind reflected on that little piece of information. Perhaps she could use pain like this more often. Block it away behind distraction and only focus on it when needed to call her healing powers forward. She embraced the pain and felt the magic itching to be put to work.

She turned to Brio and placed her good hand on the broken bone. Asher did a perfect job of rebreaking the bone in the right spots. She willed the bones to line up correctly, not needing to even manipulate them physically. In her mind's eye, she could see exactly where things needed to fit. Where the broken blood vessels should be reconnected. How to strengthen the muscles and tendons that had weakened from lack of use.

When the arm was as correct as it ever had been, she took her hand from Brio and wiped his tears. Slow, measured breaths helped her ignore her own arm and she turned to the crowd.

"Is anyone else in need of help?" She didn't know if she could bring herself to heal the pain and then cause more later. Better to get it all done now.

The crowd slowly came out of their stupor. One after another, people lined up.

Kaylee plodded a few steps in front of Asher. He refused to talk to her, and she was too exhausted from all the healing to speak anyway. She could have healed most of their aches and pains with only a smashed finger, but a couple people with internal maladies needed the amount of magic the broken arm produced. Asher would never understand her reasoning, so she wouldn't bother trying to explain.

After the crowd had stopped producing injuries or illnesses, they all rushed back to their homes and returned bearing gifts of payment. Kaylee didn't need any of the items they brought, but when she tried to refuse them, Asher whispered. "You accepted it from the potter. You should do the same courtesy for them."

Kaylee had been forced to ask the grateful people to find a wheel barrow to carry it all back to the castle for her. She had to find a different way to help them without inconveniencing Asher and without requiring their goods. Maybe she could do it as a service in the name of the queen. That would help the people to feel more loyal to her. Maybe the men in the village could fortify the castle grounds or even join the queen's army.

Kaylee shook her head. She didn't want to coerce them into anything. She wanted them to participate from their own free will. By being able to choose which side of this battle she was on, Kaylee felt more sure of herself and more willing to involve herself in the fight.

"Something's happened," Asher said from behind. "It is time to return to the castle."

Kaylee looked at him. His back was turned. She couldn't see anything odd about the castle, but Asher's body tensed as if preparing for an attack.

"What is it?" Kaylee asked.

"I heard a signal whistle."

Kaylee tilted her head up, trying to hear it. Nothing sounded out of the ordinary.

Asher looked at the man walking past them. Soon two more large men followed, and after that a couple more. Soon, men from all over the village and market area left their homes, booths, or shops and marched toward the castle.

Asher reached for her hand. She let him take it as they rushed toward whatever it was. A fear of the unknown gave her a jolt of adrenaline, allowing her to ignore the bone deep weariness healing had caused.

Inside the queen's courtyard, the men gathered together in groups of ten. One of the men in each group walked around the others as if doing a count. Asher didn't slow down, but hurried into the castle and led Kaylee up the stairs. They were met by Jayshon. "The queen desires you attend her."

Asher only nodded and continued toward the queen's wing. He knocked once on the queen's study doors and was immediately told to enter.

"What is it?" he asked.

"I've had news." She looked angry and Kaylee could see tears still in her eyes.

"Are we under attack?" Kaylee asked.

"No, that was a test," Queen Sherr said. "I wanted to see how quickly my soldiers would respond."

"What is it then?" Kaylee asked as Jenna, Lacey, and Minla entered the room.

"My queen, how can we serve you?" Minla asked.

"I need to counsel with you. I have heard from one of my spies in King Inwer's court." She held up a letter. "This was delivered to me less than an hour ago."

She motioned for them to join her at the large table in a room to the side of her office chambers. A map lay spread out. Kaylee looked at the fine details on it.

"Read it aloud," Queen Sherr said. Asher reached for the letter.

Salutations your Majesty.

This news will not please you, but must be shared regardless. Penny is dead. Her life forfeit just as yours in a failed attempt of the king's. It appears she was angry at his actions and tried to kill him immediately after she revived with her second life. The king withstood her attempt and took her second life as well. She did, however, injure him enough that he's struggling to recover. He drained Sue right away, ending her gifted life and then killing her the second time before she could retaliate.

There was nothing I could do to save them. It happened before I knew he had gone to experiment. I have been forbidden to tell the others of what was done. I doubt any of them would believe me. They seem to be enamored of him and believe him incapable of wrongdoing. None of your Sisters in Blood you suggested might be sympathetic to your cause will listen to me.

He's sworn he will not risk the trials again, but you and I know him better. He craves what Blue Blood can give him. It will happen again. I don't know when, but another of your Sisters in Blood will be next. Do what you can to stop this. I am trying to keep it from getting worse, but I believe his mind is beyond reach. Please act as soon as you can.

Your humble servant,

X

Asher looked up from the note. "The king has been drinking their blood?"

Queen Sherr nodded. "It started out so innocently, years before I was taken to him. It began when one of his new Blue Bloods chose knives to help her snap. When her blood got on his hand, he noticed the aches and the age spots were lessened there. He began experimenting on what the blood could do. He never took our blood without our permission, but it became more and more frequent as the years went by. Eventually he noticed it slowed his aging. And since he did not yet have an heir, he rationalized that he needed to stay young as long as possible."

"He still does not have an heir," Asher said.

"True. And he does not want to give his kingdom away to anyone. He wants to rule forever. Over time, he realized even drinking the blood wasn't keeping him as young as it had at first. He became obsessed. I am ashamed to admit he convinced me to let him try more. I willingly allowed him to bleed me. He sedated me so it wouldn't hurt. But he never stopped and I bled dry without knowing what was happening."

Kaylee squirmed, but Jenna asked, "What was death like?"

"It was easy. No pain. Nothing to indicate I was different, other than the fact I was no longer tired. When he realized what happened, he was shocked. It was as if he hadn't even thought of the possibility of taking too much of my blood. And then when I was no longer of worth to him, he cast me aside."

Queen Sherr leaned forward and touched the place on the map showing King Inwer's castle.

"I could see him clearly for the first time in ages. He did not seem to be in control of himself anymore. His obsession with youth and immortality had turned him from the once powerful and benevolent care of his kingdom. Something must've happened to him as he ingested our blood. Perhaps it attacked his mind. Maybe it turned him into someone else, but he is no longer worthy or able of ruling a kingdom.

"He's managed to keep his insanity hidden, for now. He's assigned his advisors and stewards to run things, but as my confidant has revealed, he is insane. I have to act."

Everyone at the table stirred. Kaylee felt revulsion at the idea of the king drinking blood. An image of Queen Sherr catching her blood in a cup that first day came to mind. Kaylee stood slowly. "My queen. I must ask something before we go any further."

All eyes turned to her.

"The first day I arrived, when you asked to see my healing power, you caught my blood in your goblet."

Queen Sherr nodded. "I can't deny I was tempted. I swirled it around in that goblet until it congealed. And even then I debated. But I swear on my last life, I did not drink your blood."

Kaylee maintained eye contact with the queen for a few more moments. She saw no lie in her countenance. She sat down and turned to the others. "I believe her and I will follow her into battle. The king needs to be stopped."

The others agreed and all eyes once again turned to Queen Sherr.

"With my knowledge of the castle and grounds, I know the best place to stage our attack. Because our soldiers are few, and there are only four of you, we will be completely outnumbered. But I've been strategizing with Asher, Tige, and Dolf for some time on where to attack." She turned to Asher.

He left the table, moving over to a shelf with scrolls on it. He selected two and brought them back to the group.

They were both smaller than the open map on the table so he laid them next to each other, covering most of the map. "This is a sketch of the king's palace. This is a map of his inner city." He leaned over the papers and proceeded to lay out the plan of attack.

Kaylee smiled. It might actually work.

There was no time for leisure over the next few days. Soldiers were gathered and armed as fully as possible. The leaders of each group of ten were instructed in their part. Having Queen Sherr's army move across the landscape all the way to King Inwer's castle, they would be stopped before even arriving near the king's borders. To counteract that possibility, the groups would break up and be sent in several different directions. They would then move without detection and meet at a rally point just off the hill near the castle. A smaller yet more specialized group would integrate themselves within the city to attack when the signal was given.

The march would take more than a month, giving the queen time to search for more Blue Bloods. Kaylee had been interacting with the women constantly, yet there was still no transfer of power. She didn't understand it. She even healed every woman of anything they had, including sunburns and skin blemishes. Though Queen Sherr never showed displeasure at the lack of new Blue Bloods, Kaylee felt miserable.

She no longer thought it a curse to have blue blood. The things Jenna, Lacey and Minla did astounded her. Jenna managed to control the wild beasts in the forest with such finesse that her animals were now a vital part of the plan. Lacey could stop entire regiments of soldiers, though it left her breathless if she did it for long. And Minla gained strength daily. At first she moved smaller objects, but she could now lift the portcullis on her own. She couldn't throw boulders yet, though Kaylee was certain she'd manage to do it eventually.

Kaylee's own ability to restore health to those injured would be invaluable. As long as she could walk among them, they'd be healed. She could heal most anyone of anything except death. Kaylee refused to think of the villager who proved she couldn't heal death. By the time she got to him and examined his wound, he was so far gone nothing short of dying herself could have pulled enough power to heal him.

The women were strong and powerful, and grateful for their abilities. If only Kaylee knew what allowed her to pass on the power, she would find more women to join them. The thought of going against King Inwer's army and more than twenty Blue Bloods in his control made Kaylee sick.

Queen Sherr encouraged Kaylee to interact with the women in the village as often as possible, but none had shown potential since Minla. They had come to accept her. Many were friendly enough to chat about their children Kaylee had healed from various things. When the last woman said her goodbyes, Kaylee turned to leave and saw Dolf. A feeling of fondness made her rush to him. He had not been around much since the queen started building her army. "Dolf." Kaylee waved as he turned.

His eyes lit up. He excused himself from the general he'd been speaking to. "Mistress Kaylee. It is so good to see you so well."

Kaylee smiled. "It is good to see you, Dolf. What have you been up to?"

Dolf smiled, showing a newly missing tooth. "I've been recruiting new soldiers and training them to fight."

"Why didn't you come to me so I could heal your tooth?" Kaylee asked. She reached up to touch his face, but pulled her hand away quickly when she realized how forward that would look.

Dolf took her hand in his and turned it over so the palm faced up. He traced his finger over the creases in her palm. He closed her fingers and let her hand go. Kaylee clasped her hands together and Dolf said. "I appreciate your concern, but there is no reason for you to feel pain just to hide this gap. Besides, I look so much more intimidating this way."

"Yes. There is that. I would hate to meet you in the forest and be kidnapped away with you looking like that."

Dolf laughed. "I'm not saying I wasn't scary looking before, but you can't deny this lends me even more credibility as a soldier."

Kaylee smile. "Thank you for your kindness to me. If it had only been Zeb, I don't know what he would've done on his own."

Dolf frowned. "He wasn't right in the head before he got hit. I was hoping that healing would have fixed him up a little, but . . ."

"Where is he now?" Kaylee asked.

"The queen gave him money and a plot of land as payment, but he cut ties with her. I haven't seen him since."

Kaylee nodded. She would very likely never see him again and found herself more than pleased with the idea. "Are you leading one of the groups?"

Dolf grinned, showing his missing tooth again. "Just got assigned yesterday. I'll be leading a group of ten through the foothills by the Aluve Mountains."

Kaylee visualized it on the map they had poured over in the queen's study. If they kept going straight along that path, they would eventually find her monastery. Kaylee shook her head. The monastery wasn't hers anymore, but living there for three years had been good for her. She felt safe and very much at peace.

"When do you depart?"

"In two days."

"So soon?"

"It is a long journey, and since we aren't going in a straight line to King Inwer's lands, we need to make good time if we plan to meet you at his front doors by the first snows."

"I wish you all the luck in the world." Kaylee reached once more for him. She placed her hand on his cheek. "Be safe. Be well. Be smart."

"Thank you." Dolf lifted his hand to touch hers and pulled it away from his face. "You be well, too. I have heard much about your healings. Don't overdo it in your trainings."

"I assure you I am not overdoing anything. I could do so much more, but that would require you all to be injured and that would just be foolish."

Dolf chuckled. "Agreed."

Kaylee patted his hand. He let go and turned to walk back to the soldiers. She felt gratitude for his help on her journey. As she watched him, she realized they had gathered an audience. Most looked curiously at the exchange, but Asher's eyes grew dark. Did he still not trust Dolf? It wouldn't do any good to ask him about it, so she turned to resume her previous path. She glanced behind her once to see if Asher had moved. He no longer looked at her, but the expression on his face as he watched Dolf made Kaylee glad Asher was staying at the castle instead of joining the troops. Of course, the odds of him traveling anywhere near another group was slim. They needed to stay inconspicuous as they infiltrated the king's lands.

CHAPTER TWENTY-SEVEN

It shouldn't bother Asher, but it did. Why Kaylee would show kindness to Dolf was a mystery to him. Asher tried to save her from Dolf as he took the knife to filet her skin, yet she'd willingly healed him and even refused to run. On their journey to Queen Sherr, Dolf had proven he was human enough, but Asher still couldn't bring himself to trust him completely. And Zeb. It was a good thing Zeb had been sent into retirement. If he had come anywhere near Kaylee again once they arrived, Asher would have killed the man. He doubted the queen would have been too upset about that, but he was still glad he didn't have to.

Asher watched as Kaylee glided across the courtyard. She hadn't turned to look at him and he was annoyed at how much that stung. She'd specifically called to Dolf and spent more than a few minutes talking to him, but she gave no indication she had even seen him until after Dolf had walked away. The dreamy look in her eye made Asher's stomach clench.

He stared at Dolf, hating himself for the jealousy growing inside. He shouldn't let Kaylee affect him so much. She could never be his. But she couldn't be Dolf's either, not while she served the queen as a Blue Blood. And since Asher would do everything in his power to keep her alive and well, he would age and soon grow too old for her to be interested in him.

He'd tried multiple times to smother his growing feelings for her. He even tried to become interested in the many women he tested each day. He'd seen plenty of beautiful and desirable women. Many made it obvious they were interested in him.

Asher blinked and shifted his feet. He didn't want Kaylee just because she showed no interest in him. He wasn't that shallow. He found her fascinating from the moment she climbed down from that tree. She had a confidence that contradicted her nervousness. Even though she didn't want to come with him, she rallied her courage and did what was best.

What a fool he'd been to take all those women to King Inwer. He should've insisted on meeting with the king more often—in taking them to him in person like he had done the first years of his service. When Lord Nirro began meeting with him and arranging his payments, Asher should've suspected. Would he have ever guessed the king was losing his mind to some strange side effect of the blue blood?

That spur of the moment agreement to come willingly with Dolf and Kaylee when it was offered was probably the wisest decision he had made in years. Queen Sherr needed to end King Inwer's rule before he killed all his Blue Bloods in his frantic attempt to extend his life.

Asher turned away from his assignment of observing the troops. He wasn't technically needed—Queen Sherr had asked him to oversee the assignments and instructions of departure. Once he'd given the information to the generals and then to the group leaders, his role was done.

Though these men were mostly inexperienced in actual combat, they followed commands well. Queen Sherr's captains and generals were all men who'd once served King Inwer and worked as the Queen's personal bodyguards. When they learned what had happened to Sherr at the king's hands, they left their posts and followed her across the country, gathering people along the way to build up this new kingdom here.

How they'd done it without garnering the attention of King Inwer mystified Asher. And because of their stealth while fleeing the kingdom, Asher knew they would be able to infiltrate the king's lands without raising alarm. King Inwer would not have enough time to fully prepare for an attack. And if they were lucky, the king would be so distracted trying to artificially extend his life, Queen Sherr could come in and end it.

"The first wave has left, each handful on a different route. In two days, wave two will go, followed by more every two days." Asher stood in front of the four Blue Bloods and the queen as well as a few of the queen's counselors.

"And they all know to be discreet?"

"Yes. We will try to raise no alarm on their journey."

Queen Sherr nodded. "There are still only four Blue Bloods. I think Kaylee is exhausted. We'll make do with what we have." She looked at the four women with her. "I believe your powers are stronger than many the king has. But do not discount their abilities."

Jenna rubbed her eyes. She looked just as tired as the other Blue Bloods. They'd been training nonstop for weeks.

Queen Sherr pulled out a worn paper with the list of the known Blue Bloods in the king's service. "Not all of them will be a threat to us. We need to be prepared for those who are. Three of them can move things like Minla can. I don't remember any of them being able to move anything as large as she can, though." She smiled at Minla.

"Two can manipulate the weather. If they see us coming, they can slow us down by bringing storms and wind. I was the weakest of the three, so King Inwer must not have worried about losing me." She shook it off and made a mark on the paper. "Two can throw fire. They will need to be neutralized immediately."

Asher knew one of them was his cousin Fran. He didn't like the thought of fighting her, but if she were loyal to the king, there was nothing they could do about it but fight.

Queen Sherr turned to Lacey. "You can probably do much against them using your control over the air. But there is one that can do what you do, and perhaps they have practiced together so they may know ways to counteract anything you might try."

Lacey nodded and Queen Sherr continued. "Four, no, three now can manipulate the earth. A couple of those can cause minor earthquakes, but wouldn't want to do that in the king's palace. He might send them out to meet us if they discover us early. One can use water. She can't create it from nothing, but she can easily manipulate any water source.

"One can affect chance, so unless she can influence the way things go for us or the king's Blue Bloods, I don't know how much of a threat she'll be. Two can make plants grow well, nothing faster than its normal timeline, just larger and more delicious or more useful. One can persuade someone to do something they normally wouldn't do. Two," Queen Sherr shook her head, "one can calm people down, get them to be more comfortable with what the king wants. One could project images into people's thoughts. She wouldn't be able to hurt you, but could make you fear something that wasn't really there."

Kaylee had counted at least fifteen they would have to be concerned about. Besides the actual guards and soldiers in the kings employ. They were outnumbered, but with a surprise attack they had a fighting chance.

They spent the next three hours discussing ways they could use the layout of the king's castle and grounds to their advantage. If they were lucky, not all of the Blue Bloods would be in the castle when they attacked. At least a few would be out on assignment for the king, unless he had changed his ways. The Queen's spy hadn't given much information about the way things were functioning besides the deaths.

At the end of the day, Kaylee could barely stay awake to finish her meal. She excused herself from the table and returned to her room. She took a moment to write a few notes in her journal then left it on the table and crawled into bed. She was asleep before the ink dried.

In the morning, she felt more refreshed than she had in days and woke to the sound of birds chirping near her small window. Kaylee quickly dressed, happy she'd insisted on some clothing that was easy enough to button and lace by herself. Kaylee tucked her journal back into the trunk next to her father's book. She wished she had more time to devote to deciphering it. Once this battle was over, she would insist on being left alone to pour over the words. There had to be a pattern to it somewhere. She traced the spiral on the center of the cover. It had been branded into the leather and was a darker color as if years of touching had left its mark. She reluctantly left the book in the trunk with her own journal and locked it. It was time for the daily testing.

As she entered the courtyard, Kaylee heard shouting. The women were all lined up as usual, but on the far side, Kaylee could see a woman she recognized as a midwife trying to get past the guards.

"Let her through," Kaylee called. When the guards stepped to the side, the midwife rushed forward carrying a bundle. Kaylee knew something was wrong with the baby and reached for her the moment the midwife arrived. "What's wrong?"

Kaylee took the wrap off the baby and saw blue around her lips and eyes. Her breaths were almost nonexistent. As Kaylee looked her over, she could see the baby's chest was sunken in. Kaylee touched the baby, and felt a shiver of power cross over them both. It startled her enough she almost dropped the baby. Had she just transferred the Blue Blood ability to this infant? Kaylee sat hard on the ground and frantically looked over the baby. She could see something severely wrong with the child, but unless she could heal whatever it was, she would never know if she had just made her a Blue Blood.

Kaylee laid the child across her lap and placed her hand on the baby's chest. The organs hadn't formed completely right. Something was off with the heart and that, in turn, affected the lungs. It wouldn't be painful to heal, but Kaylee still needed enough power to start the magic flowing. She looked around and through the growing crowd around until she saw a guard she recognized.

"Corien. Your knife." If she'd been thinking clearly this morning, she would've added her knife to her belt, but her journal had distracted her. Corien placed his blade in her hand and she slowly slid it down the back of her forearm. It wasn't deep, but stung enough to activate the power that flowed through her hands into the baby's chest. She focused her attention on the organs inside and corrected the malformations until everything was in perfect order.

Kaylee ignored the blood dripping from her arm and lifted the little girl up to eye level to check her over. Everything else about her tiny body seemed just right. Her breathing was normal and though her muscles were still weak, she looked as healthy as could be. Kaylee allowed her senses to open enough to examine every other part of the baby in case she had missed something inside. When she was sure all was right, Kaylee lowered her down into the wrap and healed her own arm.

She glanced at the knife still lying next to her where she had dropped it. Did she dare test this baby in front of all these women? Kaylee looked up to see Queen Sherr had joined them. The commotion must've interested her. When the queen knelt down next to her, Kaylee knew she had to tell her. She leaned over and whispered into the queen's ear. "I think I passed on the power again."

Queen Sherr leaned back in surprise. She looked at the baby, then up at Kaylee, one eyebrow raised. Kaylee nodded.

Queen Sherr pulled out a tiny knife from her sheath. She took the baby's foot and pressed the tip against the heel. The baby took a fast breath and let out a shriek of pain. Kaylee healed it immediately, but the blue blood was obvious. Kaylee buried her face in the blanket wrapping the baby. "I'm so sorry."

"Don't be sorry, my dear. We have one more detail to add to our study. Do you see any reason to test these other women?"

Kaylee shrugged. "I don't know. I can if you wish, but the power has already passed. I doubt there's more in me now."

"Well, in order to keep up appearances, we should test them, unless you think they should know the power has passed to this little one."

"It is your decision, Your Majesty." Kaylee couldn't look away from the baby she held. Would the baby be able to grow? According to all that happened with other Blue Bloods, they didn't age. Had she just doomed this infant to a life of stasis?

"I think we should be honest with them." Queen Sherr stood up and cleared her throat. "Thank you all for your attendance today. The testing is canceled. We've already found our Blue Blood for this session."

The crowd gasped. Some moved even closer to see the newest Blue Blood, and others stepped away as if shocked to discover it could happen to an infant. Kaylee didn't want to give the baby back to the midwife, but reluctantly agreed as long as she could go with her to the child's mother. She had to apologize.

The worried mother relaxed the second the midwife walked in the door returning her baby. "Is she all right?"

The midwife nodded. "Everything is well with her now. Mistress Kaylee healed her right away. She is breathing right and all is as it should be."

The woman sagged in relief then reached for her baby. The infant was offered the breast and eagerly took to nursing. The mother winced once then looked up at Kaylee. "Thank you so much. I am indebted to you."

Kaylee shook her head. "I have something to tell you." She moved closer to the bed and sat on the corner. She glanced at the father, who stood near the head of the bed watching his wife and child. "In the process of examining and healing your child, somehow the magical ability of a Blue Blood transferred to her. She's now a Blue Blood."

The mother relaxed her arm slightly to pull the baby back and look at her. She caressed the child's head and then looked up at Kaylee. "She'll be like you when she grows up?" The hope in her eyes was obvious and it hurt Kaylee to see it.

"I don't know. There are so many things I don't know about how it works. But there's a small possibility she'll never grow up."

The father took a step closer to Kaylee and before he could touch her, his wife grabbed his hand. "What do you mean?" the mother asked.

"Something about being a Blue Blood means we don't age. I don't know when that happens, if it is when a girl reaches a certain age. I was a Blue Blood for more than three years before my powers manifested and I've grown in that time. So she may be fine. But Queen Sherr remained the same for years until she lost her first life. I just want you to be prepared for the possibility she won't grow if she keeps her first life as a Blue Blood."

"So she'll have to die to live?" her father asked.

"I don't know. You will have to watch for signs of growth. It should be obvious in weeks whether it will affect her. My suggestion to you would be to keep her from experiencing any severe pain or trauma. If she doesn't snap and experience the change into power, she could grow with no problems. You must be very careful with her. She is completely healthy and normal in every other way that I could discern, but you'll need to treat her with the utmost care."

The new parents nodded, looking at each other and then at the baby.

Kaylee prayed it would be enough. She hated to think she had ruined this infant's life.

CHAPTER TWENTY-EIGHT

Asher felt the potential of power for only a short time and hadn't managed to get out into the courtyard for the testing until after Kaylee had left with the baby. When Queen Sherr explained to him and the other Blue Bloods, they were stunned. It was a waste that the power had been transferred to an infant. She would be completely worthless for years, if she even grew. Kaylee was so worried about the baby that she refused to talk about what happened.

And there would be no way to get her to try again with any interest. He thought she was beginning to appreciate her power and knew that by giving the power to more women their chances of success would increase, but the second wave would leave tomorrow and in a month they themselves would march to the king's lands.

His role would be simple enough. He was known by many as a bounty hunter for the king and could get into places without comment. He would travel with

Lacey as if taking her to the king. The others would follow a different path. It wouldn't look suspicious at all to have a few women traveling together with an escort or two. And even stopping at the same inns along the way would be no problem. But if they didn't find another Blue Blood in the next week, there would not be enough time to discover her ability and train her.

The idea of going against King Inwer with their small numbers made him nervous, but if everyone performed their duties correctly, they had a decent chance of success.

"But finding one now would be useless." Kaylee insisted. "We will have no time to train her, and putting someone in the middle of a battle with no experience would basically be murder."

Asher shook his head. "She would have a second life."

"And what if that is lost in the battle as well?" Kaylee said. "I will not do it. We haven't found any more since the baby, and I've tried everything I can think of to make it happen. I don't know what I did. I've healed more women than I can count so it's not related to healing. I've done it tired, I've done it rested, and I've done it early in the morning and late at night. I've even woken them all up and still nothing happens. I will not test them anymore. I'm weary of it."

"But—" Asher began.

"Enough, Asher." Queen Sherr raised her hand. "I accept Kaylee's reasoning and trust her on this. There is no way to know why it happened in the first place. And she's right. There's no longer enough time to train anyone who manifests the power."

Asher bowed his head in a curt nod as he stepped away from the table. He stopped near the fireplace and stared into the flames. Kaylee was relieved she didn't have to explain herself anymore.

"We'll be prepared to leave in two weeks. Our soldiers are more than halfway to King Inwer's lands now and the reports we've received through Jenna's birds show there has been no notice of them. Everything is working according to plan. We are only a few, but we have the element of surprise on our side. While I do not count on my Sisters in Blood to give up on the king, there is a chance they won't even fight us given the news that he's taking their lives."

"Xavier's last message to me indicated the Blue Bloods were becoming uneasy with the revelation two of their sisters were gone. It may be as simple as going in and telling them the truth. Showing them how the king has changed."

Asher turned from the fire. "I wouldn't count on that."

"I am not relying on it as certain, but I can always hope they will see reason. I don't want to end their Blue Blood life, but to stop him from draining them in a crazy attempt to live forever, I will. And Xavier's note gave me reason to believe the king's subjects would be all too happy to see him gone."

Kaylee hoped that would be true. While living among the monks, she'd heard rumors of how much he taxed his subjects. It wasn't enough to drive them into poverty, but there were many complaints about how he wanted their money but gave them nothing in return. And he had stopped taking petitions from the people, delegating that to some of his advisors who were less than sympathetic.

Queen Sherr looked at the people in the room with her. "I'm tired, and you are all even more so. We will end for now. Go do something to relax." She turned to Asher. "Tell Jayshon that there will be no more testing of the women."

Asher took a deep breath before he walked away. Queen Sherr turned to her Blue Bloods. "He means well. I think he feels strongly for each of you. I see it in his eyes."

Jenna giggled. "I wish."

All of them looked at Jenna. Lacey smiled. "You're interested in him?"

Jenna smiled. "Not really, but he is very handsome. I thought at first, when he kept looking at me before I'd changed, that he was some lecherous creep. But I know he had no interest in me that way now. He seems to be pining after some other woman."

Kaylee thought that as well. At one time she thought it might have been herself, but since arriving at the castle, he acted different. He'd always treated all women with respect. And the Blue Bloods he treated as family. It would be hard to resign herself to thinking of him as a brother since he didn't seem to want her as anything more than that. She'd always wished she had a larger family and maybe now she had one.

An idea hit Kaylee. Did it have something to do with birth order? The baby girl she'd changed was an only child right now. "Jenna, Lacey, Your majesty, do you have family?"

Jenna shook her head. "My folks died before we made it here to Queen Sherr's lands."

"Any brothers or sisters?" Kaylee asked.

"No." Jenna shook her head.

"How about you?" Kaylee turned to the others. Queen Sherr shook her head. "I had a brother, but he was killed in a skirmish in a bar before I ever changed."

Kaylee sagged as Lacey spoke. "I have a brother. He's in the fourth wave right now. My parents are both alive as well in the village."

"Why?" Queen Sherr asked.

Kaylee sighed. "I thought for a moment I may have figured out a pattern for passing on blue blood. If you have living siblings, then my theory is wrong. Unless it has to do with sisters. Do any of King Inwer's Blue Bloods have sisters, do you know?"

Queen Sherr nodded. "I know of four of them who had sisters. Keep your mind open. One day it will click and we'll know what causes it. But until then, don't worry. We'll be fine with what we have."

Kaylee tried to smile, but still felt like she'd failed.

"Go to bed early, ladies. We'll resume our regular schedule tomorrow."

Lacey and Jenna walked together to the door. Kaylee stayed at her chair until Queen Sherr noticed her. "Do you have something you want to talk about?"

Kaylee looked the queen in the eye. "Did you enjoy your life as a Blue Blood?" Kaylee asked.

"Yes."

"Do you miss it?"

"At times. I miss the feel of the power as it flowed through my veins. I miss being able to make the weather change to fit my moods. I miss being able to ensure we had enough rain for our crops. Being dependent on nature isn't always to my liking, but we've been fortunate here. The sea brings us rain regularly. I miss knowing that I had the power to ensure good traveling weather for our needs."

Kaylee traced her finger on the route they would take.

"But my power did not define me as a person. What I could do was wonderful in its own way, but what I can do now is still of worth. I have my intelligence and I've been forced to do things with only my own charm, and charisma, and knowledge. Look at what I've accomplished. I started out with a few soldiers and my own personal guards, and now I have an army I'm willing to pit against a kingdom that's ruled uncontested for close to a century."

Kaylee looked at the king's land on the map. The queen moved closer to her. "I'm also relieved to know I can live my life the way I want to. I never want to force my Blue Bloods to do my will. I want you to make your own choices. I want you to develop a sense of right and wrong. And I want the people in my realm to know that if a Blue Blood steps out of line, they can do something about it."

Kaylee looked up and met the queen's eyes.

"If any one of you starts to do something you shouldn't, I will not condone it. I will hold you accountable. And though some of you are very powerful and could do a lot of damage, I want the people I rule to know they can stand up against the Blue Bloods and hold them to a higher standard. I would not hesitate to end your power if you misuse it."

"But how could you hope to ever stop someone more powerful than you?" Kaylee asked.

"Exactly the way I am doing it now. Planning, finding those who'll support me, and going after them when the time is right."

Kaylee took the queen's hand in hers. "It's my honor to serve you. If you ever require more of me than I'm giving, let me know. I am yours to command because I know you will not misuse me."

"Thank you, child." Queen Sherr squeezed Kaylee's hand. "Now go do something for yourself. You deserve it."

On the way to her rooms, Kaylee took a detour and found herself in the kitchen's garden. She loved the way the freshly turned dirt blended with the variety of herbs. She longed to get down on her knees and weed the garden, to feel the strength of each root as it held its tenuous life. The dirt giving way beneath her knees as she crawled forward. Though Kaylee was happy here, she longed for the simplicity of her life with the monks.

As she looked out over the garden, she reflected on all the healing she'd done for the queen's subjects. Many had avoided death by infection. Wounds that would've crippled or pained people for months had been set right. She'd even saved the life of more than six who would've died within hours of their injuries.

She felt more valuable and pleased with herself than she had her entire life. She could do so much more with her healing power than she could as her regular self. Perhaps being a Blue Blood was not a curse. It did require a huge sacrifice on her part, but the good far outweighed the bad.

It was time to get to work. She would go to her notes and not leave them until she figured out what caused the change to occur.

CHAPTER TWENTY-NINE

Asher ran through the corridor. "Up! Everyone rally. We're under attack!" He ran past every door before they opened. He didn't stop to answer the questions shouted. "Get everyone who can fight to gather in the dining hall."

By the time he got to the queen's chamber she'd opened the door and stood there in her night robe.

"What is going on?"

Asher took a quick breath. "I felt them. They have Blue Bloods. They must have come for us."

"Just Blue Bloods?" Queen Sherr asked. "Maybe they are—"

"Not just them, there is an army with them. King Inwer has sent an army against you."

"But how could he know?" Queen Sherr clutched her robe closed near her neck.

"I don't know, but they're here. What's your command?"

Queen Sherr looked at him with wide eyes. He knew this was not something they ever thought would happen. With most of her soldiers on the march toward King Inwer's castle, they didn't have much to protect themselves. Asher opened his mouth to speak when Queen Sherr pulled herself together and took over.

"We'll fight them off. My Blue Bloods are ready. We have an advantage by knowing what King Inwer's Blue Bloods can do. They know nothing of us."

"But what about your soldiers?"

Queen Sherr looked down the hallway for a moment. "Have Jenna send out a message with her birds. She'll know what to tell them to locate each group. They may be too far for us to call back, but we can try. In the meantime, we'll gather all those in the village inside the castle walls and protect ourselves from the inside. Send a messenger. Now. Then we'll meet in the dining hall to discuss our plan."

She turned around and closed the door to her room. Asher rushed off to fulfill his commands.

Queen Sherr stood regally in front of her people. Asher watched as she commanded attention from the crowd. More than five hundred people gathered in the courtyard. They quickly decided the dining hall would not fit everyone. Torches lit the area as two servants held torches near Queen Sherr so she could be seen.

"We'll be under attack before this time tomorrow. King Inwer has somehow learned of us and sent an army. Most of our soldiers are gone, but we are not defenseless. We have our own Blue Bloods, who will do everything in their power to protect us. One regiment of soldiers remains, and most importantly, we have you."

The crowd murmured. Asher caught a few words of surprise and doubt.

Queen Sherr raised her hand. "I know you have fear. I respect that. I honor it. But you also have courage. We left King Inwer's rule because of all he did wrong. We wanted freedom from his tyranny and madness, but more importantly, we wanted to stop him from ruling forever. If we let them defeat us now, there will be no hope for the future generations. He's close to figuring out the agelessness of the Blue Bloods. It cannot happen. We won't go easily. We'll triumph over this attack and we'll stop him.

"Each of you will have to save yourselves and your family. I know you can do it. General Levas will organize you into regiments. He'll appoint captains over you. You will obey with exactness every command given you. Failure to follow orders could lead to not only your death, but the deaths of countless others."

Queen Sherr bowed her head. "I do not want to frighten you, but I can't impress this on you in any other way. We are fighting for our lives. And for the lives of your children. And for your right to live as you want to."

Asher watched her as she continued to motivate the people in front of her. He could see them own their fear and embrace the courage they had to fight for their lives. He once again thanked his fortune that he could serve with her.

Asher looked out over the landscape at the gathering army. Jenna, Lacey, Minla, and Kaylee stood near him.

"Do we have a chance?" Minla asked.

"Of course we do," Jenna said.

"A very good chance?" Minla asked again.

Asher turned to look at the four women who carried the hopes of a kingdom on their shoulders. "You can do so much to stop them before they even get close to us. Stopping their army before they breach our doors will mean less battle for the villagers inside."

Lacey nodded. "And we do still have one regiment of soldiers."

Minla didn't speak, but Asher could tell she wasn't convinced.

"We'll do our best. We knew when we started this plan that our chances of success depended a lot on our talents and a lot on luck. We'll just have to make sure we don't need too much luck by doing everything we can first."

They all fell silent once more as they watched the dawn turn to full morning. Though the army was larger than they expected, they still had hope. A shout from a turret above made Asher look out toward the army. A lone rider approached the castle at a walk. He held a white flag up. When he got closer, they heard the request of safe passage. Asher looked at the women and when Kaylee scowled, he looked at the messenger again. He leaned over the edge of the wall, but it didn't change the fact that it was Zeb approaching.

"What has he done?" Asher turned from the wall and rushed down the stairs. He had to get to the queen before Zeb did.

Queen Sherr was surrounded by soldiers and Asher was relieved to see her look of surprise when he arrived. She hadn't been told of the messenger yet.

"There is a lone rider coming from the army. It's Zeb."

Queen Sherr's eyes narrowed to slits and she pressed her lips tight together. "He's coming as a messenger?"

"He's holding a white flag and has requested a safe passage."

The queen nodded and motioned for Asher to take care of it.

Asher sprinted back out to the courtyard and found the guards manning the gates. "There's a rider out there who wishes to speak to the queen. I will question him from the tower. On my command, you may open the gates just enough for him to walk in. He will not bring in his horse."

The soldiers nodded their understanding and Asher rushed back to the top of the wall. The four Blue Bloods watched Zeb as he approached. Asher glanced at Kaylee. She no longer looked angry, but slightly wary of the man below. When he got a little closer, Jenna took a deep breath. "I know him. He was a creep when he was in the castle before. Wouldn't stop looking at me with those dark eyes."

Lacey leaned closer, but didn't seem to recognize him.

As Zeb got within arrow range, he slowed his horse and stopped. "I request safe passage. I have a message for the queen."

"You are granted safe passage on one condition," Asher called from his position.

Zeb sneered at Asher. "And what is that condition?"

"That you walk in without your horse and you strip down to just under clothes. Not even your boots. And leave those knives of yours on the horse." Asher glanced at Kaylee. She hadn't flinched at the mention of the knives.

Zeb cursed loud enough for Asher and the Blue Bloods to hear. Jenna gasped, but Lacey giggled. She turned to Asher. "He's got a bit of a temper doesn't he?"

"That he does," Kaylee said.

Asher pursed his lips together as he waited for Zeb's response. Finally Zeb dismounted from his horse and began to strip off his outer clothes. He wore a thin layer of chain mail under his shirt. It was obvious he wasn't happy to do it, but he was soon in just his long underwear and socks. He spat on the ground. "Can I approach now?"

Asher shouted his agreement and Zeb took a step forward. Asher hollered down. "And when you get to the gate, be expecting us to check you for hidden weapons."

Zeb shook his head and reached behind him quickly and pulled out a knife. He placed it in the saddle bag of the horse.

"That's unfortunate," Asher said. "I was hoping to add another of his knives to my collection." He pulled out the bone-handled knife and examined the blade playfully. "He does have some of the best."

Kaylee paled a moment.

Asher could've kicked himself for his flippant comment. He turned to Lacey. "Will you come with me? If he tries something, we need to be able to stop him before he gets too far. He'll want to speak directly to the queen, but with his past behavior I'm not going to take any chances."

Lacey nodded. Asher turned to the others. "You're welcome to come as well, or you can remain up here and watch for any mischief." Asher stopped in front of Minla. "It may be best for you to stay here. You can use your power to move objects in the way of an attack. Or you could even deflect anything shot at us."

Minla nodded. "I'll stay."

Jenna looked back at the army across the expanse of land. "I'll stay as well."

Kaylee looked at Zeb as he neared the castle. She didn't speak, but turned and descended the steps into the courtyard.

CHAPTER THIRTY

Kaylee studied Zeb as he entered the gate. He didn't look much different than before, except, of course, for being dressed in his underwear. They looked grimy, like he didn't care enough to wash them more than once a month, if that. Kaylee was glad he was unarmed, although she didn't think he would actually attack her.

Asher must have had a good reason for insisting he come in almost naked. His underclothes were long enough to cover past his knees and he wore a loose fitting shirt that wasn't tucked in all around.

Asher insisted on checking Zeb for weapons and Kaylee knew it was important, but she wished she hadn't come. After months of not seeing Zeb, she had thought she was over the trauma he'd brought her, but she shivered as she remembered the crazed look in his eye every time he tested her healing powers.

Zeb stood before them in the company of an army stationed less than an hour's march from the castle.

They would be at the mercy of this army if things didn't go well.

"Why have you come?" Asher said.

"I have a message for the queen," Zeb said. He held a rolled piece of paper in his hand. Asher reached for it, but Zeb pulled it back. "I will see her in person. I must wait for her response."

Asher considered Zeb for a moment, and then he motioned for him to follow. He instructed two of the guards to accompany them.

Kaylee looked at Lacey, wondering why they needed guards. Perhaps he didn't want to give away their secret of more Blue Bloods. She followed behind the guards and watched for any sign Zeb would try to bolt. Lacey walked just in front of Kaylee. She would be able to stop him if he tried anything.

Zeb glanced behind him, meeting Kaylee's eyes. He looked her over from head to toe in one quick motion, making Kaylee feel sick. She feared his message to the queen had something to do with her.

Queen Sherr sat on her throne and stared at Zeb with disappointment in her eyes. Kaylee saw the power and authority radiating from Queen Sherr in her element. Zeb even seemed to take a moment to compose himself when he saw her.

"Why have you returned to my realm with an army?" Queen Sherr asked. Kaylee moved closer to the queen. She stayed down on the main floor, close enough to help if Zeb did something crazy.

"I bring news from King Inwer." Zeb held the letter before him. Queen Sherr looked at it. He cleared his throat. "It's important."

Queen Sherr made no move to retrieve the letter, nor did she give instructions for her guards to hand it to her. Kaylee smiled inside at the snub.

Zeb broke the seal of the letter and opened it up. He glanced at the queen, then the guards around him, and cleared his throat again. "The king wishes to inform you of his knowledge of your betrayal."

"And who, I wonder, gave him the information?" Queen Sherr said, raising one eyebrow. Zeb ducked his head for a moment, staring at the paper in front of him. He seemed to be trying to find an important place to start. Kaylee realized he couldn't read after he cleared his throat a third time.

"He wishes for you to return to his company. He will give you a reward for finding a Blue Blood with healing power. You are both to return to him, escorted by his honor guard."

Asher snorted. "Honor guard?" He shook his head. "You call three thousand men an honor guard?"

Zeb tried to hide a smile, but Kaylee could see the same small twitch to his lip that indicated he was excited about something. Had they hidden a larger army somewhere? She would have to mention it to the queen.

Zeb held the letter toward Queen Sherr again. "If you would read his kind words, you will see for yourself that he wishes for your safe return."

Queen Sherr motioned for Asher to take the paper. He brought it to her and she scanned it. An incredulous smile crossed her lips. "You think this letter is kind?" She set it down on her lap. "King Inwer is a fool. I will not deliver myself to him. I will not allow my Blue Blood to be placed in his care, and I will not submit my people to his rule."

Queen Sherr leaned back against her throne. "You may return and tell King Inwer I decline his invitation to return to his lands. He will have nothing of mine ever again."

Zeb blinked in surprise. "You're refusing his offer?"

Queen Sherr glanced at the letter. "His 'offer' is nothing more than veiled threats. And I can't tell you how shamed I am that you would fall for his lies. That you would go to him and tell him of me. What were you thinking, Zeb?"

Zeb recoiled at first, but then leaned forward, making the guards grab him by the arms. "You are no better than a tyrant yourself, Sherr. I offered all I had in your service and you sent me away. I went searching for more Blue Bloods for you and tracked some down, but I wanted to know if King Inwer would pay more for them than you. He was very interested to know that Asher had deserted him and gone to an upstart queen who dared to build a kingdom. He was also thrilled to hear about a Blue Blood that could heal."

Zeb's words got louder the more he talked. "King Inwer offered me so much more than just a small plot of land to live out the rest of my life on. I've been given more power and authority than you could dream of holding yourself."

Queen Sherr remained motionless, but Kaylee saw her anger rising as Zeb ranted. Had he been this way before his head injury?

"I will take back your answer as well as the spoils of war when my army wipes out your little resistance."

Asher placed a blade against Zeb's throat. Kaylee hadn't even seen him pull the knife. "How will you do that when you're dead?"

"Kill me now, and the army will descend upon you within twelve hours, killing everything in its path."

"And if we let you go?"

"Then we'll be more selective in our fighting. Only those who raise up weapons against us. We'll prevail and I will take Kaylee to his majesty."

"Asher," Queen Sherr said. "Put the knife down. We will not kill him here. Though he doesn't deserve to live after his betrayal, we'll allow him to return to his camp. We have more honor than that."

Asher pressed the knife to Zeb's skin. A small trickle of blood escaped under the blade. "You gave up much when you left this wise queen for a fool of a king."

Zeb blinked. As Asher pulled the knife away, Zeb pressed his hand to his own throat. Lacey handed him a handkerchief and he dabbed at the blood. He looked at the red stain on the white cloth before he lifted his eyes to Kaylee. "One last time?"

Kaylee shook her head. "What's the use? You'll be missing your head come morning."

Zeb glared at her. Queen Sherr said, "Take him back outside the castle. He has my refusal to deliver."

"I pity your choice, Sherr. Things would've been so much better for your people had you accepted the king's offer."

"My people would rather die than subject themselves to the rule of one like Inwer."

"Well, isn't it just lucky for them they'll get their wish." Zeb took one last look at Kaylee and turned around. The guards escorted him out, followed by Lacey and Asher. Kaylee remained with the queen.

"Do you think we can survive the attack on our people?" Kaylee asked.

"It will be a fierce battle, but if you can heal the wounds of our women and children and soldiers, we'll have a much better chance than if we fought on our own. And under the king's rule, all of our people would be subject to his harsh laws and excessive taxes."

"There is more to his army than just the three thousand our scouts have named."

She nodded. "And I'm sure there are many Blue Bloods. Asher felt them out there. He isn't sure how many, but he can sense more than fifteen."

"Will they kill for the king?" Kaylee asked.

"I am afraid so. He has one Blue Blood he treats better than the others. She can convince people to do something they wouldn't normally do. So any of my Sisters in Blood who had any love or concern for me would no longer feel that. We should expect no mercy from them. It is a war and we will have much to answer for when it's done, but I intend to make King Inwer pay for his sins. He will not take you or the others and twist you to his own personal use. You will be as free as I can possibly make you." Queen Sherr rose from her throne. "Even now, you are free to do as you want. But if you go to King Inwer, I will have no choice but to end your life. He cannot have your power of healing. It will be the one that will bring him closest to immortality and I will not let him have that."

Kaylee shook her head. "I'm yours to lead. I swore to serve you and will not break that promise. I have no desire to go with Zeb and his honor guard." Her lips fought a smile.

"King Inwer always was a pompous fool." Queen Sherr snorted and took Kaylee's hand. "You may be the difference between success and failure. And it will be hardest on you."

Kaylee saw the concern in the queen's eyes and felt she had found a true friend. "I will do everything in my power to keep us all alive."

"Do what you can, but don't give it all. We need you for more than just this battle."

She kissed Kaylee's cheek and motioned for her to go. "I have much to do before tomorrow. Please go rest so you are at your strongest. I'm afraid we're going to need you to be in top form."

Kaylee left with the pressure of hundreds of lives in her hands.

Asher slept fitfully during the remainder of the night after they'd done as much as they could to prepare for the coming battle. He'd never been involved in a war before. Although he was comfortable with a sword and a bow, he would much rather have left all the fighting to the soldiers as planned. With them gone, every able-bodied person needed to help keep the army from breaching the castle gates. They'd made huge strides in repairing and fortifying the castle, but weak spots that could be broken through with little effort remained.

He wasn't usually a dreamer, but Asher had been haunted by visions of the castle in ruins and more bodies than he could count. He'd hoped the surplus of bodies in the dream was more than there were people in the village. That would indicate his dream was just a nightmare, not a vision of the future. He'd heard of Blue Bloods having visions, but he wasn't one.

Asher shook off the remaining concern and belted his sword on his waist. His quiver of arrows was full, but he knew it wouldn't last long in a fight. A second quiver hung over his chair with more on the wall. He prayed his aim would be true. He glanced one last time at his room. He hoped to return that evening, but if not, he would do his very best in the service of his queen.

On the wall of the castle the archers lined up, ready to shoot on command. Extra stones had been piled in addition to the supplies already there. If they ran out of arrows, they would throw the stones on the advancing army as they reached the castle walls. The soldiers were ready, but he could tell they were nervous. Most of them were new in the queen's service and had never seen battle before. King Inwer always ruled with the threat of attack, but had never sent his army in a full battle either. His rule had been mostly peaceful up until now.

"Any sign of advance?" Asher asked the scout with a looking glass.

"There is movement in their camp, but they don't look like they are ready to march yet. We still have time."

Asher nodded. "Are the fletchers still making arrows?"

"As fast as they can, but it takes time for the feathers to set right and not all of the wood is the right kind. Those will be our last resort."

Asher glanced at the men lining the wall. "Don't worry much. You'll get a chance to use your bows, but I think our Blue Bloods will be able to make a huge dent in their army before most of them reach our walls."

"I hope so, Lord Herst. I truly hope so."

Asher excused himself and descended the stairs to the main courtyard. He needed to find the women who would do so much to save them. He saw no sign of them in the queen's study, nor in the throne room. He doubted they would have remained in their rooms. Asher pulled the medallion from under his shirt. He closed his fist around it and willed it to tell him what direction they went. Not all were together. He turned to the left and followed the stronger pull.

He wished Kaylee had been able to transfer the power to more than three, and a baby. He shook his head in disappointment. The baby would be worthless to them, yet he hoped she would grow to eventually be a Blue Blood. If he was lucky, he'd live long enough to see it happen. Asher clamped down that thought. They would prevail. They had to.

He found Lacey and Minla in the kitchens, eating as if nothing concerned them. He stared in surprise. He almost spoke, until he saw the tightness around Lacey's eyes. She didn't look like she'd slept much. Minla bowed her head to Asher, and he nodded in return.

"How are your plans for this morning going?" Asher asked.

"We've found lots of places to slow down the attack, but until we know for sure where they're coming from, we're just guessing and hoping," Lacey said.

"I tested my strength to see how far out I could move an object. They will have to be less than one hundred yards, but I can disturb the ground and make the rocks shift under their feet. The closer they get, the more I can do."

Lacey nodded. "I have to see them clearly to be able to hold them in the air. I haven't done more than a few men at a time, so I don't know how many I can stop. And once I look away from them, they're free to move again. It will slow them down enough that the archers should have a better shot."

"That will make them happy," Asher said. "Have you seen Jenna or Kaylee?"

"Jenna was on the south side of the castle. She's been trying to reach the animals in the forest." Minla pointed the direction.

"Kaylee was with the queen last I saw. They were hoping to find one more Blue Blood this morning."

Asher shook his head. "I don't feel any potential out there. Do you know where they were looking?"

Lacey thought for a moment. "Check the servant's wing."

Asher thanked the women. Taking a biscuit off the tray, he popped it in his mouth. Normally they tasted divine, but Asher couldn't help wondering if this were his last meal.

He walked through the castle. Servants rushed around as if not knowing what to do. He spoke kindly to them, encouraging them, giving them the confidence he knew they needed. As he passed, each person calmed down and slowed their walk. They moved with more purpose. Now if only he could convince his heart that things would be fine.

He found Kaylee and Queen Sherr talking to the women in the hallway. He could see each of them had been tested already as they held their fingers looking at the prick. Red dots were all he saw.

Queen Sherr looked only slightly disappointed, but Kaylee had tears in her eyes.

Asher closed the distance between them and smiled at the servant women. "Thank you for your willingness to try. But don't worry. I've been talking with our Blue Bloods and they're ready to fight. They'll stop most of the attack before they even reach our walls."

Queen Sherr looked at him in surprise. Kaylee gave him a smile that pierced his heart. She had looked sad and heartbroken before. At last he found a gleam of hope in her eyes.

"If you will excuse us, I must speak with the queen." Asher looked at the women ranging in age from around fourteen to somewhere in their early fifties. "Go report to your stations. They have not begun their march yet, but our scout has seen movement in the camp."

Each woman bowed to Queen Sherr and then to Kaylee. Nodding to Asher, they moved away. Asher turned to the Queen. "What were you thinking, testing them today? There is no time for them to learn anything."

"They came to us," Kaylee said. She watched the women as they disappeared out of the hallway.

"They wanted to be tested this morning?" Asher asked.

"They wanted to do as much as they could to help. They were even willing to go through torture to snap if we happened to find one this morning."

Asher regarded his queen once more. "Forgive me for my impertinence."

"No need. I could see you had their best interest at heart. And you probably knew none of them had the potential."

Asher nodded. "I felt nothing new. I can sense the four current Blue Bloods, and that infant. And far to the east I can sense the king's Blue Bloods. I am not sure of the count."

"Well, until I can see their faces, I will not know what powers they have." Queen Sherr looked thoughtful. "If only I could have a moment to speak to each of them. One by one. I am sure I could convince them to join me. If Liliana has persuaded them to follow the king, then we will have a terrible fight on our hands."

"Your Blue Bloods here are not powerless. They will do much to keep the soldiers away. When they do make it to our door, we'll have a much better chance of survival."

Queen Sherr nodded as the horn blew, signaling the army had advanced. "It's time."

CHAPTER THIRTY-ONE

Kaylee didn't have much to do at first. She watched in horror as the army advanced. When they reached the location Minla could affect, they began to stumble and trip over the ground, which heaved and roiled beneath them. Immediately, one of King Inwer's Blue Bloods retaliated by sending an earthquake. It wasn't overly strong since it apparently had to start just in front of the woman wielding the power, but it sped forward lifting more and more of the ground in front of it.

Lacey screamed in fright, but focused her attention on the moving ground. She strained with the effort, beads of sweat popping over her forehead, but she managed to build a wall of air that stopped the debris from slamming into the castle's outer walls. Her air couldn't stop the quake. It still rumbled beneath them, making the very foundation shake.

Lacey staggered for a moment, calling for Asher to join her. "I'll hold her still. Shoot her!"

Kaylee saw the woman who had sent the earthquake struggle to move, but Lacey's power over the air held her fast.

"She's not in range!" Asher looked sick at the thought of shooting a woman, but they must stop her from sending another earthquake. They would never survive if she knocked the castle walls to the ground.

"Minla!" Lacey shouted.

Minla rushed over to them.

"Can you reach her?" Lacey panted with exertion, not breaking eye contact with the Blue Blood she held.

"Not with any certainty. But maybe . . ." Minla focused hard on the woman. Kaylee watched in amazement when the woman lifted from the ground and pulled forward. Minla gripped onto Kaylee's arm and sagged as if carrying an actual physical weight. She brought the woman closer, over the heads of the soldiers marching in front of her. The woman screamed in terror. Minla gathered strength as the woman drew closer to the castle.

She lowered her to the ground. As soon as the woman touched the earth, another rumbling started.

Kaylee shouted, "Lift her back up!"

Minla immediately pulled her back up and the earthquake eased, but didn't stop. The earthquake rumbled under the castle walls again but wasn't as strong as before.

"Shoot her!" Lacey shouted.

Asher pulled the arrow back. Air hissed as the bow string shot it straight into the woman's chest. She collapsed to the ground. The army surrounding her stopped in amazement that their Blue Blood was gone.

Asher cringed. Kaylee wished she could do something to comfort him. But there was no time. The army would advance again. It came close enough now that their arrows would soon reach the queen's army. Kaylee would be needed.

The king's soldiers seemed shocked that the army they faced had the ability to fight back. Another woman stepped forward and the ground rumbled again. She stayed farther back than the first. The soldiers split ranks and stayed far back as well.

"Minla, can you bring her forward?" Lacey asked. "I'm having a hard time trying to wrap her in air."

The ground vibrated beneath them. Ripples of earth crashed forward. Lacey struggled to keep the boulders from beating against the castle walls, but this quake shook much more than the previous one. And the vibrations never stopped.

"Do something," Lacey grunted.

Asher took aim with his bow once more, aiming high into the air. Kaylee could see the arch as it shot into the sky and came down short of the woman creating the tremors. He tried once more, pulling the arrow back as far as the bow would bend and shot it again, still falling short.

Jenna looked out into the trees. She must have called something out because birds scattered from the treetops and headed straight for the woman. They dove at her, and soon she cowered beneath the onslaught. She fell to the ground, hidden by hundreds of birds. Shouts from the soldiers around her sounded horrified. A huge gap formed in the earth under the fallen woman. The resulting earthquake knocked down most of the king's army.

Boulders and dirt bounced, revealing the path of the earthquake.

"It's going to hit the wall!" an archer shouted.

Kaylee could see the crack as it worked its way toward them. It split wider and wider as it came. "Get off the wall!" Kaylee shouted.

Everyone scrambled to the stairway, but only half of the archers made it off before the wall shook violently. Kaylee felt as if she were riding a choppy horse and bounced down the stairs, falling on people as she went. Those behind her fell as well. When the rumbling ceased, she found herself buried beneath bodies and pieces of the wall. Kaylee felt pain in her ankle and pain in her shoulder. She healed the ankle quickly, knowing she'd need to move fast but left her shoulder. The pain and the nerves should allow her powers to flow enough to heal anyone injured in the quake.

Kaylee felt boulders lifting away from the pile. She looked up to see Minla standing on a section of wall that had not collapsed. She lifted the stones from those they had fallen on and threw them toward the oncoming soldiers. Screams of pain from the advancing army proved the boulders found their mark.

Kaylee crawled through the wreckage and touched every person she found. She didn't even ask permission to heal, just delved into them to see where they hurt and fixed whatever was wrong. None of them were more serious than broken bones and some crushed organs, but she soon healed them. Each man gathered up what he could for a weapon and ran to meet the oncoming hoard.

The twang of bowstrings and the thuds of resulting hits punctuated by screams or gasps played a strange symphony. The rumbling hadn't started again, and Kaylee wondered if the woman causing the earthquakes had been killed by the birds. She shuddered at the thought. She hoped she wouldn't have to see the results of that attack.

Soon, arrows found their marks in Queen Sherr's soldiers. Kaylee moved quickly between each person, crossing the courtyard and then working her way back. The pain in her shoulder soon turned numb. She could no longer feel it. The power diminished with the pain and she found she couldn't heal as quickly as before. Kaylee healed her shoulder and pulled her knife free from her belt. She sliced her arm and wrapped it loosely to prevent the loss of too much blood.

She didn't worry about bleeding to death over the course of her healing. Once she took care of that wound, her blood would be replenished and she'd receive most of her strength back. She just didn't want to lose too much of it too quickly or she'd be forced to heal it again.

The wounds she touched were severe, but nothing she couldn't handle. The most difficult part was pulling the arrows out of the wound before she could heal it. More than once she had to break the shaft and pull it out from the back.

Each man she healed kissed her hand and then jumped up to fight again. The first fatality came as a shock. The arrow had gone into the eye socket. She found no life in the body. Kaylee tried to ignore it, but the pain of losing a soldier was greater than what she felt in her arm.

The next person she touched was healed before she even had a chance to pull the arrow from his leg. He stood up immediately and looked down in shock at the shaft protruding from his thigh.

"I'm sorry. It healed too soon. I'll have to pull it free then heal you again."

The man smiled sheepishly and Kaylee grinned back. She flinched when the man staggered forward with an arrow through the chest.

She caught him just before he fell on her and helped lay him down. She pulled the arrow from his chest and sealed the wound, and then turned to his leg and broke off the back end, yanking it clear to heal his fresh wound.

Too many men fell wounded as the enemy approached the fallen castle walls. Minla grunted more and more as she threw heavier boulders from the remaining pile. Kaylee took a moment to survey the area. Jenna commanded the animals. More than one riderless horse trampled the king's soldiers. When a bear's roar echoed through the troops outside, many of the enemy soldiers stopped and stared. They scattered as the bear charged through their midst.

Birds of all sizes darted in and around the army still mostly outside the castle walls. Jenna wouldn't be disappointed in her abilities now. She was more valuable than she'd ever thought possible.

Kaylee looked for Lacey and saw her still on top of the castle wall where she'd been before the quake knocked down a portion of it. Asher was there with her. He looked like he was picking off people she pointed at. Kaylee wondered who they were targeting and hoped, yet feared, it was the Blue Bloods.

Kaylee turned her attention back to the soldiers struck by arrows. It pleased Kaylee to know that each of the men she healed would have a chance to live another day. If they could survive this one being shot many times over. When she reached a man whom she had healed more than four times, Kaylee looked him in the eye as she healed him.

"If I didn't know any better, I'd say you were enjoying this."

The man chuckled. "Who wouldn't enjoy being touched by a beautiful woman like you?"

Kaylee blinked in surprise. The man chuckled again. "Besides," he said, "how many men get to live again after wounds like I've had?"

"Well, do try to be careful. I've got lots of others to deal with besides just you. Don't purposely get hit. It's not a competition, you know."

As Kaylee healed her wound and sliced a new gash over her arm, the man cringed. "What was that for?"

Kaylee shook her head. "You can't have all the fun, now." She bent down and healed a man with two arrows in him, one in the leg and one in the shoulder. He got up and rushed forward with his bow and arrow, positioning himself behind a pile of rubble Minla hadn't moved yet.

Kaylee looked back at the man she had been joking with earlier. He didn't smile but looked at her with new understanding. "I'll be more careful."

"Thank you."

Asher glanced at Lacey. She was tired. But she didn't ease up at all. She'd erected a pocket of air beneath them that kept arrows from reaching them from below. She'd left most of the area in front of them open so that Asher's arrows could fly. A few archers from King Inwer's army had gotten close to hitting them, but so far they had managed to avoid being struck by any arrows.

How Lacey could hold a shield of air and still manage to stop the march of a large portion of the king's army astounded Asher. He felt almost guilty picking off the captains of the king's army as they were stuck in Lacey's air. Without their leaders, Asher hoped many of the men would be confused and give up the fight, or at least make mistakes and be easier to defeat.

Asher saw many of the Blue Bloods the king sent. He could only count seven, maybe eight women including the two who had caused the earthquakes. From the vibe on his medallion, he had expected more, but he only saw five women now. He recognized three of them. Candari could manipulate the weather like Queen Sherr. Fran was skilled in fire. And Tasha could move objects like Minla. He hadn't seen any indication she'd tried to move anything yet. Perhaps she wasn't as strong as Minla, or maybe they were still strategizing.

They were far enough out of range that Asher couldn't reach them with his arrows. Minla couldn't grab them with her power to bring them closer either.

They'd done something to stop the animals from reaching their staging area. Jenna had sent birds and all sorts of critters, but it was almost as if they had bounced away from them. Maybe they had someone like Lacey who could create a barrier of air.

Asher spotted another captain, but knew he was too far away to reach with his arrow. He wished he could tell Jenna which ones to send her animals after, but she'd managed to stay on the wall on the other side of the fallen stone. She couldn't come down, since the ladders as well as the stone steps built into the wall had fallen away.

Asher focused his attention back on who he could hit. A flash of light ripped past him. Lacey screamed. He turned to see her fall to the ground fifteen feet below, engulfed in flame. When she went over the edge, the shield she had been holding vanished. An arrow zipped past Asher. A second arrow struck him in the side and he crouched down.

The soldiers who had been stuck in Lacey's trap rushed forward. Asher shouted for the archers to prepare for a stronger attack. They rushed to meet their foe and Asher hurried down the ladder. He looked for something to smother the flames and found a flag. He pulled it down from the post and covered Lacey with it.

The smell of charred flesh was overpowering. Lacey was almost unrecognizable. Tears stung his eyes. "Kaylee!" he shouted. He hoped she was close enough to help. "Kaylee!"

Asher leaned closer to Lacey. "Hold on. You'll be just fine. Kaylee can help you."

Lacey's left eye was burned beyond recognition. Her right eye tried to focus on Asher, but he could see her fading fast. He stood up and shouted for Kaylee just as she reached his side. She dropped immediately to her knees and placed her hands on Lacey.

She flinched back as if surprised. Asher had never seen her react that way to touching someone she meant to heal.

She looked at Asher with shock on her face. "I don't know if I can do it."

Lacey twitched and tried to grab Kaylee's hand. She struggled to speak, but Asher couldn't hear the words. Kaylee leaned closer and placed a hand on Lacey's face. The burns eased a little. Lacey's mouth was able to form the words.

"I will be fine." She gasped for a moment and then a smile broke out on her cracked lips, making them bleed a strange blue through the charred skin. "Tell Jenna I have her beat."

Kaylee blurted out a laugh and then sobbed as Lacey started to convulse. At first Asher couldn't understand what was happening, until he realized Lacey was laughing.

Kaylee lifted her head and looked at Lacey. "I'm sorry. I can't heal you. I don't have enough power to do it."

Lacey's hand tightened on Kaylee's. "Thank you for this gift. I really enjoyed it." The last came out in a whisper. She was gone.

Asher stared at Lacey's motionless body. The black, charred skin blending with purple and then pink flesh. It shouldn't have happened. He should have been able to stop it. He knew Fran could use fire.

Asher reached down and patted Kaylee. "She's gone. We have more to do." He turned to go. When Kaylee touched his side, the wound he'd forgotten in the midst of all the heartache was gone completely.

Kaylee didn't say a word, but left to continue healing. Asher looked once more at Lacey, wondering if she would return to her Red Blood life in the middle of the battle. He pulled her body against the wall and hoped she'd be undisturbed until she rose again.

Asher moved with purpose. He climbed the ladder to the top of the wall and examined the enemy. He held a shield up to keep the arrows from reaching him. Minla was still throwing rocks, but instead of taking aim, she moved every piece of rubble she could find and flung it over Queen Sherr's army, hitting whatever it lit on in the ranks of the king's soldiers.

The king's Blue Bloods were still too far away to hit with anything they could use. They had to stop them somehow. Asher quickly descended the ladder and sprinted across the open area, barely managing to avoid being hit. He shot three soldiers with his arrows. As he crossed the threshold of the still standing wall, Asher grabbed a fallen ladder. He had to pull a dead body off the ladder to lift it, but he placed it against the wall and climbed up. He had to get to Jenna.

Jenna squeaked in surprise when Asher climbed up next to her. She didn't have a lot of room up on the top. She remained hidden behind a section of the battlement. She could see enough of where she needed to send her animals to attack.

"Why are you here?" Jenna asked. She looked over to where he and Lacey had been on the other side. She looked back at Asher. "Where's Lacey?"

"She's gone."

"What?"

"A fireball hit her. Didn't even see it coming, it was so fast." As if that was the magic word, another fireball shot into the midst of the soldiers. Screaming and panic took over and Asher had to shout over the terror. "Smother the flames!"

A few men dropped to the ground and rolled around in the dirt. A couple who had not been hit grabbed whatever they could find to wrap around those still struggling. Kaylee rushed into the group. She'd been hit as well—a charred arm hung to her side. He nearly vomited at the sight, but Kaylee still moved and healed each man she came in contact with.

Asher forced the fire victims out of his mind and turned to Jenna. "You have to find a way to stop them."

"I've tried. They have something preventing any of my animals from reaching them."

"Is it air like Lacey's?" He saw another fireball shooting through the air. "Incoming!" He shouted to the men below. They dove out of the way. Only a few were hit this time.

"The response I'm getting from the animals make me think they are being thrown back, almost. Like they're caught in something and then tossed away again."

Asher peeked at the king's Blue Bloods. He shouted to the men to avoid another fireball. He looked back at the Blue Bloods and saw one he thought might be like Minla. She must be stopping them and tossing them back. She didn't take her eyes off the animals, and that made Asher even more sure she was stopping them.

"Have you tried sending them from behind?" Asher asked.

"I have the birds going at them from all directions." She looked like she was lost in her own thoughts. "I can sense a couple of wild cats in the forest behind them. I'll try to summon them closer. And in the meantime, I'll see what a stampede of horses can do to shake things up."

Asher squeezed her shoulder. "Do what you can. We have to stop Fran. She's going to kill us all if she keeps throwing the fire."

Jenna nodded and Asher climbed back down the ladder. It felt odd to wish for the death of his cousin.

CHAPTER THIRTY-TWO

Exhaustion began to set in. Healing didn't take strength. It took pain. But pain took her strength, and Kaylee wondered how much longer she could keep this up. She'd healed each of Queen Sherr's men at least twice, some more than half a dozen times. The one she had joked with had finally been killed before she had a chance to reach him the ninth time.

As she healed another man, she surveyed the area. More were wounded than still fighting, but more were alive than dead. It was a miracle they had lasted this long. She knew her power was invaluable and once again, Kaylee felt happy to have it. Each man she healed showed their gratitude. She knew she wanted to save people for the rest of her life.

She didn't want to ever have to do it on a battle field after today, but she wanted to live her long, ageless life healing those who suffered.

The loss of Lacey as a Blue Blood was tragic. They felt the effects of her being gone immediately as the fighting became more intense. Kaylee saw Queen Sherr watching from a high tower as the battle began and knew she wanted to be down here fighting, but Asher had forbidden it.

When she'd tried arguing, Asher said, "If we lose our head, we'll die. You must stay out of harm's way and lead from a safe place." Kaylee knew it was true and didn't envy the queen at all. It would be torture to stay out of the battle, knowing so many died to save your cause. But the last time Kaylee looked toward where Queen Sherr stood, the window had been empty.

Kaylee wondered if she'd joined the women within the castle itself. If they didn't manage to defeat the army outside the castle and even into the courtyard where fighting with swords would soon occur, then the women and younger boys would do their best to stop them from reaching the children and the Queen who were secreted in the center of the castle.

Another fireball broke out across the courtyard, but it only hit a couple people. They were becoming used to the sound it made and managed to get out of the way. Kaylee rushed to the people and healed them. She'd only lost three to the fireballs. Most hits had not been direct like Lacey's and the power of the fire must have been less. She still had to use a lot of power to heal those burns, but the burn on her arm had begun to lose its intensity. She placed her hand on her arm thinking to heal it, but changed her mind and pulled on the charred flesh, peeling it back until it reached the unburned purple flesh.

The pain made her knees buckle. She fell to the ground awkwardly. She stood up and staggered toward her next patient and healed him immediately. She moved on to the next casualty. Kaylee found that as she healed each person after having lost one, she wouldn't even need to feel the pain of her injury. The sorrow and pain of death was enough. It would be nice to close her mind to the horror of battle, but in order for her healing powers to work, Kaylee had to feel it all.

She found solace in the relief each person felt when she healed their wounds. As the battle grew closer and closer, Kaylee heard death screams of the men in the king's army. Though she didn't want to heal them, she wished she could ease their suffering. Or that she could shut out the pain of their cries. There would be no relief for them. The sorrow she felt almost overwhelmed her.

Another fireball shot overhead, but before it hit the ground, it fizzled out and was gone. Kaylee looked up to see Jenna jumping up and down on the top of the wall.

Jenna's scream was primal. "Take that you horrible creature!" she shouted. Asher rushed up the ladder. She heard Jenna holler, "I got her. She's not going to stop any more of my animals."

When Asher pulled Jenna close in an embrace, Kaylee felt a stab of jealousy. She didn't understand where it came from. Asher wasn't hers. And she wasn't his. She didn't want any man. Ever.

Kaylee turned away from the scene above her and focused on healing those she could find. Minla caught her attention, and she rushed over to the woman. Minla held onto the wall and panted as she focused on another boulder. Kaylee touched the older woman on the shoulder and felt the bone-deep weariness.

"Minla, you must rest. You'll give yourself a heart attack."

Minla shook her head. "I must do what I can."

"But if you fall, we'll be worse off. You have to slow down. Take a few breaths."

Minla looked at Kaylee. "You're one to talk."

Kaylee glanced at her arm where Minla's gaze rested. "It no longer pains me."

"Then why haven't you healed it?" Minla asked.

Kaylee shrugged. "I forgot about it." She placed her hand on her charred skin and felt the life return to it as the power flowed through her fingers.

"If it doesn't hurt, then how did you heal it?"

Kaylee took Minla's hand as she offered it. "I feel enough pain seeing all of this. I think I could heal most anything."

Minla squeezed softly. "I never wish to see something like this ever again."

Kaylee nodded. "Amen."

Asher surveyed the scene before him. Their odds had never been good to start with, no matter what he had said to the others. Now that Jenna's wild cats had attacked the Blue Bloods and stopped them from sending fire balls with no chance of retaliation, they might have a chance after all.

With Kaylee healing the soldiers and archers over and over again, it was almost as if they had a full army. Asher cursed under his breath. Why had they never considered the possibility of being attacked at home? They'd sent almost every able-bodied man across the hundreds of miles separating Queen Sherr's lands from King Inwer's. And since most of their soldiers had gone along the sidelines and through unpopulated areas, the likelihood that any of those troops had seen King Inwer's army wasn't great.

When Queen Sherr's group never showed up in their meeting place in a few weeks, the soldiers would have no idea what happened. It was unlikely they would stage an attack against the king without Queen Sherr's command.

Asher looked at Jenna again. He hoped her messages sent with birds had reached the armies, but they would be too far away to return in time to help. Maybe they could bury the dead. Or possibly avenge them, though that thought did little to comfort him.

If they could keep the Blue Bloods from fighting, then eventually with Kaylee healing Queen Sherr's soldiers, they might be able to outlast the army King Inwer sent. But Kaylee didn't look like she could keep up that pace much longer.

She staggered between the men she healed. They jumped up immediately and fought until being struck again. Some even moved over to her for healing and then shot their arrows again and again.

Asher saw a couple of young boys running around the courtyard, pulling out the arrows from the dead and finding the discarded ones if they were still usable. They rushed them over to a man who examined them and set the usable ones aside. The boys then delivered more arrows to the archers.

Asher had been restocked twice now and hoped they could continue holding off the advancing army. Minla still threw boulders at the enemy, but they were fewer than before with less power behind them. She looked even more exhausted than Kaylee.

Jenna stood on the top of the tower still, hiding behind the stone. She wore a heavy leather chest armor.

If any of those archers aimed true, the leather wouldn't stop it completely. She'd started to act slightly crazed. Asher wondered if Jenna suffered some sort of side effect from constantly connecting to the minds of her animals.

King Inwer's soldiers had killed all of their horses when they realized they were being trampled by them. Asher knew those horses and many of Jenna's wild beasts had taken out close to a tenth of the army. And their arrows had taken another fourth, but King Inwer's army was still too strong for them to defeat.

Asher hated to think that the women inside the castle would eventually have to fight. Asher climbed the wall where he and Lacey had stood. He found a place to observe the condition of the army. Inwer's men seemed just as tired as the queen's. Asher looked for the Blue Bloods. One of them was still behind their army and Asher wondered what she was doing. She stared into the sky. He thought he recognized her from the description Queen Sherr had given. It was probably Candari, who could affect the weather. Would she bring a storm on them? Could she do it in a way that would hurt them and not her own army? Any storm she brought would force her soldiers to fight in the same conditions, so he hoped she wouldn't be any threat for now. But where were the other three he had seen?

Asher scanned the army below him. They hadn't reached the castle yet. Minla's boulders and the arrows from his archers kept them back for now. The gap in the earth wasn't huge, but it did seem to slow their advance. Jenna's animals still occupied a lot of their attention as well.

A movement off to the side caught Asher's eye. At least ten soldiers held double shields up surrounding a small group of people. Asher aimed and struck the lower leg of one of the soldiers. He stumbled and fell behind, but before the other soldiers could close the gap he'd left, Asher saw the skirts of women. The Blue Bloods were advancing.

"Stop them!"

Kaylee felt herself slipping. She didn't know how many she had healed or when she last felt the physical pain of her own injury, but she had nothing left inside her. Kaylee placed her hand on the man in front of her. She knew everything about his injury and what it would take to correct it, but she had no power to call forth. Kaylee took the knife from her belt and cut her arm just below the other wound. She stared at her arm in surprise—she felt no pain.

Kaylee looked at the man, the fear in his eyes apparent as he seemed to realize she was unable to help.

Kaylee tried again, yet only felt a small trickle of power. Had she used it all up? Was she empty? She placed her hand on her own injury and healed it immediately. Both gashes on her arm were gone. The only sign they ever existed was the blue blood that stained her clothes. She slid the blade's edge across her arm again. Nothing. Kaylee touched the man anyway, hoping she could heal him. Still, she felt nothing. She was useless to them. Kaylee touched a different man, and still nothing. She knew what they needed but the power to heal was gone.

Kaylee's eyes filled with tears. The faces before her blurred. She willed herself to pull the power forward. Nothing. Despair overcame her. She collapsed. She felt herself being caught by a couple men before she hit, but she was out before they eased her to the ground.

"Asher!"

He turned at his name and saw a soldier pointing toward a group gathered in the east corner of the courtyard. He looked to the soldier to ask what it was then he saw Kaylee's dark green dress. She lay on the ground.

The soldiers surrounding her were still injured and Asher saw the panic rising in the ranks. Asher rushed down the ladder praying that Kaylee wasn't dead. They needed her. If those Blue Bloods managed to break through the army's defenses then they could wreak havoc among the queen's people in the castle.

"Hold them away!" Asher shouted to the captain closest to him. "Do not let them reach the walls."

The captain saluted and issued more commands. Asher sprinted across the courtyard, not caring that he was in the line of fire. He had to get to Kaylee. Though he had no idea what he could do if she succumbed to her wounds.

The soldiers parted as Asher approached. Kaylee only had one small wound on her arm. She breathed but lay completely motionless.

"What happened?" Asher asked.

"She healed everyone she could find, but suddenly she couldn't anymore. She healed herself, cut her arm, and tried again, but nothing." The soldier speaking shook his head. "She looked terrified just before she collapsed."

"Did she say anything?" Asher asked.

"No."

Asher quickly checked her body for any hidden wounds. Maybe she'd been shot and not noticed it. Asher's hands found nothing to indicate she was injured more than her arm. He pulled out his medallion from his shirt and held it close to her. He felt a small vibration, just enough to make Asher sure she was still a Blue Blood. Even if the dark blue blood oozing from her wound hadn't told him that much already.

"Bind her arm," Asher commanded.

Someone rushed away and returned with some bandages. As they cared for her, Asher debated on what to do. They had to have her help, but if she were unconscious, nothing could be done.

"Take her into the castle. Take her to the kitchens and tell Cook to try to revive her. She needs rest and time to recover."

A couple of the less wounded soldiers picked her up and gently carried her through the small doorway that led to the castle. Asher watched them go, praying for her recovery. They would be lost without her.

"Quickly bind your wounds and return to your posts. We aren't through yet."

The soldiers nodded and immediately carried out his orders. Asher turned to the front of the courtyard. More and more soldiers fell by the arrows hitting them, but even then they continued to return fire through the missing wall.

Jenna screamed in rage and staggered for a moment. Asher feared she'd been hit, but she stood again and roared in frustration. He could only imagine she'd felt the pain of one of her animals as it was slain. She appeared to be in a trance of sorts. He only hoped she wouldn't lose her mind to the animals she was connected with. Those beasts were doing more and more to take out the army. Without Jenna, their cause was lost.

Minla sagged against the wall to her back, but she still threw boulders occasionally. They were smaller, but she managed to hit her mark more often than not. Asher wondered how she aimed so well, but then it occurred to him that the king's army was large enough she had high probability that each rock would hit someone.

Asher looked at the queen's army. Less than sixty archers remained. He didn't know if he should call a retreat into the castle walls themselves or if they should maintain the courtyard for as long as possible. Asher doubted he'd be able to get Jenna to leave while her animals still fought. And he couldn't abandon her. Minla might collapse from exhaustion soon. If that happened, he'd have to send men to retrieve her and get her into the castle.

A horn blasted through the air, followed by three shrill blasts from a different horn. The vibrations hurt Asher's ears. Silence followed. The queen's soldiers paused as a voice reverberated off the walls.

"I call a cease-fire!" The woman's voice was beautiful. It sounded like joy, and Asher wished to hear it again.

"Cease fire!" Asher shouted, but there was no need. None of his soldiers lifted an arrow. None of the king's soldiers took advantage of the lull.

"I would speak to the one in command," the woman's voice said.

All eyes turned to Asher. He turned full circle and realized he was the closest thing to a leader they had. A smile tugged at his lips. Jenna looked at him and shook her head. Minla closed her eyes and slowly slid down the wall. A tiny voice in the back of his mind told him to see to her, but when the beautiful voice spoke again he forgot about Minla.

"I vow no harm will come to you. Step out and speak with me."

Asher took a step forward. Jenna shouted something at him, but Asher couldn't understand her rough words. Jenna looked over the edge of the castle wall and shook her head.

"Don't," Jenna said.

Asher shook his head. "It will be fine." He looked around the courtyard. "See to the wounded." Asher pointed at Minla. "Take her inside." He didn't wait to see if anyone would follow his orders. It almost didn't seem to matter right now. He wanted to get to the woman who called for him. If they could stop this battle with words, it would be worth it. There shouldn't be any more death. And Kaylee would have time to recover.

Asher moved to the edge of the wall where the center had crumbled during the earthquake. The king's soldiers watched him, but none of them had their weapons up. They looked alert enough, but not ready to attack.

As Asher turned the corner, he saw the woman who had called to him. "Liliana," he whispered.

"Hello, Asher," she said. "I wondered when I would see you again."

CHAPTER THIRTY-THREE

When Kaylee's eyes fluttered open, she found Cook and a few of the kitchen servants fussing over her.

"What happened?" Kaylee asked.

"The soldiers brought you in here."

"Why?" Kaylee asked. "Are they still fighting?"

The girl closest to the door shook her head. "I don't hear nothing anymore."

Kaylee struggled to sit up, but Cook pushed her gently back down. "You need to take it easy."

"I'm fine," Kaylee said. She pushed Cook's hand away and sat up, feeling a strange tightness on her arm. She glanced at it, surprised to see it wrapped in white cloth. It was stained blue with her blood. Kaylee touched her arm and felt the healing power flow through her hand. She unwrapped the bandage and dropped it onto the floor as she stood up.

"I have to get back out there," Kaylee said. "They need me."

Cook crossed her arms over her chest. "You won't be able to help them if you're too exhausted." She took Kaylee by the shoulder and made her sit in a chair. "You eat a couple bites of this bread and have some soup."

The cook turned to the girl by the door. "Colie, go see if you can find a wounded soldier." Cook turned back to Kaylee as Colie left the kitchen. "Unless you can heal him, you aren't leaving. Got my orders from the queen herself."

"Where is Queen Sherr?" Kaylee asked.

The kitchen door opened and Colie led a soldier into the room. She took his hand, pulling him toward Cook and Kaylee. He looked surprised until he saw Kaylee awake.

"Try it," Cook said.

Kaylee placed her hand on the soldier's arm, just below the wound where an arrow had gone through. She felt what needed to be done just as before, but she had no power. She pulled her knife out. Since slicing her arm no longer seemed to help, Kaylee stabbed her left hand, feeling the knife hit the table as it cut through her flesh. She stared at her hand. She felt nothing. She touched the man and tried to bring power forward, but nothing happened. Kaylee grabbed the knife and stabbed her hand twice, with still no feelings. She was empty.

"Can you heal him?" the cook whispered.

Kaylee shook her head.

Colie stared at Kaylee's hand. "Can you heal yourself?"

Kaylee placed her good hand on the stab wounds and felt the power flow. She didn't understand how it could work for her, but nothing for others. "I'm sorry," she whispered to the still injured soldier.

"Don't worry about it. I'll heal in time." His eyes didn't look hopeful. He turned to leave, and the cook offered Kaylee another plate of bread.

Kaylee shook her head, pushing the plate away. "I have to go help."

"You can't help." Cook tried to stop Kaylee.

She held her hand up. "I may not be able to heal anyone anymore. But I can fight. I feel no pain now, and I can use a weapon. I'll heal myself when injured. I have to help." She moved to the door, relieved when no one tried to stop her.

Asher couldn't believe he'd worked out a way to get the fighting to stop. Liliana had been given authority from the king to call a truce. Asher knew King Inwer had kept Liliana close to him as an advisor because of her ability to produce calmness and get people to think rationally. Her Blue Blood power was a wonder. Asher only wished they had spoken first instead of the army attacking.

Liliana explained so eloquently how a misunderstanding started the attack. Celeste, one of the Blue Bloods who could manipulate the earth, had been overzealous to show her strength. She'd never been given permission to attack.

It all seemed so reasonable.

Asher wandered the halls, looking for Queen Sherr. Liliana wanted to talk with her. He could solve all of the problems. Asher felt a strange tingle on the top of his head. He wanted to scratch it, but he knew from trying moments ago that it didn't help.

Asher's hand went to the top of his head. He rubbed it anyway but the tingle remained, as if it were under the skin. He shook his head, trying to dismiss the confusion he felt. He looked around the almost empty hallway and wondered where everyone went. A maid dashed from one room down the hallway, carrying a bundle of rags and bottles with some ointment. She bumped into him, stammered an apology, and then rushed on. Where would she be going with them? Asher shrugged. He focused on the hallway and realized he was near the queen's chambers. That was it. He needed to speak to her. He had something important to tell her.

Now if he could just remember what it was. He scratched harder at that annoying tickle on his head.

Absently and without any real thought, Asher pulled the sword from its sheath. It was important to have his weapon ready. He felt it.

Asher opened the door to the queen's chamber with ease. Why was that strange to him? He couldn't figure it out. Asher stepped into the room and walked around it. He saw no sign of Queen Sherr. Maybe she was making her rounds of the castle. Asher left the room without closing the door, his sword gripped tightly in his hand.

Kaylee touched every soldier she passed as she walked through the makeshift hospital that had taken over half of the kitchen's butchering area. It was almost surreal to see soldiers lying on the counters where the kitchen servants usually cut up the meats brought from the stock yard.

Though she could feel their wounds and knew the extent of each injury, she was still helpless to heal them. She whispered her apologies to each one, but soon found herself instructing the servants who tended to the injured how to best try to heal from the outside using their needles, thread, bandages, and poultices. Cook followed her out and told Kaylee she would see to the care of each wounded soldier.

Kaylee nodded her agreement and found herself taking a bite of a roll she didn't know she held. Kaylee looked back at Cook to see her nodding in approval. A young serving girl burst through the doorway carrying a bundle of more rags and some bottles of ointment. Cook took them from her. Kaylee turned to go.

"Lord Herst looked lost," the girl said.

"What?" Cook asked.

"Lord Herst. He was wandering the hallway above. Headed to the queen's wing."

Kaylee turned to the girl. "Was he injured?"

"Not that I could see, but he kinda just stared at me as I passed. I didn't stop to ask him anything because Cook told me to get back here with these things."

Kaylee patted the girl on the shoulder. "I'll go look for him." She needed to know what happened and who had called a cease fire. There was no more fighting right now and Kaylee was grateful for it, but she didn't trust it. Something was wrong.

As Kaylee left the impromptu hospital, she found herself face to face with Queen Sherr.

"What is going on?" Kaylee asked.

"I don't know. I was watching the battle from my chambers above. I couldn't see what caused it to stop, but then Asher left the courtyard and went around the corner of the wall. He came back and commanded the wounded to be brought in and treated. He told the other soldiers to stand down. None of them could explain why either. They said he entered the castle and haven't seen him since."

Kaylee looked at the soldiers in the courtyard. They looked alert, but none held their bows ready to fire. She let her gaze sweep King Inwer's soldiers, who still remained outside the courtyard. They were so much closer than before.

"This has to be a trick. They will attack us at any moment," Kaylee whispered.

"My thoughts exactly. I must speak with Asher and see what possessed him to do this."

"A servant girl said she saw him near your wing of the castle. Maybe he went to consult with you," Kaylee said. She hesitated a moment. "I have bad news."

Queen Sherr looked at Kaylee.

"My powers have changed."

"How?" Queen Sherr asked.

"I can no longer heal others. I feel no pain of my own wounds. Without the pain, I can't heal them. I can still heal myself, but nothing else." Kaylee hung her head.

Queen Sherr lifted Kaylee's chin. "I do not blame you. There was no way to know what would happen in a situation like this. Think of the good you've done. You've healed so many of my soldiers. Without you, we would have been wiped out completely by now."

Kaylee blinked back the tears. She knew she didn't deserve this praise, but she felt so much gratitude for it anyway. "I can still fight if it comes to that. I am still yours. Command me as you need."

"Go find Asher." Queen Sherr looked up toward where her wing of the castle was.

Kaylee nodded and turned to go. "Where are Minla and Jenna?"

Queen Sherr pointed behind her. "Jenna is still on the castle walls. She growls at anyone who approaches her, so everyone has left her alone. She has a bunch of birds close by as well." Queen Sherr turned to the door where Kaylee had come from. "Minla is unconscious in there. No signs of injury. I believe she's just exhausted."

Kaylee nodded. She knew it was bound to happen with how much effort Minla had put into throwing those boulders. Almost none were left to litter the ground beneath the broken section of wall.

"Any signs of the king's Blue Bloods?" Kaylee asked. "Have you been able to discern who came with him?"

"Candari is out there trying to figure out what to do with the weather, but she was never one of the king's smartest. She had lots of power to her storms, but not much for strategy." Queen Sherr pressed her lips together. "I can only assume the two who caused the earthquakes were Elin and Sorine. Fran was throwing the fireballs." She shook her head. "It's too bad they had to be killed. I would have loved to speak to them, perhaps convinced them to join me."

"Did you see any more?"

"I saw three others, but couldn't see them clearly enough, nor did they show any sort of power to indicate who he had sent."

"Perhaps you should hide," Kaylee said. "We don't know what else to expect, but we need you to be safe. You have to lead us."

Queen Sherr nodded. "Bring me Asher. I'll be in the throne room." She turned to her guards, and together they left quickly. Kaylee glanced once more at the soldiers still standing at attention and felt her stomach drop. Something was truly wrong.

Running footsteps echoed off the halls. Asher turned quickly, bringing his sword up. Kaylee stopped in her tracks and stared at him.

"Where is Queen Sherr?" Asher asked. Seeing Kaylee made it clearer to him that he needed to find the queen.

"She's in her throne room. She sent me to find you."

Asher brushed past Kaylee and she turned to keep up with him. "What happened out there?"

"A cease fire." Asher spoke over his shoulder.

"How?" Kaylee asked.

Asher felt irritation at her many questions. "We don't have time for that. Why aren't you healing the soldiers?" Asher snapped. He could see the shock on Kaylee's face and wondered why she seemed upset. He brushed it off and rushed through the hallway. If he had thought about it, he should have realized the queen would be in her throne room if not in her chambers.

His scalp itched. He rubbed it, finding no relief from the irritation. He'd been sure he would find her hidden in the higher rooms of the castle, not down in the throne room where anyone could find her. He told her to stay hidden. What was going on?

Asher registered Kaylee further behind him. She panted as if running was difficult for her. He tried to ignore her, but a small blossom of compassion formed in his chest. Asher nearly dropped the sword when the itch on his head intensified. He scratched vigorously at his scalp, and was surprised to see blood under his fingernails. He touched his head and pulled his fingers away to find them red with the sticky blood. He wiped it on his shirt front and pressed on.

He was running out of time. He had to get to the queen. If Asher didn't deliver the message to the queen, Liliana wouldn't maintain the cease fire for much longer. He had to save the soldiers and anyone else who followed Queen Sherr.

He barreled through the hallway, forgetting Kaylee once more. One guard stood at the entrance to the throne room. It was Dolf's brother Tige, the queen's most trusted guard. He could easily get past him, but he needed to be sure Tige didn't interfere. Asher slowed his approach, acting as if everything was fine. The guard nodded to Asher as he passed. Asher took his knife from his belt and struck Tige on the back of the head with the hilt, dropping him with one swift motion. Asher opened the door and saw the queen pacing before her throne. She stopped and faced him, a look of relief on her face. Asher took the knife and threw it straight into the queen's chest.

CHAPTER THIRTY-FOUR

Kaylee couldn't keep up with Asher. She tried, but her lungs burned. Her heart beat harder than she'd felt in months. The crazed look in Asher's eye in that brief moment he glanced back worried her. She wished she'd been able to stay right with him.

Kaylee turned the corner and started toward the throne room. A guard lay crumpled on the floor. Had the enemy broken the cease fire and attacked? Kaylee couldn't hear any signs of battle at first, but the ring of clashing swords echoed in the hallway. Kaylee pulled her knife from her belt. It wasn't long, but she could still fight with it. She ran as fast as she could and threw open the door.

Asher fought with one queen's guard. Another lay on the floor dead. A third was unable to stand from an obvious wound in his leg. Kaylee couldn't understand why the queen's guards would have turned on her. She looked for the queen and felt her chest collapse in fear as she saw her leaning against her throne, a dagger in her chest. She looked at Kaylee with wide eyes, and then stared at the fighting men.

Kaylee rushed to the queen and dropped to her knees. "What happened? Why did they attack?" Kaylee placed her hand on the queen's chest and felt the damage beneath her ribs. The dagger had punctured a lung and cut through a major vessel near the heart. Kaylee prayed her power would work this time. She took her knife and stabbed it into her thigh. No pain, but Kaylee tried to heal the queen anyway. They needed her. As much as she wished it, she had no power left.

They would have no way to stop King Inwer if the queen died today. Kaylee looked to Asher wishing he could help, but he fought fiercely with the remaining guard. Kaylee turned to the queen. For the first time, she noticed the intricate handle on the blade. She knew this knife. Zeb had used it on her many times.

Kaylee looked around for Zeb. Had he managed to sneak into the castle? There was no sign of anyone else in the room but the guards, Asher, and the queen. Kaylee's heart stopped for a moment. Though it had been Zeb's knife, it had a new owner. She pulled her hand away from the queen and looked at Asher. He wasn't fighting to save the queen. He was fighting against her.

The last guard held his own, but Asher fought with a ferocity Kaylee had never seen before. She knew he was good with a bow and a knife, but she had never seen him fight with the sword. He looked equally matched with the guard. She looked at the guard on the ground. Asher had stopped the other two as well.

Queen Sherr gripped Kaylee's hand. The queen struggled to breathe. The words she spoke were almost too soft to hear. "Stop him."

Kaylee turned to the queen and tried once more, unsuccessfully, to heal her. "How?" she asked. "Why did he do this?"

Queen Sherr shook her head. Kaylee tried again to heal the queen, stabbing her leg again, lower down. There still was no pain, but she tried anyway. Queen Sherr took Kaylee's hands off her chest and struggled to place them on Kaylee's own wounds.

"Stop." She struggled for breath once more. "Heal." Another breath. "Yourself."

Hot tears stung her eyes as she obeyed her queen. She cursed her lost ability and wished she could heal others instead of herself. Queen Sherr needed to live. If the knife remained in her chest, it would block the bleeding of the nicked vessel. The tissue surrounding the knife began to swell. The queen was in no immediate danger of death, but Kaylee could sense how much pain it caused her to breathe and speak.

Kaylee heard a grunt and turned to see the guard drop to his knees, holding the blade of Asher's sword as he looked at it sticking in his gut. As Asher yanked the blade free, Kaylee's vision turned blue. She was on her feet one moment and staring into Asher's eyes the next. She buried her own blade deep into his side. With rage, she pulled the dagger out and slammed it in again. Asher grabbed her hand with his and stopped her from pulling it out a second time. She grabbed at his chest, trying to push him back. Her hand got tangled in the medallion he always wore.

"Why?" he gasped.

Kaylee stared at him in shock. How could he ask that? He crumpled before her, one hand holding the knife as she released the handle of it, the other hand holding onto her as he fell. She staggered a moment and tried to pull back. His medallion broke away from its chain as she clutched it in her fist.

Asher's eyes closed tightly. When he opened them again, he looked at her with such betrayal in his eyes. "Why did you do this?"

Kaylee's confusion swallowed her anger. "Why did I? You killed the guards. You killed Queen Sherr."

Asher's head lifted in shock. He looked over at the queen and got to his feet. He staggered forward but Kaylee pushed him back. "Leave her alone!" she shouted.

"What happened?" Asher's face drained of color.

"You tell me." Kaylee pointed at the queen. She was still alive, but not for long. "That's your dagger!"

Asher shook his head. "Impossible." He collapsed to the ground and struggled once again to get to his feet. He half crawled, half dragged himself closer to Queen Sherr. Kaylee watched in confusion as he got nearer. It looked as if her words completely stunned him.

"My queen," Asher grunted as he got closer. Kaylee watched him like a hawk as he reached her, but he was no threat to the queen now. "What have I done?"

Queen Sherr struggled to open her eyes. She stared at him with a look of sadness and longing, looking just as confused as she felt. Asher looked devastated. Kaylee was sure something happened that she didn't understand.

The door opened. Kaylee spun around and dove for Asher's bloody sword. It was heavier than she expected, but she would not be weaponless.

"Ah, Asher, I see you've fulfilled your assignment." A tall, strong woman stepped into the room, followed by Zeb and two other women.

"Liliana," Asher whispered, "you did this?"

"No. Of course not." She smiled. "You did."

Asher blanched.

"Although I may have suggested you fulfill your assignment from King Inwer."

Kaylee turned to Asher, feeling more pain than she thought possible. "You've been working for him all this time?"

Asher shook his head. Of course he'd deny it. But why did he seem so genuinely upset about the queen?

Liliana laughed. "Why do you act so surprised?" She glanced at Zeb, who had a sick gleam in his eyes. "Do you really think one of King Inwer's most trusted advisors would really turn coat and join the rebel Dead Blood?" Liliana narrowed her eyes, looking at Queen Sherr as if she were garbage. "He has been here for the king and sent Zeb to warn us about Sherr's foolish aspirations. He told us about your wonderful gift."

Asher shook his head in denial. Kaylee didn't know what to believe. He seemed horrified, but she couldn't deny he'd fought the queen's guards and stabbed Sherr.

Zeb's eyes darted between Liliana and Asher. Kaylee studied him closely as Liliana continued to speak. Zeb didn't seem to understand, making Kaylee believe Liliana was lying.

"Enough." Kaylee shifted the sword in her hand. "Why are you really here?"

Liliana looked Kaylee over for a moment. She glanced at the other women behind her, who remained quiet. One of them looked at Queen Sherr with confusion in her eyes. The other seemed to be staring at something behind Kaylee's shoulder.

"We are here to escort you to the true king." Liliana took a small step forward. She moved hesitantly, as if approaching an injured animal. "You will be treated well in his kingdom. He will grant you everything your heart could desire."

Kaylee shook her head. "I had that here."

Liliana chuckled and looked around the castle. "You think this place is worthy of you? Your queen is a fraud. And her army is pathetic. By the grace of our king, he has ordered all of you spared if you will come to him."

"You lie."

Liliana blinked, surprised Kaylee didn't believe her.

"You are the one who can convince another to do what she says. I will never trust a word out of your mouth."

Liliana's smile turned to a sneer. "I doubt that." She pulled out a small tube and placed it to her lips. "If you won't come of your own free will, I'll bring you by force." She took a quick breath and blew into the tube.

Kaylee felt something hit her shoulder. She looked down at a tiny needle sticking out of her sleeve. She plucked the needle out and tossed it away. Liliana blinked in surprise and blew again. Kaylee ducked and tried to lift the sword. She had to stop Liliana. There had to be some way she could heal Asher and Queen Sherr, but that wouldn't happen if she was gone.

Another small needle bumped into her, this time into her thigh. Kaylee felt a strange numbness in her side. It might be a poison or a sedative. Kaylee placed her hand on where she'd been struck and tried to heal it away, but couldn't tell if it worked. The sword was still too heavy to be of any use to her. As the poison spread, she felt weaker by the moment. Kaylee remembered the medallion she still held in her hand. She yanked off her belt and folded it in half, making a small pocket for the medallion to rest in. It wasn't the same as the sling she'd used, but it was close.

Kaylee spun the belt around, faster and faster until just the right moment and let the medallion fly. It flashed in the light from the window and struck Liliana in the neck. The Blue Blood's hands flew to her throat. She croaked and coughed and stumbled forward. Kaylee looked for something else to fight with, but only swords were available. She turned to Asher in time to see him pull her knife from his side and throw it at Liliana. The knife hit her in the soft spot just below her sternum.

Liliana looked down in surprise and pulled the knife free. She dropped it, holding her hand to her stomach. When she pulled it away, blue blood dripped from her fingers. Kaylee knew it was a fatal wound. Liliana looked up at Kaylee once more and tried to speak, but fell forward, dead.

The other Blue Bloods stood in silence, watching Liliana in the pool of blood that still oozed from her.

Kaylee recognized they were no threat. She looked for Zeb, but he was no longer in the room. She hadn't even noticed when he fled.

Kaylee turned to the two behind her. The amount of blood spilling to the floor proved Asher had only moments left to live. Kaylee's heart broke. The anger and sadness battled with her pain as she watched him dying in front of her. She placed her hands on him, hoping she could do something to stop him from dying. As her hands found the wound, she felt the power once more.

The emotional pain of losing him and of being the one to kill him were more than she could bear. She allowed the power to flow from her, taking her strength and her health and pouring it into him. Her heart ached with the betrayal, and the confusion that had plagued her for the last half hour. She looked into his eyes and knew he felt the same thing. She understood exactly what Liliana had done to him and Kaylee felt his horror as he realized what he'd done under that spell.

Kaylee searched his wound, finding the punctured bowels and organs she'd slashed and then stabbed again. She willed his to heal and felt hers break apart as if exchanging lives. She felt his health increase and his heartbeat return to normal. The clammy skin beneath her hands felt warm once more.

She pulled her hands away from him and placed them on the queen. She was still alive, but just barely.

Kaylee felt the sorrow and heart ache and despair of knowing that she was their only hope—if Queen Sherr didn't make it, the king would win. She had to heal her. Kaylee's breath came quick. Almost as if she weren't able to get enough air. She felt the tightness in her chest that the queen had felt as all the blood filled her lungs. Kaylee pulled the injury from the queen and exchanged her healthy lungs and whole heart for the queen's damaged ones.

In one final effort, Kaylee took the blade's handle and pulled it out of the queen's chest. Queen Sherr gasped in a quick breath and placed her hands on her chest. Kaylee smiled at the look of surprise in her eyes. She dropped the knife and lay down, her head resting on the queen's thigh.

Kaylee's soul floated. Her body didn't pain her anymore. She couldn't feel a thing. Finally, all the pains were gone. Kaylee looked to the queen and realized she could see her from a completely different viewpoint. She gazed down on the scene. Asher bowed his head over her damaged body. Though she couldn't hear anything, his body shook as he sobbed. Queen Sherr tenderly smoothed the hair off of Kaylee's forehead and looked at Asher with a gentle smile.

Kaylee watched her Blue Blood body change. She didn't know how long it would be before her spirit returned and she could resume her red-blooded life once more. For now, she was free.

EPILOGUE

Kaylee sat at her desk, idly running her finger over the swirling pattern on the cover of her father's book. She hadn't even known it was missing until Dolf brought it back with him a few days ago. He'd found it in Zeb's pack when the queen's army returned to Egera from Inshansi after receiving the written message on Jenna's bird. Kaylee didn't ask for the details of Zeb's fate, but she knew he would truly never bother them again.

If Zeb had taken it, it must mean it was important. Kaylee still couldn't decipher what the jumble of words meant.

She traced the pattern over and over again, feeling the strange ridges as if they were branded into the thin leather. Kaylee opened the book and scanned its pages, hoping for a clue. No one would've gone to the effort to write so much in an old book like this without it meaning something. Kaylee touched the familiar symbols in the corners. Each one was at the top corner on the outer edge of the page. Sometimes the symbol repeated for many pages, but then would change to a new symbol. Kaylee was sure the words found under the same symbols were related to each other. Like a chapter or a journal entry. She looked closer at the pages. In places, the faded ink was almost unreadable.

Kaylee set the book on the table and pulled a second candle closer to her. As she read each word, she looked for anything odd about the page. Soon she realized there was a tiny swirl connected to the beginning of one word on each page. Every one was in a different location on the page, but each page had one.

Could this be the starting point? She flipped back to the first page.

Kaylee read the first word attached to the swirl. *This.* She read the line from left to right, but the words didn't make sense. She stared at the word again. The letter S was longer than most others on the page. It crossed over another word. *book.* The K also had an elongated stem that crossed a word on the line below it. *is* followed by *my* and *attempt* and *to* then *document* . . .

Kaylee's heart beat quicker as she realized the words were beginning to make sense in this order. She rushed through the words, following the connections, only needing to back up and start over a few times.

The journal, as Kaylee soon understood, belonged to a Blue Blood named Silva—over four hundred years ago. She detailed how, with the help of another Blue Blood, they had discovered the way to pass on their powers to other women. People had feared them so much that they hid to protect themselves from angry mobs who would come after them.

They didn't want the ability to be lost and had decided to imbue this book with power. Using the blood of both women, they mixed it together and added a touch of magic from their gifts. In doing so, they lost each gift as they wrote it down. But having lived for more lives than they cared to count, they were each willing to do so.

Kaylee couldn't believe the Blue Bloods had started out having more than one power. She continued deciphering the text.

After writing the book, they wandered the land searching for a place to hide their sacrifice. They didn't want the magic to be gone forever. When they found a queen who understood their plight, they entrusted it to her.

She read it and, through the gifts embedded in the book, became a Blue Blood then passed the power on to others after each reading.

Kaylee finally understood why she had passed on the power to Jenna, Lacey, Minla and the baby. Kaylee put the book down and stared. Should she tell the queen?

Jenna had taken days to return to normal. Minla recovered after a week. Lacey returned to her red-blooded life and claimed she was happy enough to stay that way. Kaylee missed the power she once held. She wished to heal all Queen Sherr's soldiers who remained wounded, as well as King Inwer's who had surrendered when Liliana died.

Kaylee looked out the small window of her room onto the courtyard. The enemy soldiers agreed to stay and serve Queen Sherr once the driving force for their attack was gone. Kaylee didn't think it wise, but since she no longer had any power, she didn't dare say much to the queen. Soldiers loyal to the queen watched them while they built up the outer wall of the castle grounds and fortified the city against future attacks.

Queen Sherr spent most of her time in her wing of the castle speaking with her Sisters in Blood as well as providing a life for those former Blue Bloods like Kaylee.

Kaylee returned to the book and followed the swirl once more. A shiver shot up her arm, reminding her of when she'd passed on the power to the other Blue Bloods.

Kaylee held her hand up in the narrow stream of light from her window. She didn't know what had happened, but Kaylee felt different. She pulled out the knife she refused to stop carrying and pressed it against the side of her thumb.

Her blood wasn't blue. But it wasn't red either.

Dear Reader,

I hope you enjoyed reading *Burden of Blood*. Please consider posting a review or rating on Amazon or Goodreads. Reviews help spread the word. It's the best way to say "thank you" to any author.

If you have questions or comments, please feel free to contact me at authorlaurabastian@gmail.com

Thanks for reading.

Laura D. Bastian

ACKNOWLEDGMENTS

I definitely need to thank my husband for this book. And the fact that he says it's his favorite one of mine has nothing to do with it. He's been more supportive of my writing than I could have hoped for when I first started on this endeavor years ago.

I need to thank my oldest for being so caught up in this story as I was explaining it to my husband on a road trip that when I got to the place where I hadn't written anymore, she begged me to keep going. Well sweetie, here it is.

I need to thank NaNoWriMo for the awesome idea of writing a novel in a month. No this wasn't finished in a month, and it took me some time to tweak it to my satisfaction, but I for sure got this story going during November one year not so long ago.

And a special thanks to Betsy Love for sparking the idea. Throwing rocks at Kaylee was exactly what I needed to get the magic flowing and discover the magic deep within her.

ABOUT THE AUTHOR

LAURA D. BASTIAN grew up in a small town in central Utah and now lives in another small town in northern Utah. She always loved stargazing and imagining life out-side her own little world. A graduate of Utah State University with a degree in Elementary and Special Education, Laura has been using that training as she raises her children and writes make believe worlds. You can usually find her on her laptop either typing away, or on social media interacting with friends when she's not playing in her garden

You can connect with Laura on her website, www.lauradbastian.com, and find her other books on Amazon!